THE BABY-SITTERS CLUB®

BOY-CRAZY STACEY

**DON'T MISS THE OTHER
BABY-SITTERS CLUB GRAPHIC NOVELS!**

KRISTY'S GREAT IDEA

THE TRUTH ABOUT STACEY

MARY ANNE SAVES THE DAY

CLAUDIA AND MEAN JANINE

DAWN AND THE IMPOSSIBLE THREE

KRISTY'S BIG DAY

ANN M. MARTIN

THE BABY-SITTERS CLUB®

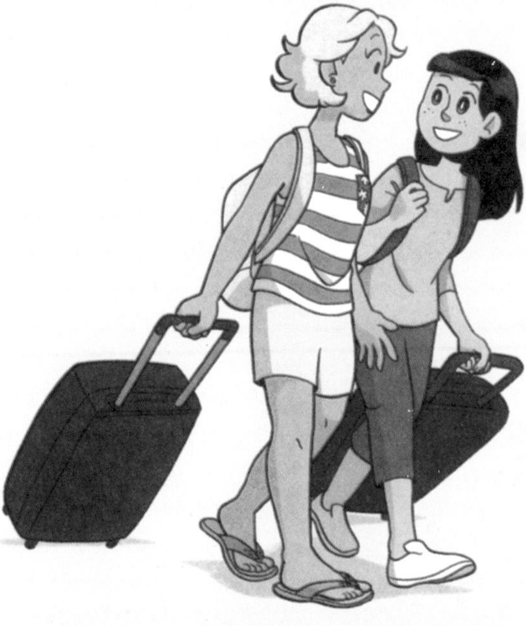

BOY-CRAZY STACEY

A GRAPHIC NOVEL BY

GALE GALLIGAN

WITH COLOR BY BRADEN LAMB

graphix

An Imprint of

SCHOLASTIC

Library of Congress Control Number: 2018953576

ISBN 978-1-338-30452-7 (hardcover)
ISBN 978-1-338-30451-0 (paperback)

10 9 8   21 22 23

Printed in China   95
First edition,September 2019

Edited by Cassandra Pelham Fulton and David Levithan
Book design by Phil Falco
Publisher: David Saylor

This book is for June and Ward Cleaver
(alias Noël and Steve) from the Beav
A. M.M.

For Mon, Dad, Lori, and all
our childhood beach adventures.

And for Patrick, who I forgive for pretending to be
a sea monster and grabbing my ankle that one time.
G. G.

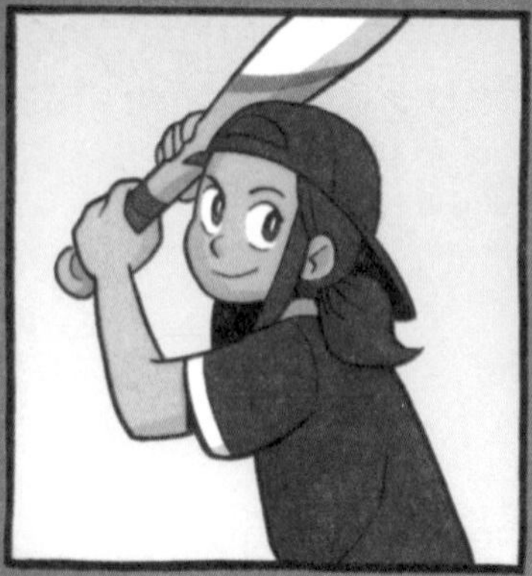

KRISTY THOMAS
PRESIDENT

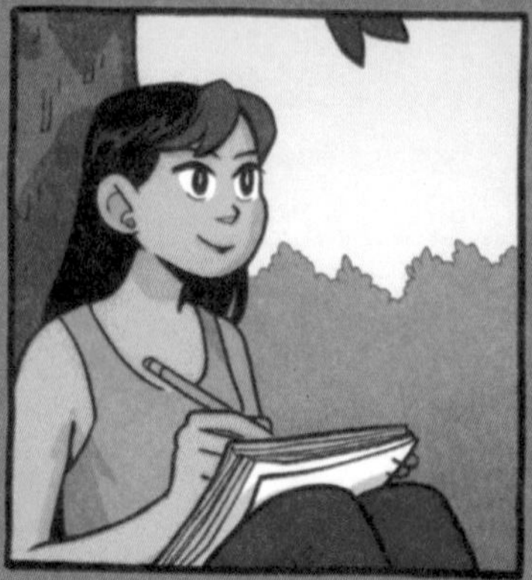

CLAUDIA KISHI
VICE PRESIDENT

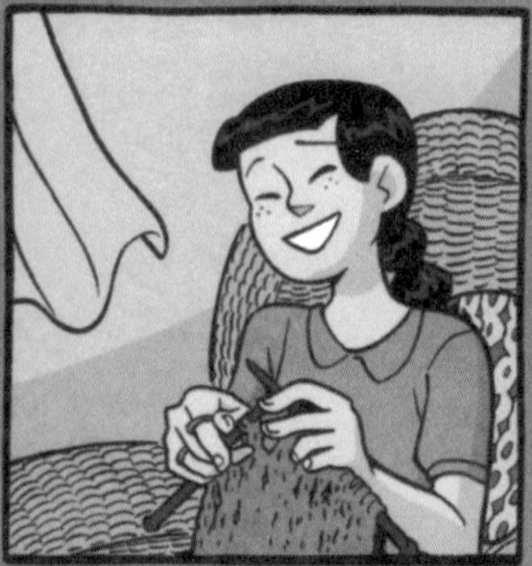

MARY ANNE SPIER
SECRETARY

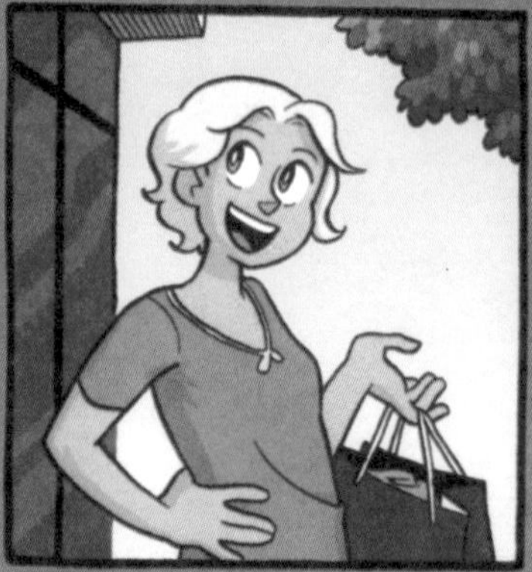

STACEY MCGILL
TREASURER

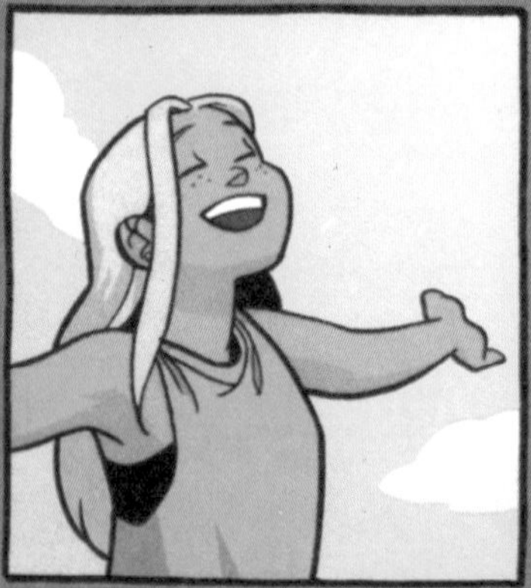

DAWN SCHAFER
ALTERNATE OFFICER

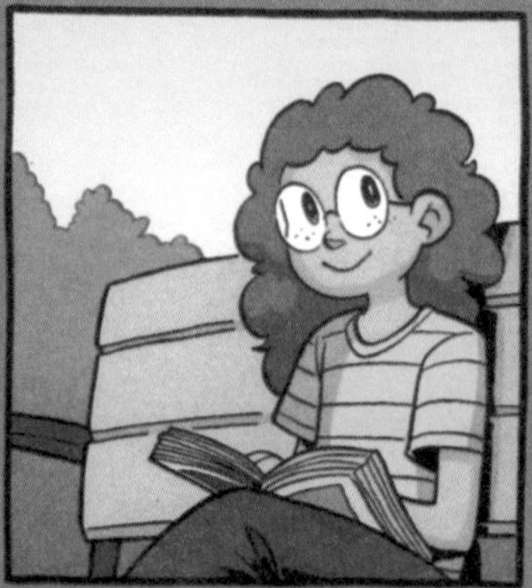

MALLORY PIKE
JUNIOR OFFICER

CHAPTER 1

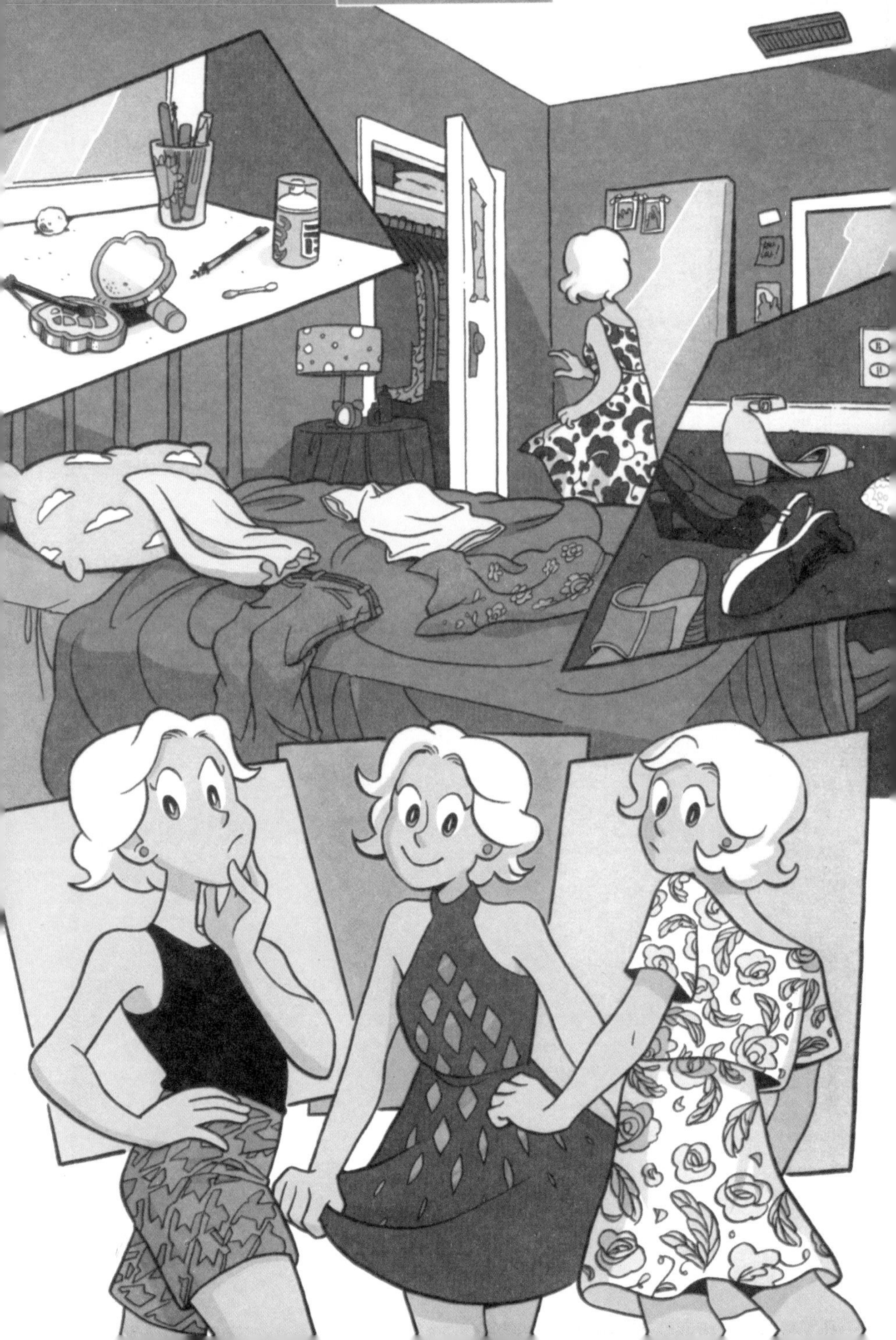

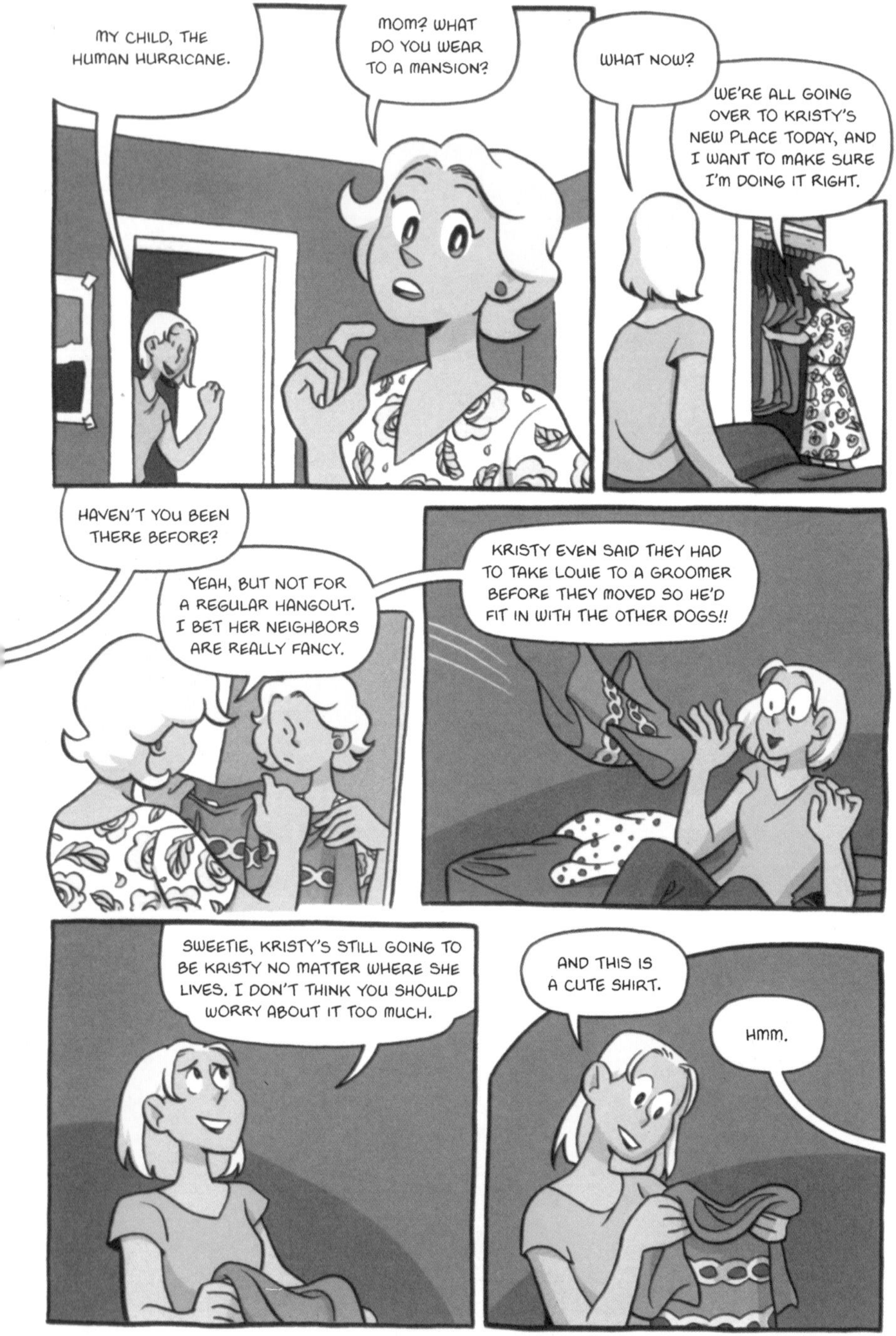
MY CHILD, THE HUMAN HURRICANE.
MOM? WHAT DO YOU WEAR TO A MANSION?
WHAT NOW?
WE'RE ALL GOING OVER TO KRISTY'S NEW PLACE TODAY, AND I WANT TO MAKE SURE I'M DOING IT RIGHT.
HAVEN'T YOU BEEN THERE BEFORE?
YEAH, BUT NOT FOR A REGULAR HANGOUT. I BET HER NEIGHBORS ARE REALLY FANCY.
KRISTY EVEN SAID THEY HAD TO TAKE LOUIE TO A GROOMER BEFORE THEY MOVED SO HE'D FIT IN WITH THE OTHER DOGS!!
SWEETIE, KRISTY'S STILL GOING TO BE KRISTY NO MATTER WHERE SHE LIVES. I DON'T THINK YOU SHOULD WORRY ABOUT IT TOO MUCH.
AND THIS IS A CUTE SHIRT.
HMM.

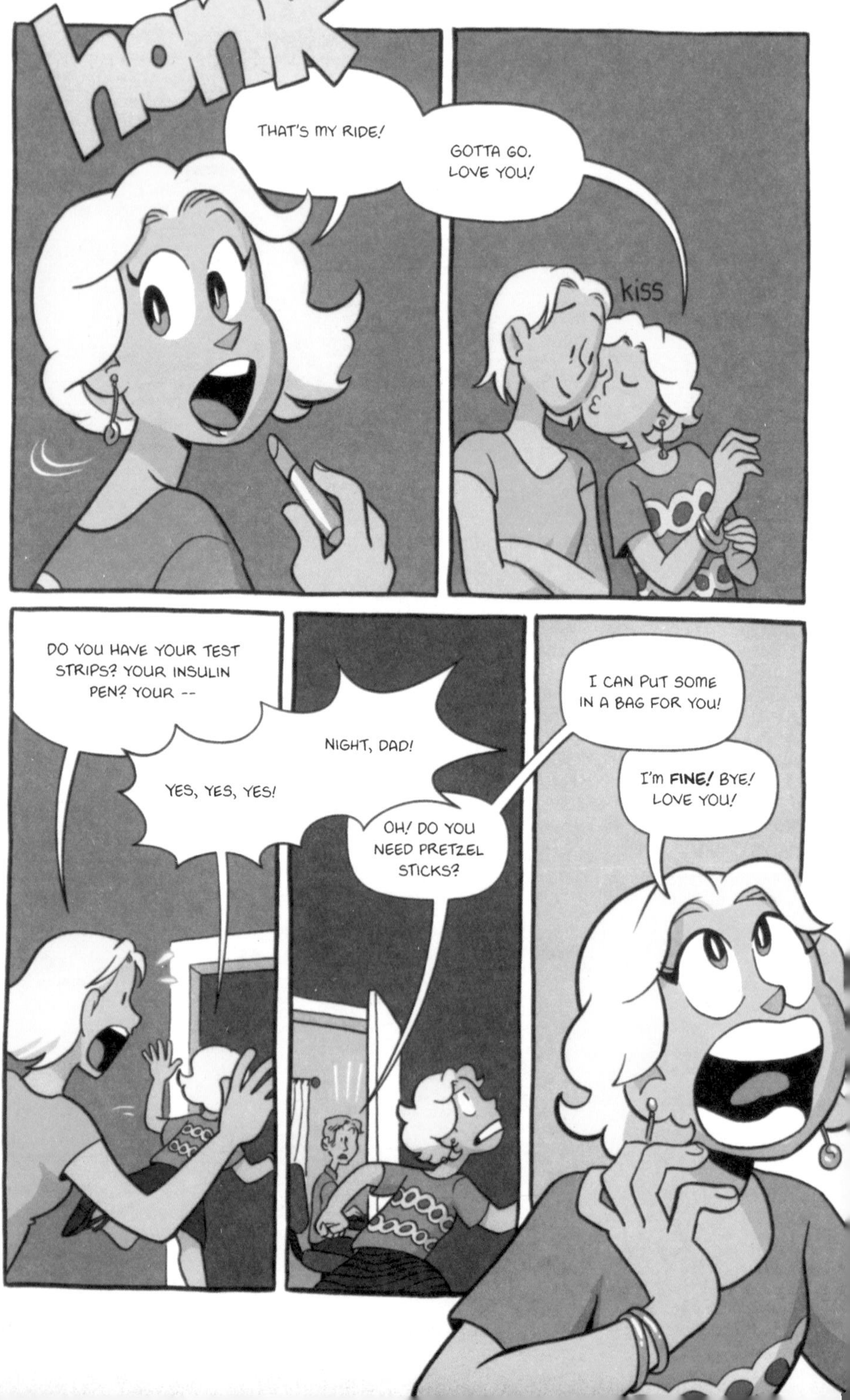
honk
THAT'S MY RIDE!
GOTTA GO. LOVE YOU!
kiss
DO YOU HAVE YOUR TEST STRIPS? YOUR INSULIN PEN? YOUR --
YES, YES, YES!
NIGHT, DAD!
OH! DO YOU NEED PRETZEL STICKS?
I CAN PUT SOME IN A BAG FOR YOU!
I'm **FINE!** BYE! LOVE YOU!

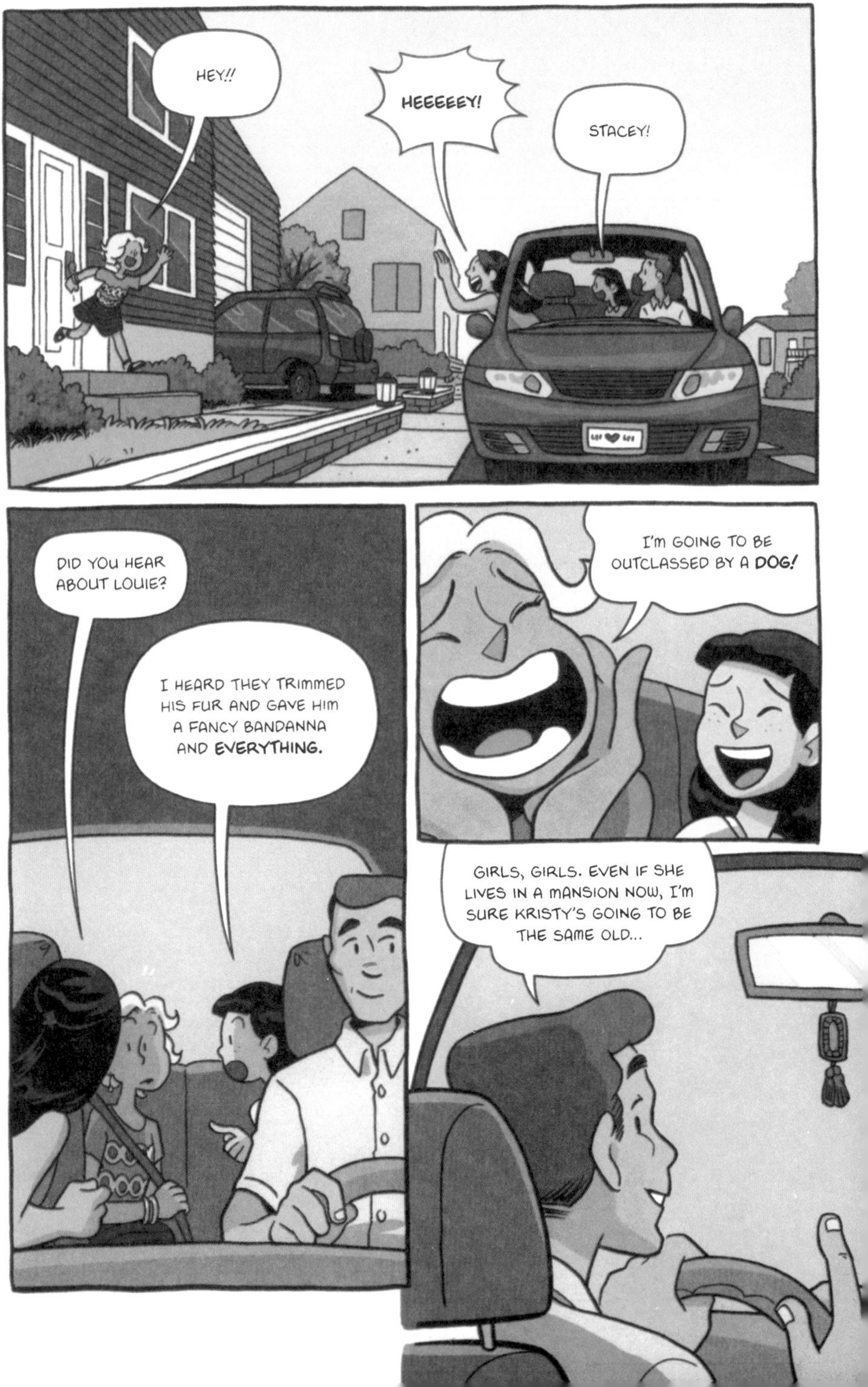
HEY!!
HEEEEEY!
STACEY!
DID YOU HEAR ABOUT LOUIE?
I HEARD THEY TRIMMED HIS FUR AND GAVE HIM A FANCY BANDANNA AND **EVERYTHING.**
I'M GOING TO BE OUTCLASSED BY A **DOG!**
GIRLS, GIRLS. EVEN IF SHE LIVES IN A MANSION NOW, I'M SURE KRISTY'S GOING TO BE THE SAME OLD...

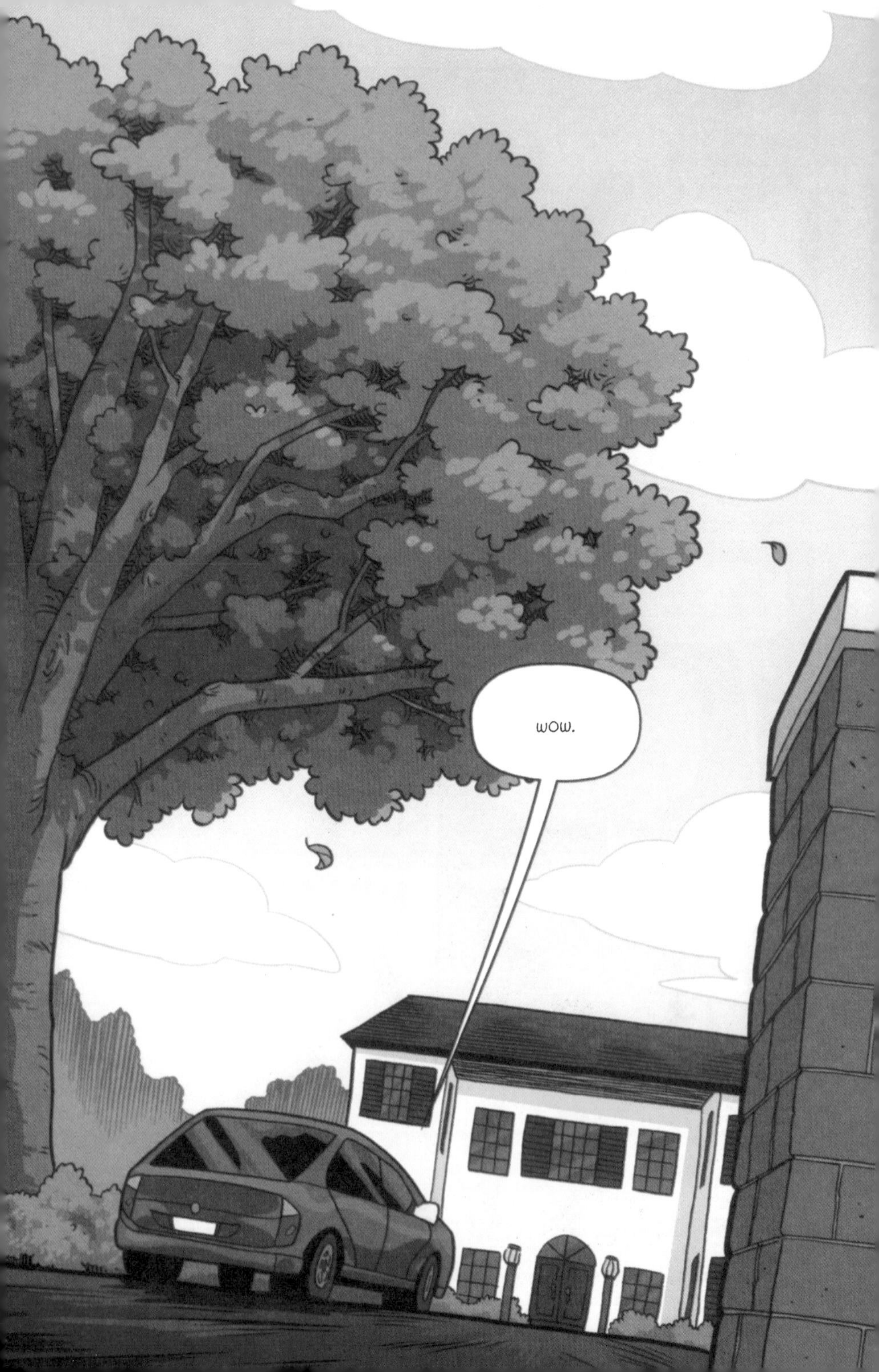
WOW.

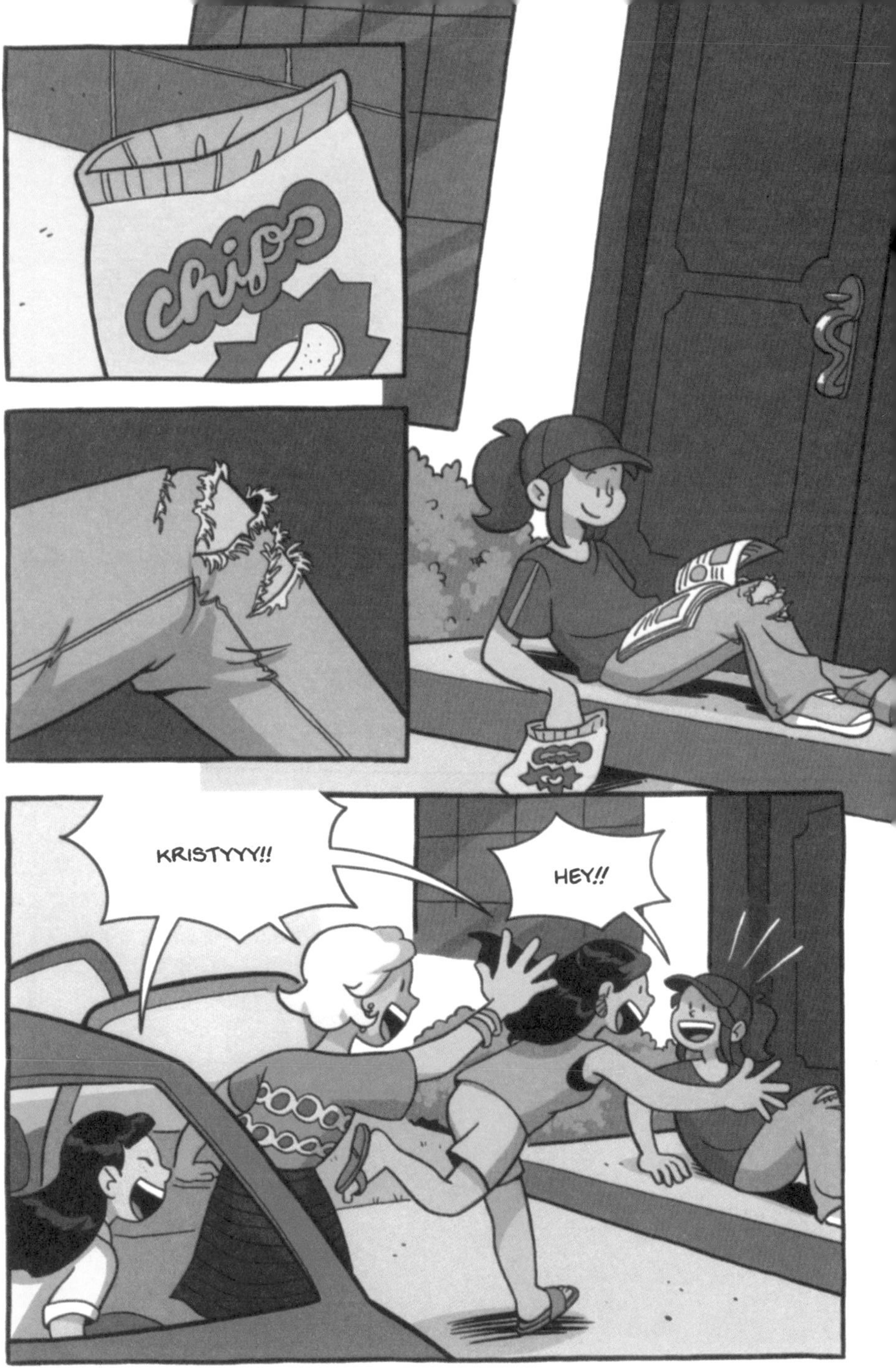
chips
KRISTYYY!!
HEY!!

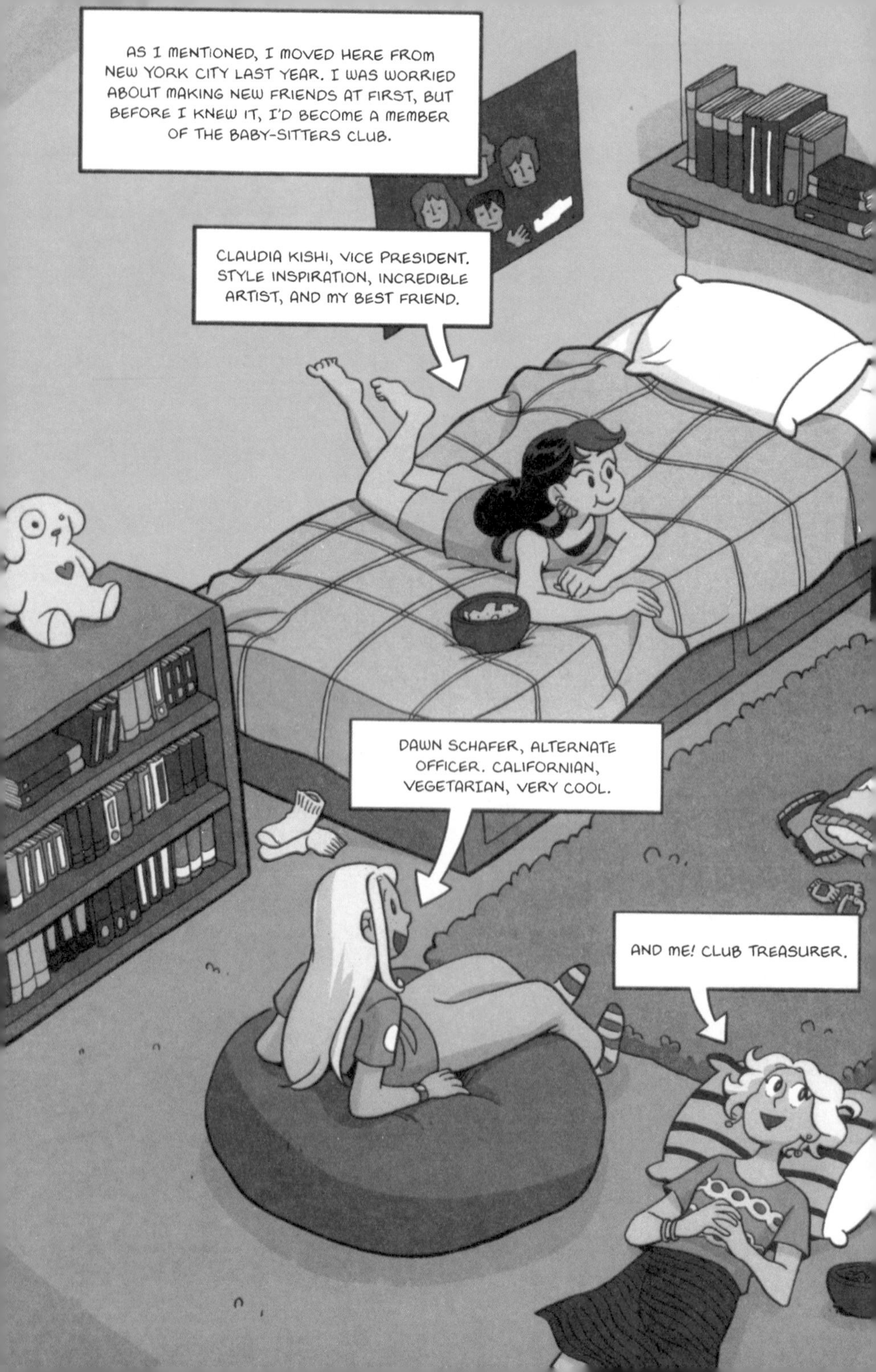

AS I MENTIONED, I MOVED HERE FROM NEW YORK CITY LAST YEAR. I WAS WORRIED ABOUT MAKING NEW FRIENDS AT FIRST, BUT BEFORE I KNEW IT, I'D BECOME A MEMBER OF THE BABY-SITTERS CLUB.
CLAUDIA KISHI, VICE PRESIDENT. STYLE INSPIRATION, INCREDIBLE ARTIST, AND MY BEST FRIEND.
DAWN SCHAFER, ALTERNATE OFFICER. CALIFORNIAN, VEGETARIAN, VERY COOL.
AND ME! CLUB TREASURER.

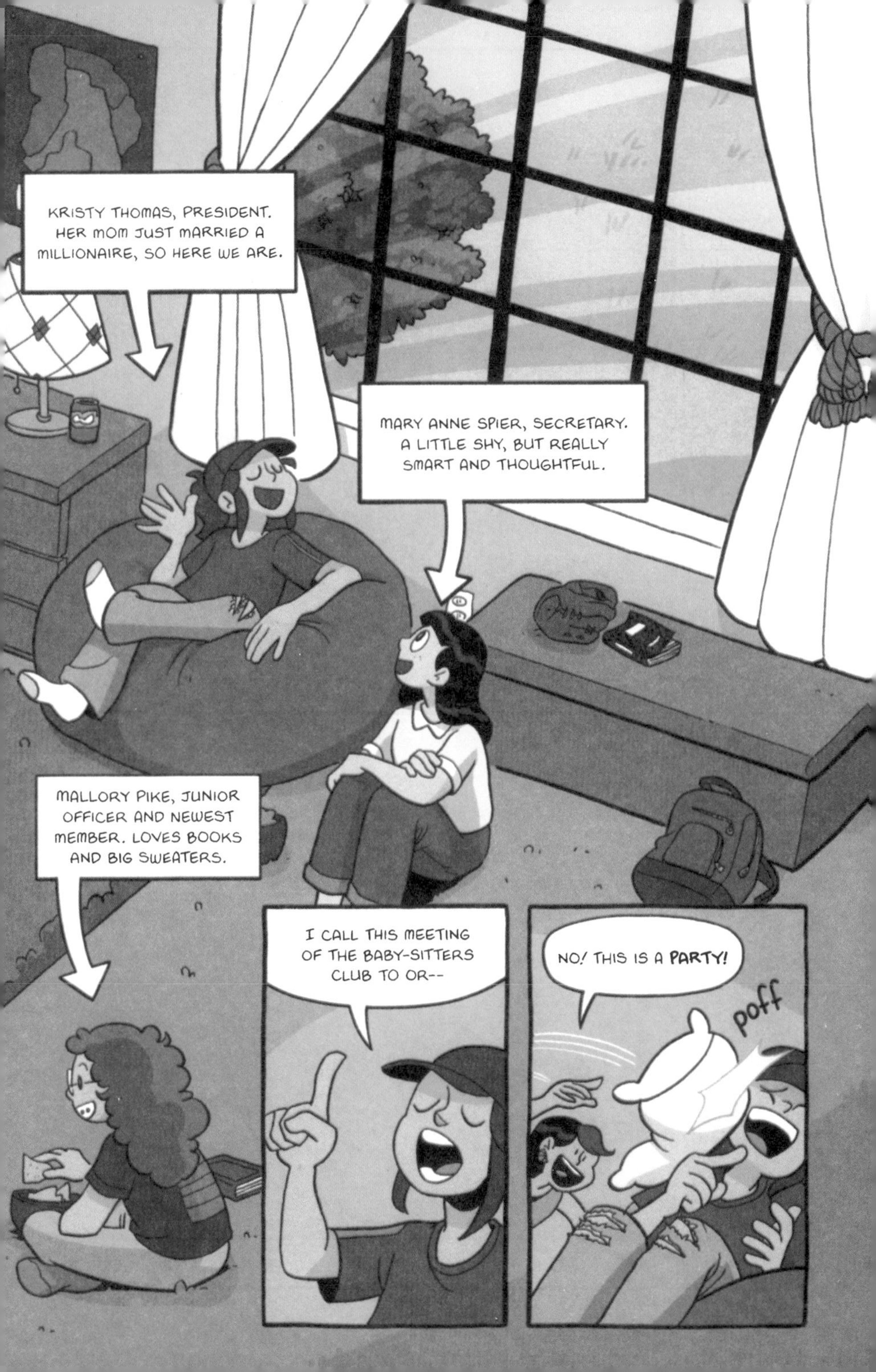
KRISTY THOMAS, PRESIDENT. HER MOM JUST MARRIED A MILLIONAIRE, SO HERE WE ARE.
MARY ANNE SPIER, SECRETARY. A LITTLE SHY, BUT REALLY SMART AND THOUGHTFUL.
MALLORY PIKE, JUNIOR OFFICER AND NEWEST MEMBER. LOVES BOOKS AND BIG SWEATERS.
I CALL THIS MEETING OF THE BABY-SITTERS CLUB TO OR--
NO! THIS IS A **PARTY**!
poff

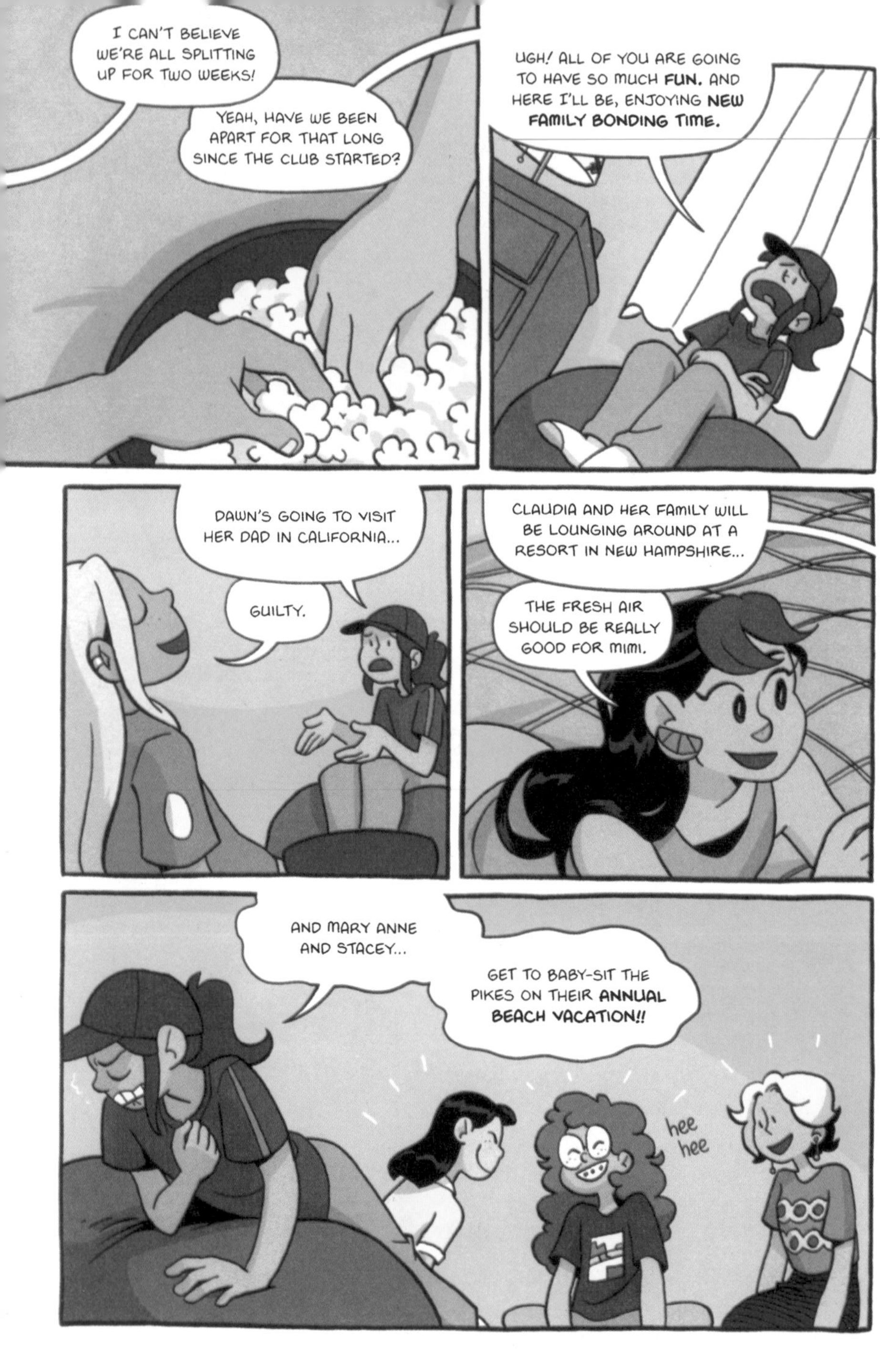
I CAN'T BELIEVE WE'RE ALL SPLITTING UP FOR TWO WEEKS!
YEAH, HAVE WE BEEN APART FOR THAT LONG SINCE THE CLUB STARTED?
UGH! ALL OF YOU ARE GOING TO HAVE SO MUCH **FUN.** AND HERE I'LL BE, ENJOYING **NEW FAMILY BONDING TIME.**
DAWN'S GOING TO VISIT HER DAD IN CALIFORNIA...
GUILTY.
CLAUDIA AND HER FAMILY WILL BE LOUNGING AROUND AT A RESORT IN NEW HAMPSHIRE...
THE FRESH AIR SHOULD BE REALLY GOOD FOR MIMI.
AND MARY ANNE AND STACEY...
GET TO BABY-SIT THE PIKES ON THEIR **ANNUAL BEACH VACATION!!**
hee hee

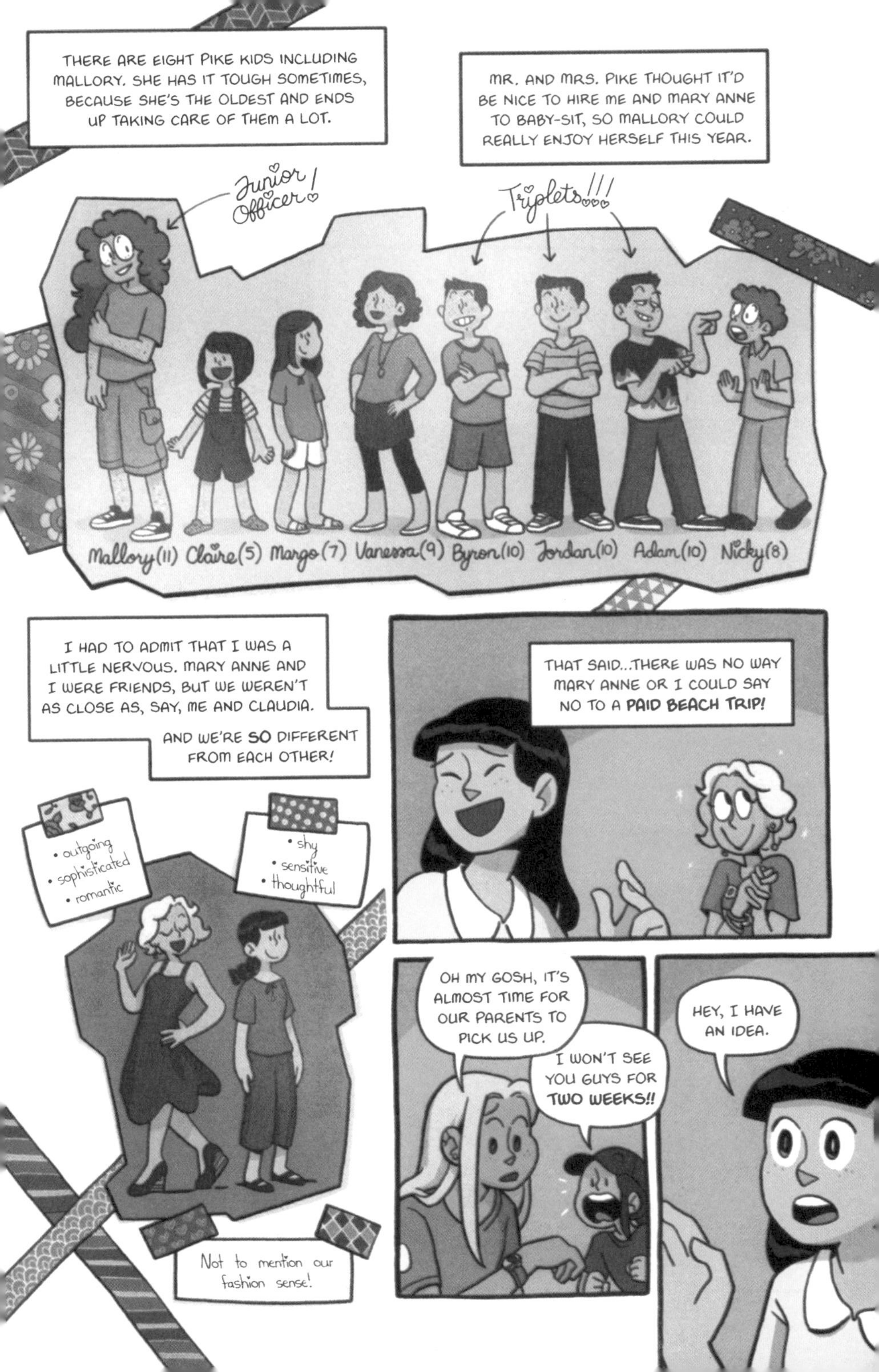

THERE ARE EIGHT PIKE KIDS INCLUDING MALLORY. SHE HAS IT TOUGH SOMETIMES, BECAUSE SHE'S THE OLDEST AND ENDS UP TAKING CARE OF THEM A LOT.
MR. AND MRS. PIKE THOUGHT IT'D BE NICE TO HIRE ME AND MARY ANNE TO BABY-SIT, SO MALLORY COULD REALLY ENJOY HERSELF THIS YEAR.
Junior Officer!
Triplets!!!
Mallory (11) Claire (5) Margo (7) Vanessa (9) Byron (10) Jordan (10) Adam (10) Nicky (8)
I HAD TO ADMIT THAT I WAS A LITTLE NERVOUS. MARY ANNE AND I WERE FRIENDS, BUT WE WEREN'T AS CLOSE AS, SAY, ME AND CLAUDIA.
AND WE'RE **SO** DIFFERENT FROM EACH OTHER!
• outgoing • sophisticated • romantic
• shy • sensitive • thoughtful
Not to mention our fashion sense!
THAT SAID...THERE WAS NO WAY MARY ANNE OR I COULD SAY NO TO A **PAID BEACH TRIP!**
OH MY GOSH, IT'S ALMOST TIME FOR OUR PARENTS TO PICK US UP.
I WON'T SEE YOU GUYS FOR **TWO WEEKS!!**
HEY, I HAVE AN IDEA.

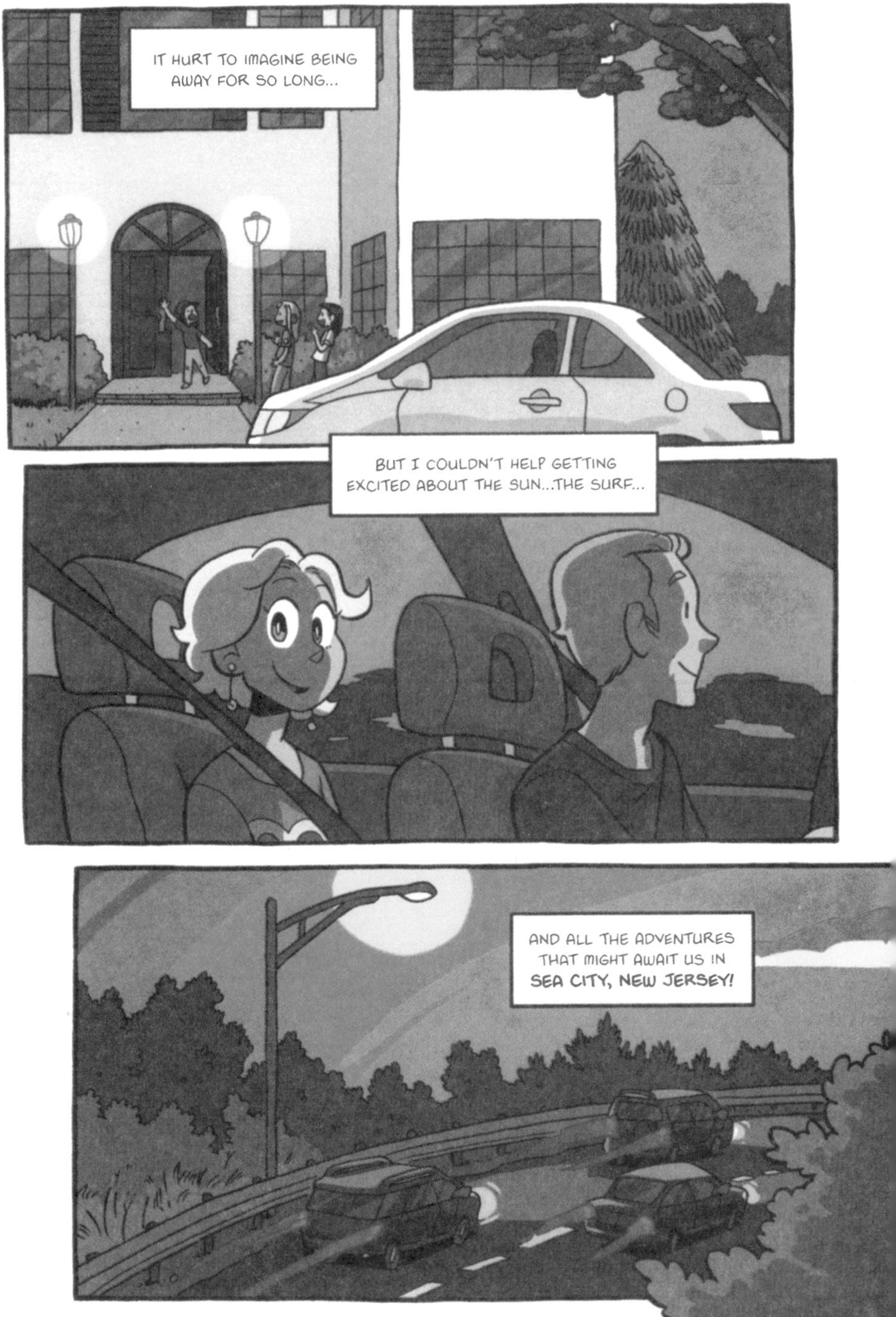
IT HURT TO IMAGINE BEING AWAY FOR SO LONG...
BUT I COULDN'T HELP GETTING EXCITED ABOUT THE SUN...THE SURF...
AND ALL THE ADVENTURES THAT MIGHT AWAIT US IN SEA CITY, NEW JERSEY!

CHAPTER 2

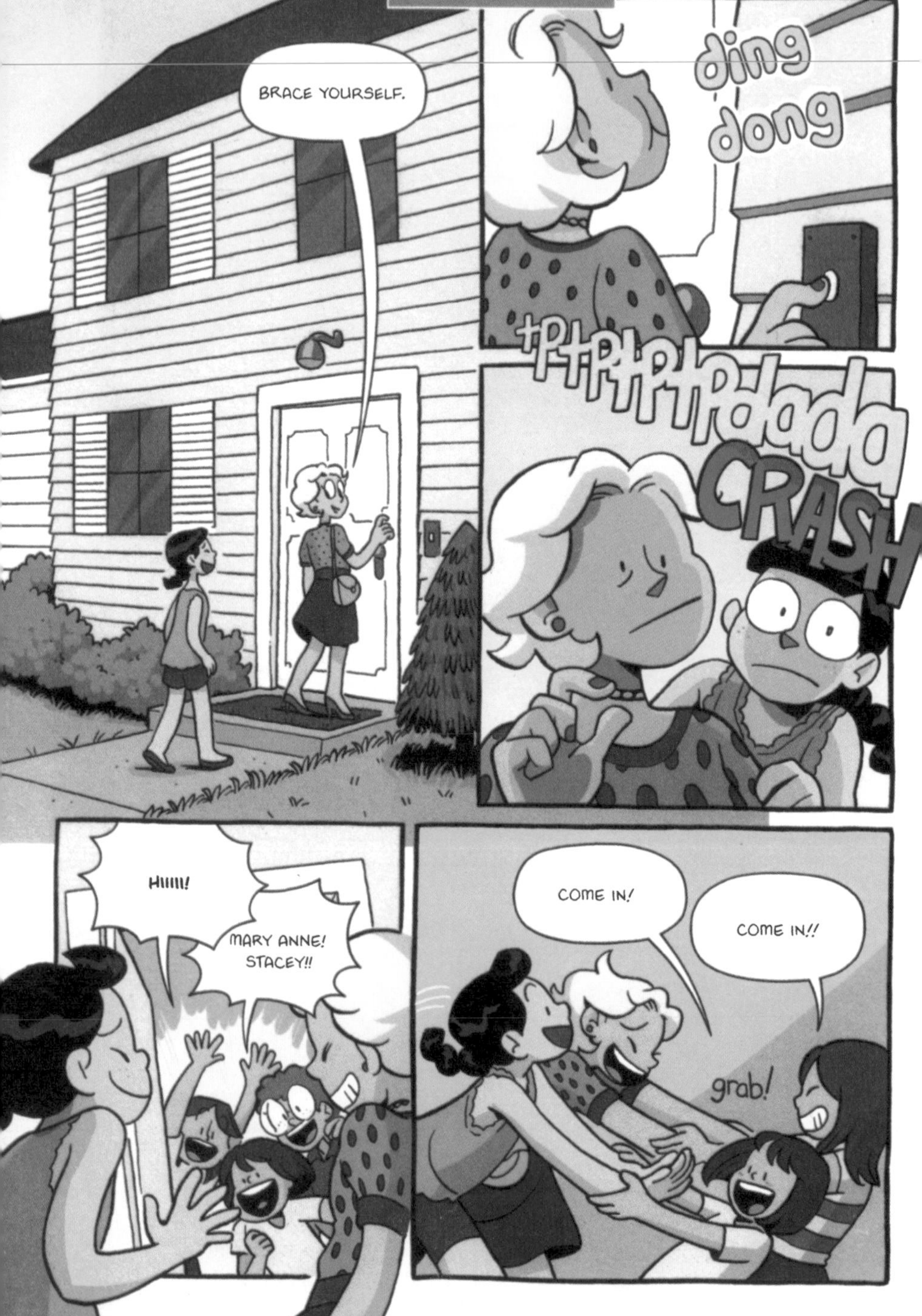
BRACE YOURSELF.
ding dong
CRASH
HIIIII!
MARY ANNE! STACEY!!
COME IN!
COME IN!!
grab!

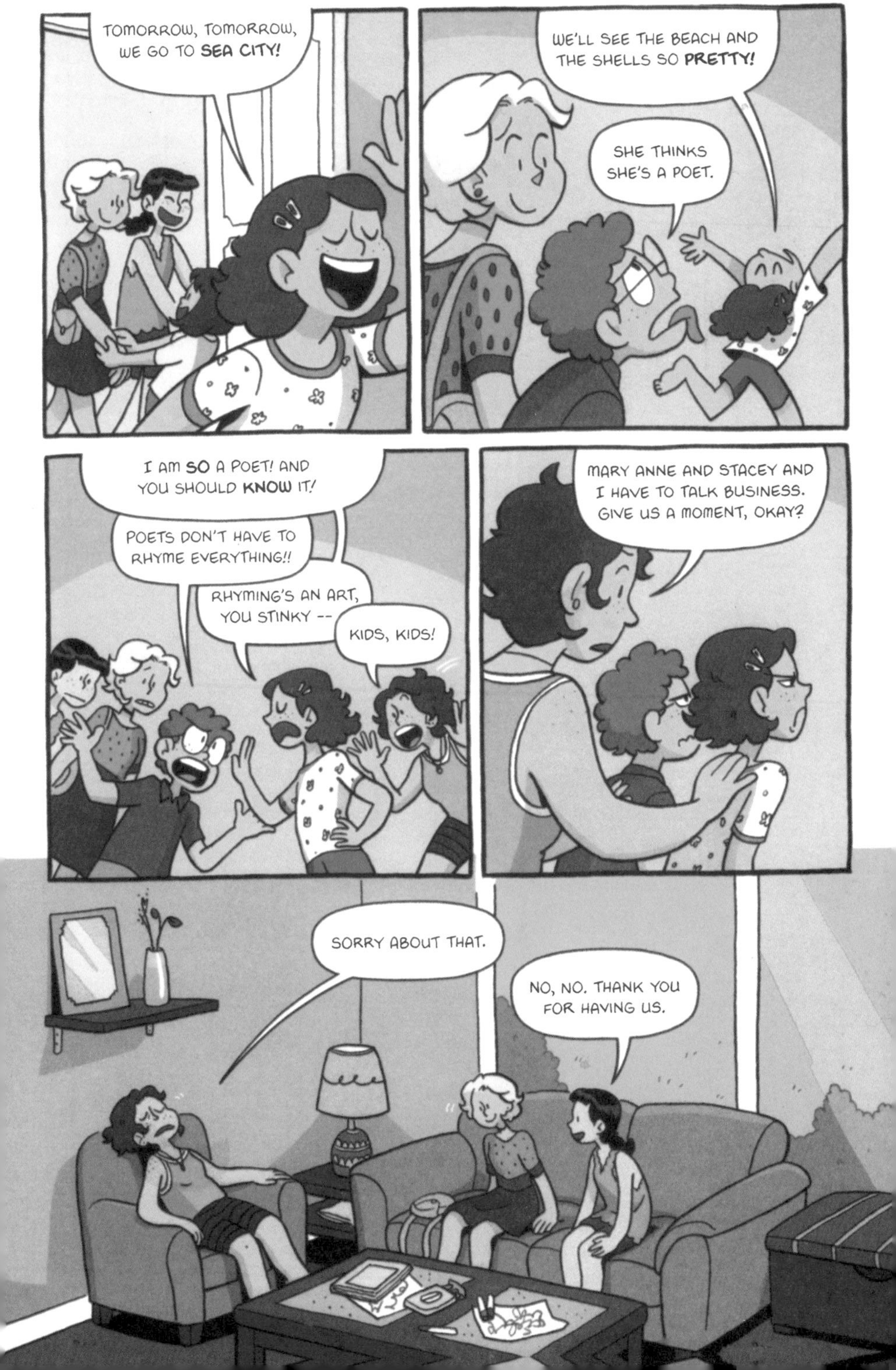

TOMORROW, TOMORROW, WE GO TO **SEA CITY!**
WE'LL SEE THE BEACH AND THE SHELLS SO **PRETTY!**
SHE THINKS SHE'S A POET.
I AM **SO** A POET! AND YOU SHOULD **KNOW** IT!
POETS DON'T HAVE TO RHYME EVERYTHING!!
RHYMING'S AN ART, YOU STINKY --
KIDS, KIDS!
MARY ANNE AND STACEY AND I HAVE TO TALK BUSINESS. GIVE US A MOMENT, OKAY?
SORRY ABOUT THAT.
NO, NO. THANK YOU FOR HAVING US.

I ASKED YOU OVER HERE TODAY SO WE COULD TALK ABOUT WHAT YOU'LL BE DOING IN SEA CITY, AND SET SOME GROUND RULES.

MOSTLY, YOU'LL JUST BE GIVING MR. PIKE AND ME A HAND SINCE, OF COURSE, WE'LL BE THERE, TOO.

BUT WE WOULD LIKE A LITTLE TIME TO OURSELVES AS WELL.

THERE WILL BE AFTERNOONS OR EVENINGS WHEN WE'LL GO OFF TO DO THINGS ON OUR OWN. THAT'S WHEN YOU'LL BE IN CHARGE.

THERE'S A LOT TO SEE AND DO IN SEA CITY, AND YOU SHOULD BE PERFECTLY SAFE ON YOUR OWN. JUST KEEP A CAREFUL EYE ON THE CHILDREN WHEN YOU'RE CROSSING THE STREET.

AND WE HAVE ONE BEACH RULE.

ABSOLUTELY NO GOING IN THE OCEAN, NOT EVEN WADING, BEFORE NINE A.M. OR AFTER FIVE P.M. THAT'S WHEN THE LIFEGUARDS ARE OFF DUTY.

ASIDE FROM THAT, THE KIDS CAN SWIM AS MUCH AS THEY WANT AS LONG AS THEY STAY IN FRONT OF THE LIFEGUARD STATION. OKAY?

OKAY.

nod

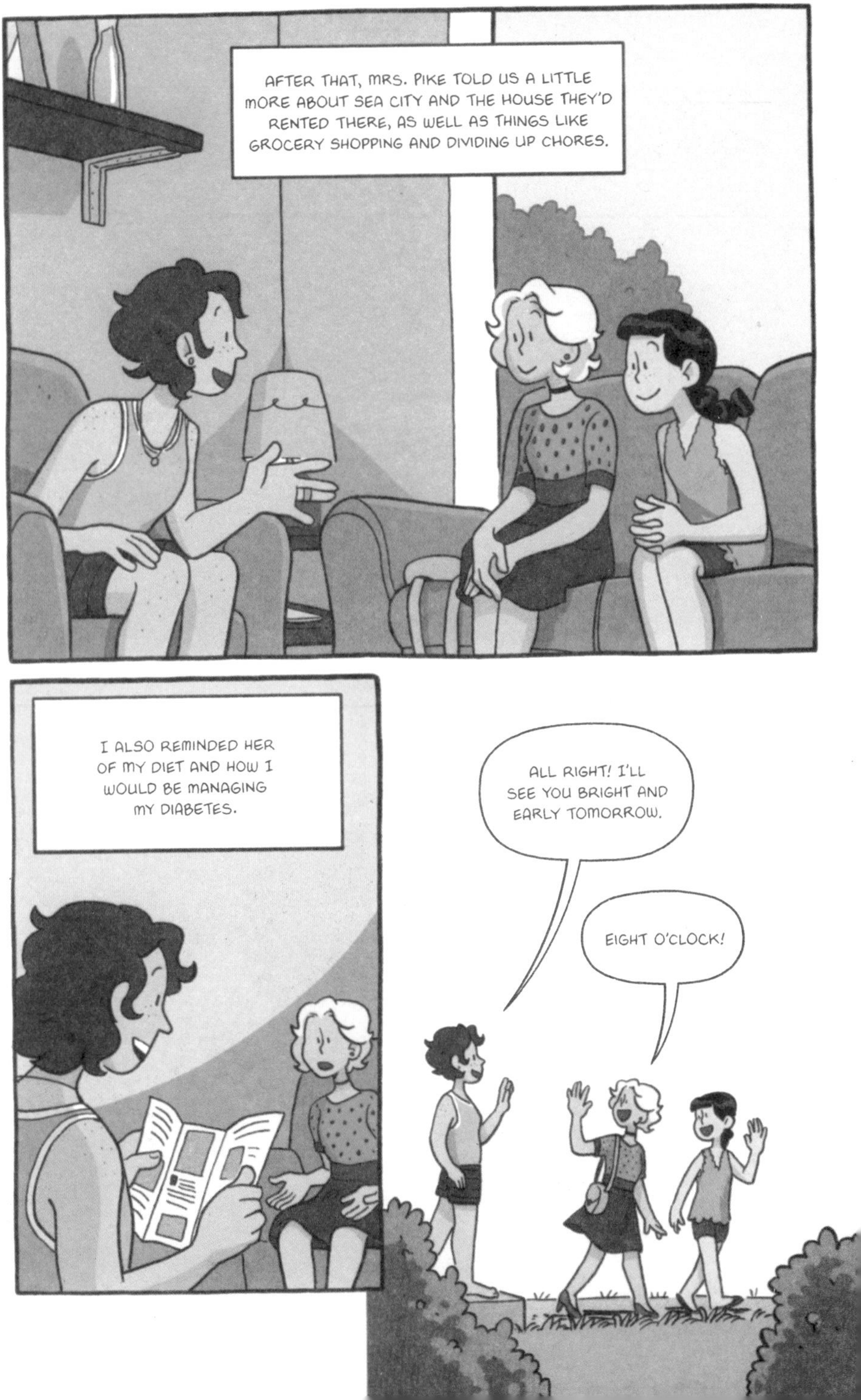
AFTER THAT, MRS. PIKE TOLD US A LITTLE MORE ABOUT SEA CITY AND THE HOUSE THEY'D RENTED THERE, AS WELL AS THINGS LIKE GROCERY SHOPPING AND DIVIDING UP CHORES.
I ALSO REMINDED HER OF MY DIET AND HOW I WOULD BE MANAGING MY DIABETES.
ALL RIGHT! I'LL SEE YOU BRIGHT AND EARLY TOMORROW.
EIGHT O'CLOCK!

AND WITH THAT, IT WAS TIME TO GO HOME AND PACK.
stacey's two
cute tops
SUNSCREEN!
no BURN
SPF 60
(don't forget!!)
toiletry bag
NY
bikini!!
strappy heels

...eek beach bag

sundresses

a good book

sweater

(just in case)

diabetes travel kit

embroidery

flip-flops

shorts & jeans

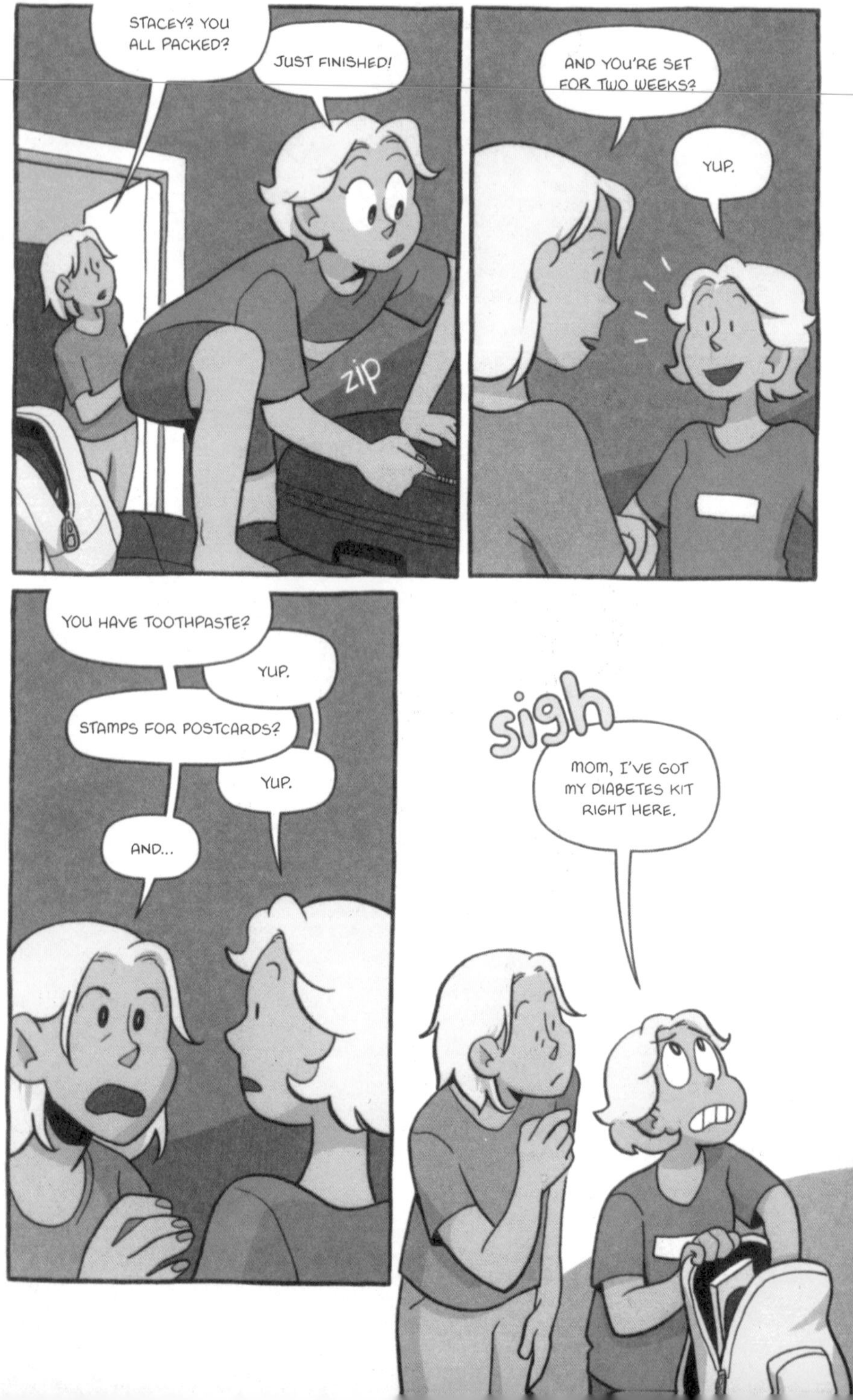
STACEY? YOU ALL PACKED?
JUST FINISHED!
zip
AND YOU'RE SET FOR TWO WEEKS?
YUP.
YOU HAVE TOOTHPASTE?
YUP.
STAMPS FOR POSTCARDS?
YUP.
AND...
sigh
MOM, I'VE GOT MY DIABETES KIT RIGHT HERE.

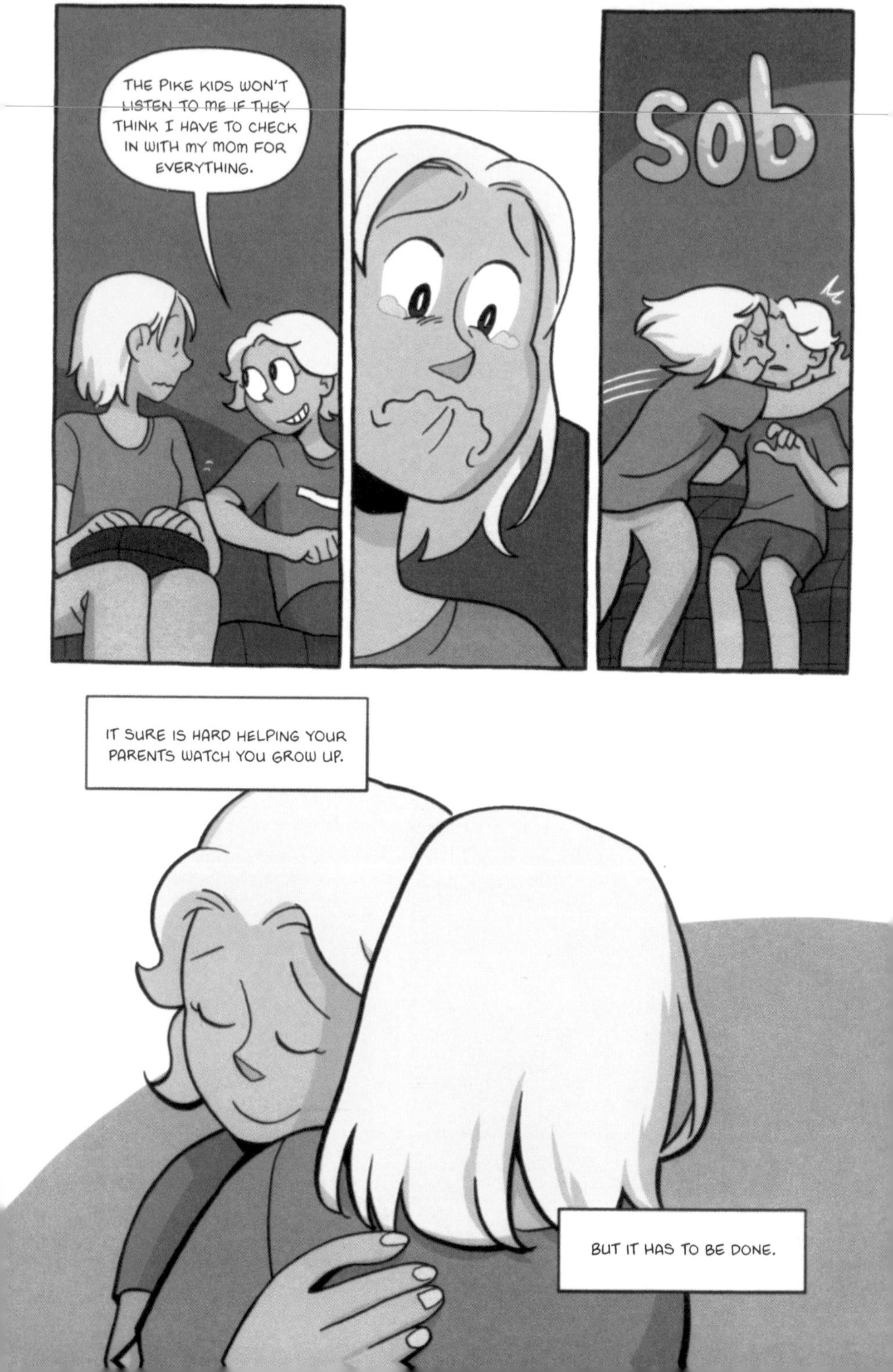
THE PIKE KIDS WON'T LISTEN TO ME IF THEY THINK I HAVE TO CHECK IN WITH MY MOM FOR EVERYTHING.
SOB
IT SURE IS HARD HELPING YOUR PARENTS WATCH YOU GROW UP.
BUT IT HAS TO BE DONE.

Saturday afternoon

Dear Kristy,

Hi'! We made it. The drive down here was wild, but we arrived unharmed. Do you like this postcard? Mary Anne and I found a drugstore with all these cards. Here are some things to put in the Baby-sitters Club Notebook:
Sometimes the Pike kids get carsick. Claire is still in her silly stage. She calls her mother "Moozie" and her father "Daggles." That's all for now. More tomorrow! Bye!

Luv,
Stacey

Kristy Thomas

1210 McLelland Rd.

Stoneybrook, CT 06800

CHAPTER 3

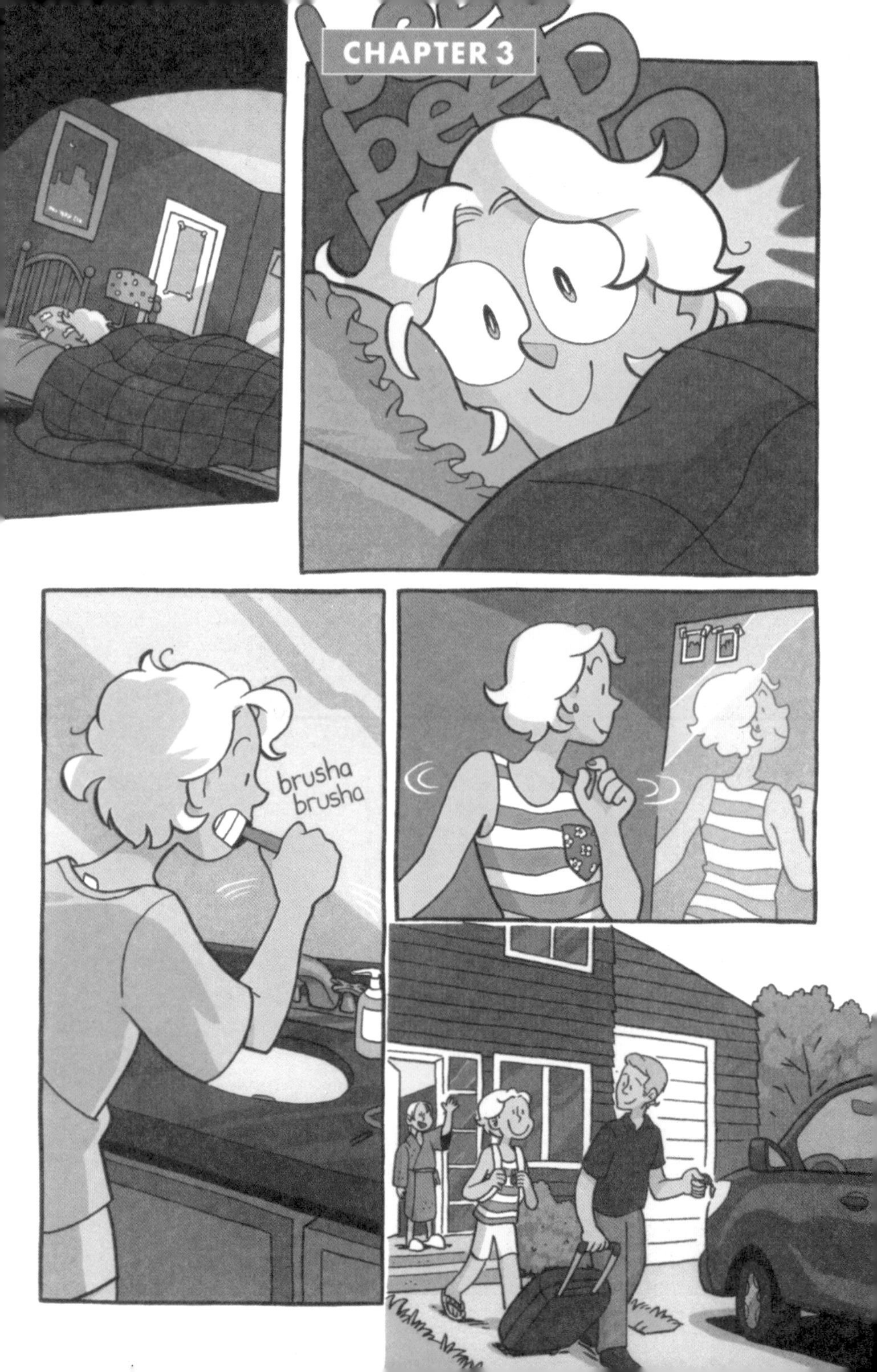
brusha
brusha

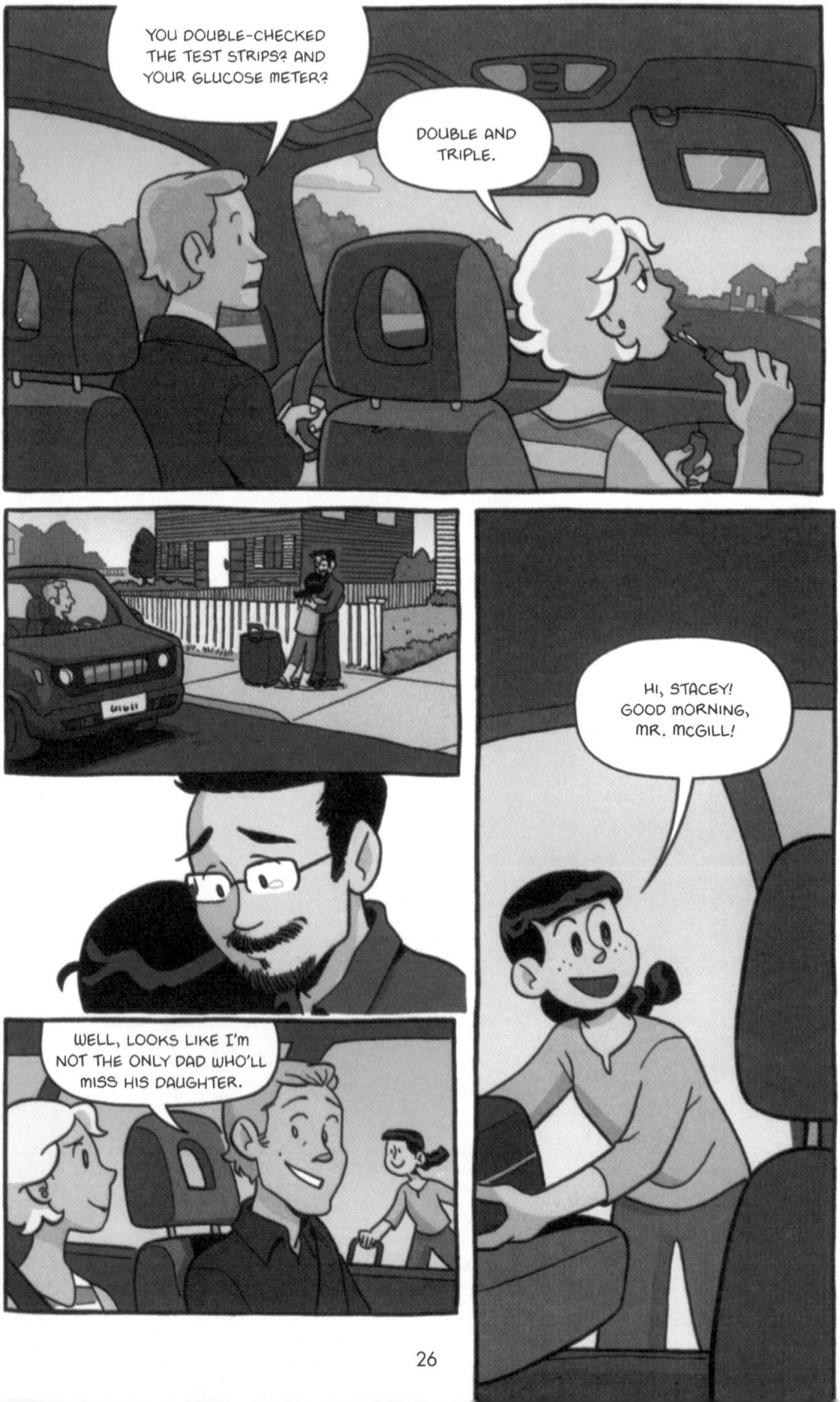
YOU DOUBLE-CHECKED THE TEST STRIPS? AND YOUR GLUCOSE METER?
DOUBLE AND TRIPLE.
HI, STACEY! GOOD MORNING, MR. MCGILL!
WELL, LOOKS LIKE I'M NOT THE ONLY DAD WHO'LL MISS HIS DAUGHTER.

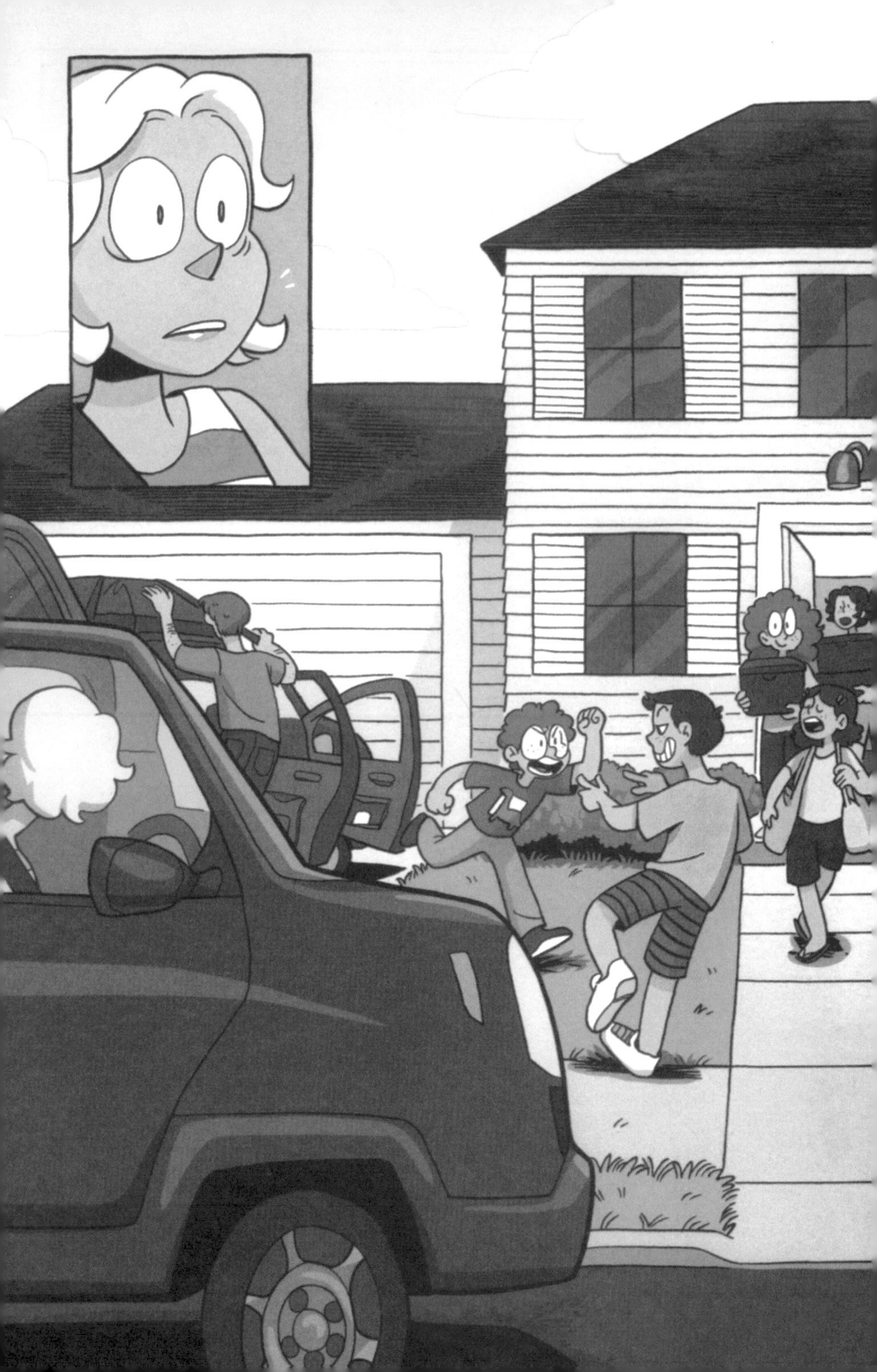

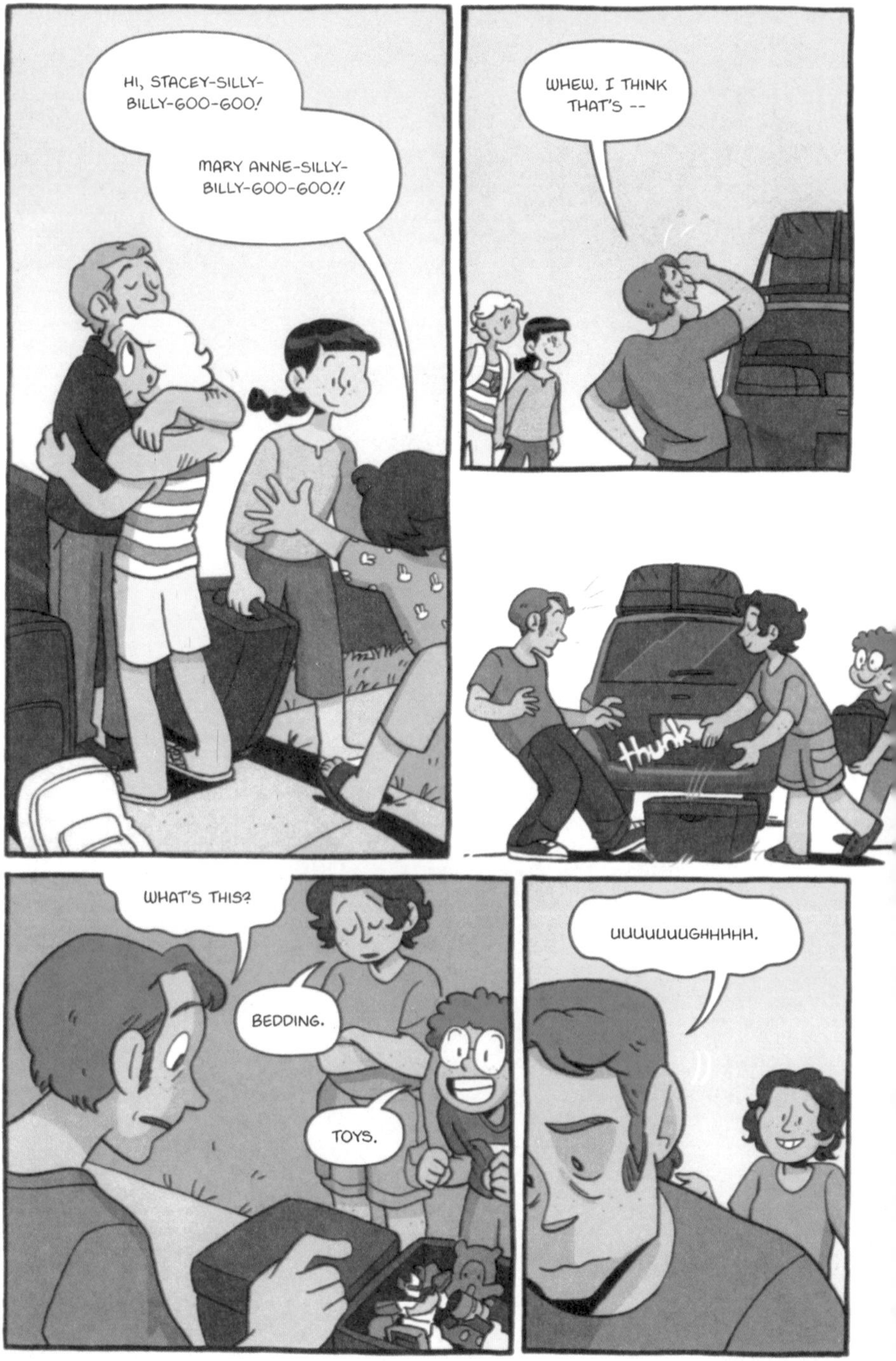
HI, STACEY-SILLY-BILLY-GOO-GOO!
MARY ANNE-SILLY-BILLY-GOO-GOO!!
WHEW. I THINK THAT'S --
thunk
WHAT'S THIS?
BEDDING.
TOYS.
UUUUUUUGHHHHH.

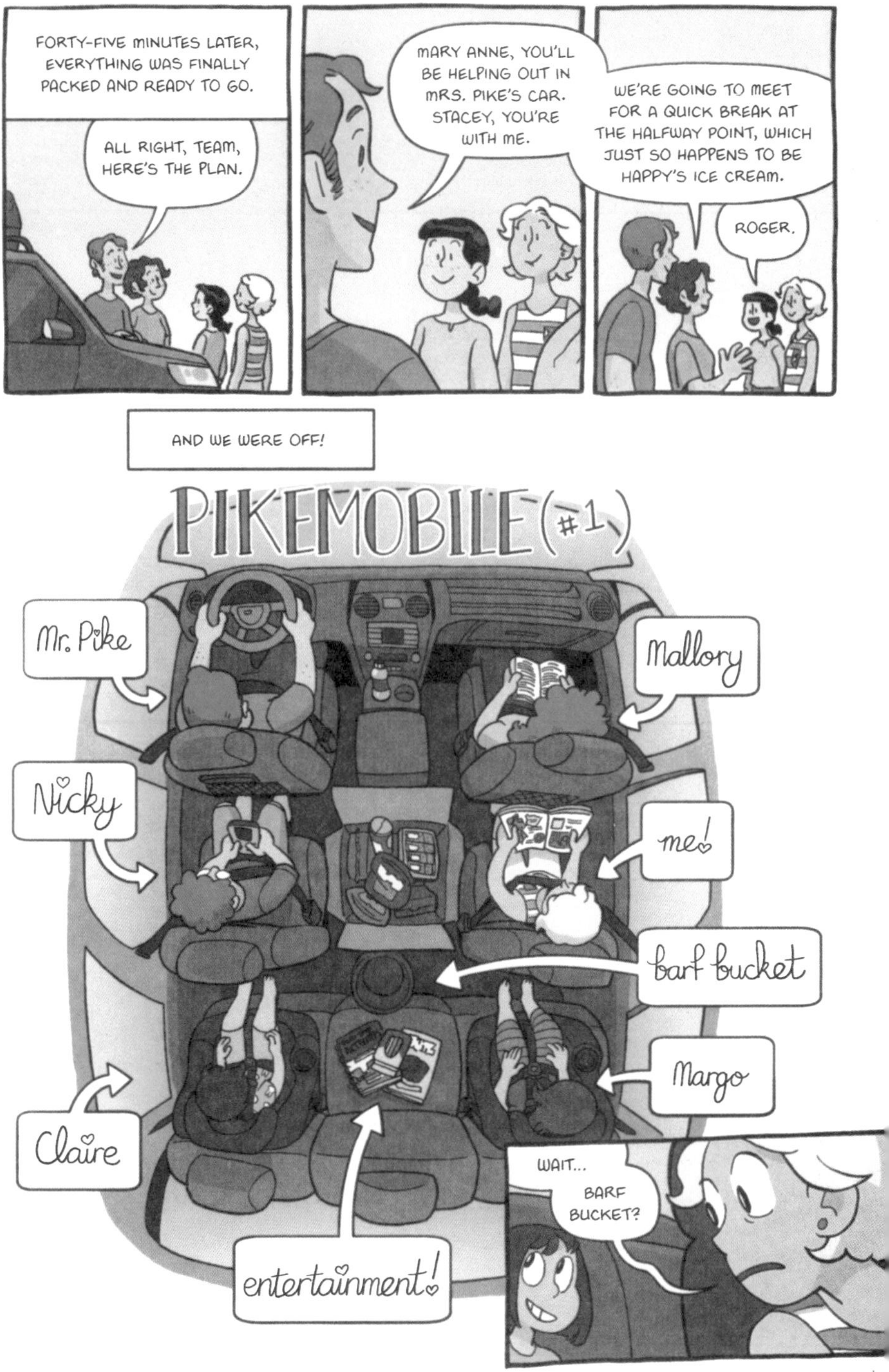
FORTY-FIVE MINUTES LATER, EVERYTHING WAS FINALLY PACKED AND READY TO GO.
ALL RIGHT, TEAM, HERE'S THE PLAN.
MARY ANNE, YOU'LL BE HELPING OUT IN MRS. PIKE'S CAR. STACEY, YOU'RE WITH ME.
WE'RE GOING TO MEET FOR A QUICK BREAK AT THE HALFWAY POINT, WHICH JUST SO HAPPENS TO BE HAPPY'S ICE CREAM.
ROGER.
AND WE WERE OFF!
PIKEMOBILE (#1)
Mr. Pike
Mallory
Nicky
me!
barf bucket
Margo
Claire
entertainment!
WAIT...
BARF BUCKET?

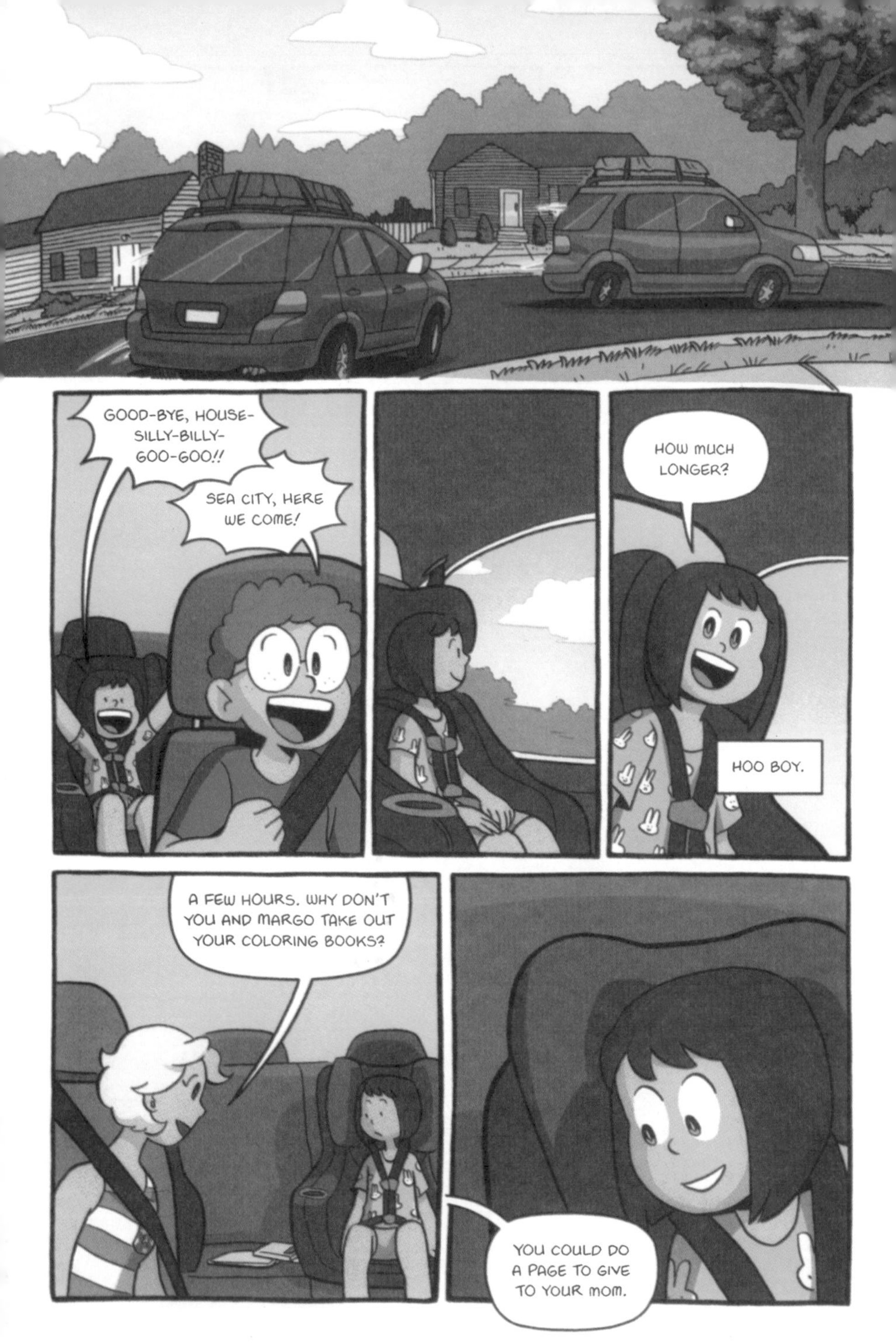
GOOD-BYE, HOUSE-SILLY-BILLY-GOO-GOO!!
SEA CITY, HERE WE COME!
HOW MUCH LONGER?
HOO BOY.
A FEW HOURS. WHY DON'T YOU AND MARGO TAKE OUT YOUR COLORING BOOKS?
YOU COULD DO A PAGE TO GIVE TO YOUR MOM.

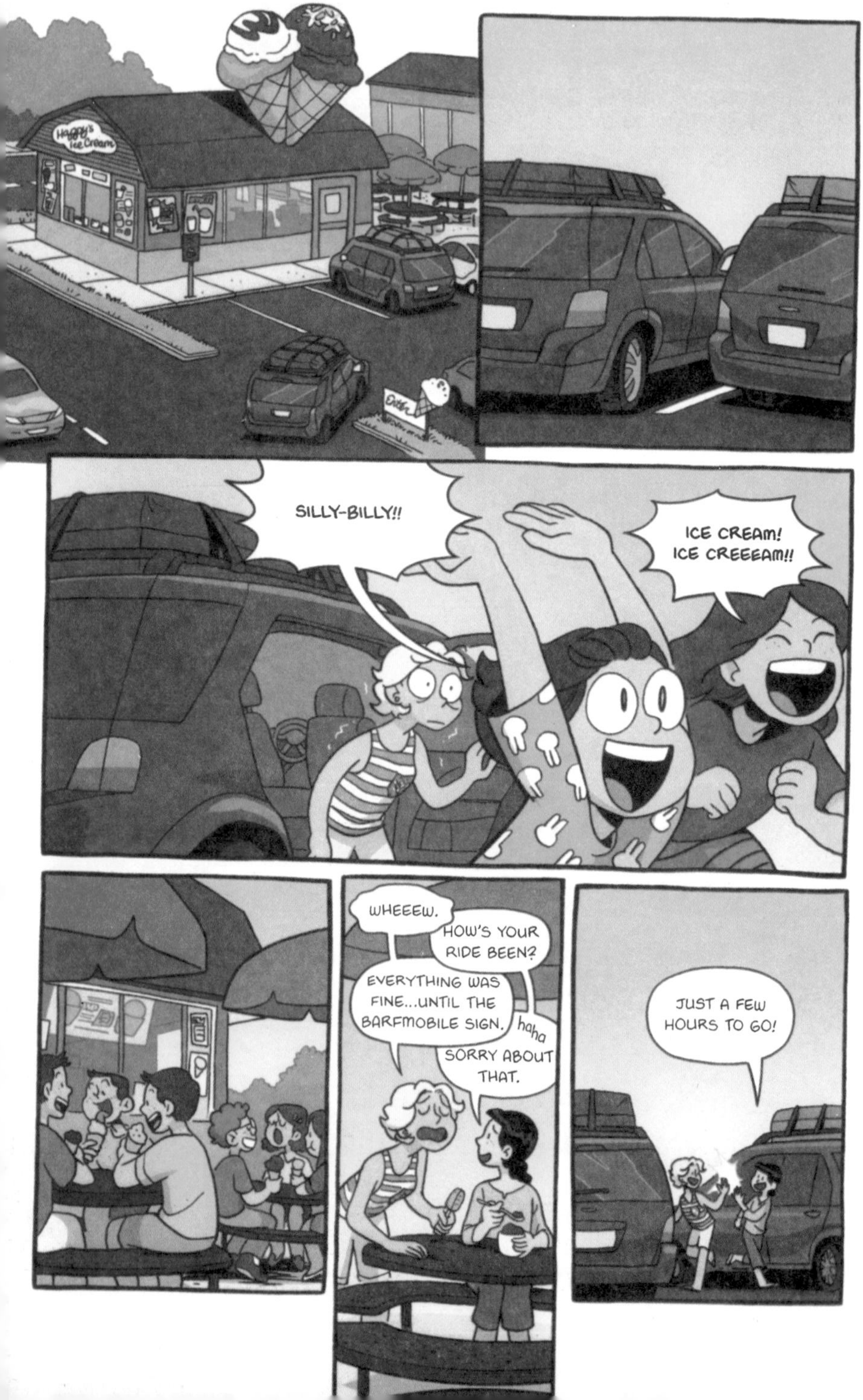
Happy's Ice Cream
SILLY-BILLY!!
ICE CREAM!
ICE CREEEAM!!
WHEEEW.
HOW'S YOUR RIDE BEEN?
EVERYTHING WAS FINE...UNTIL THE BARFMOBILE SIGN.
haha
SORRY ABOUT THAT.
JUST A FEW HOURS TO GO!

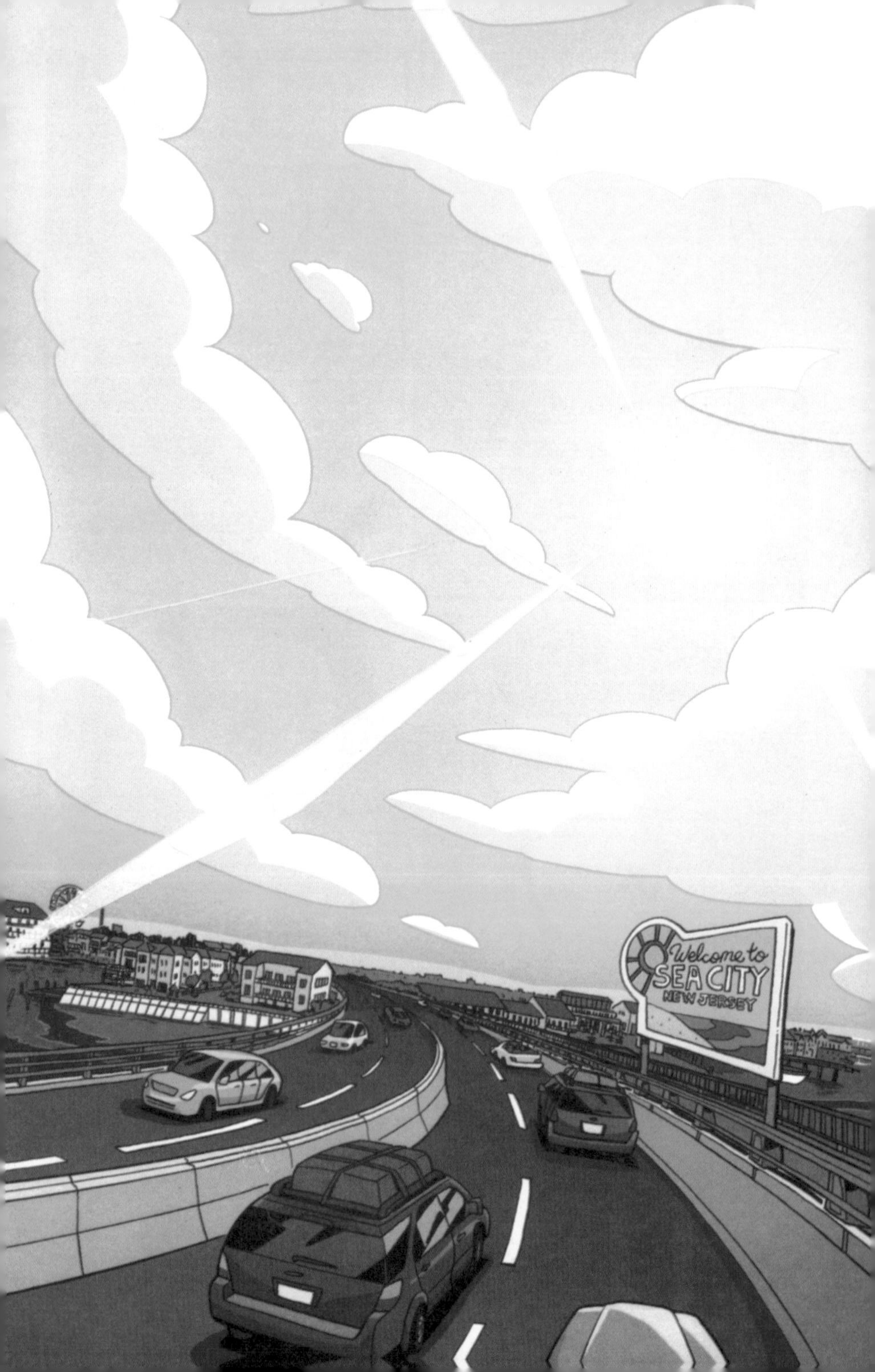
Welcome to
SEA CITY
NEW JERSEY

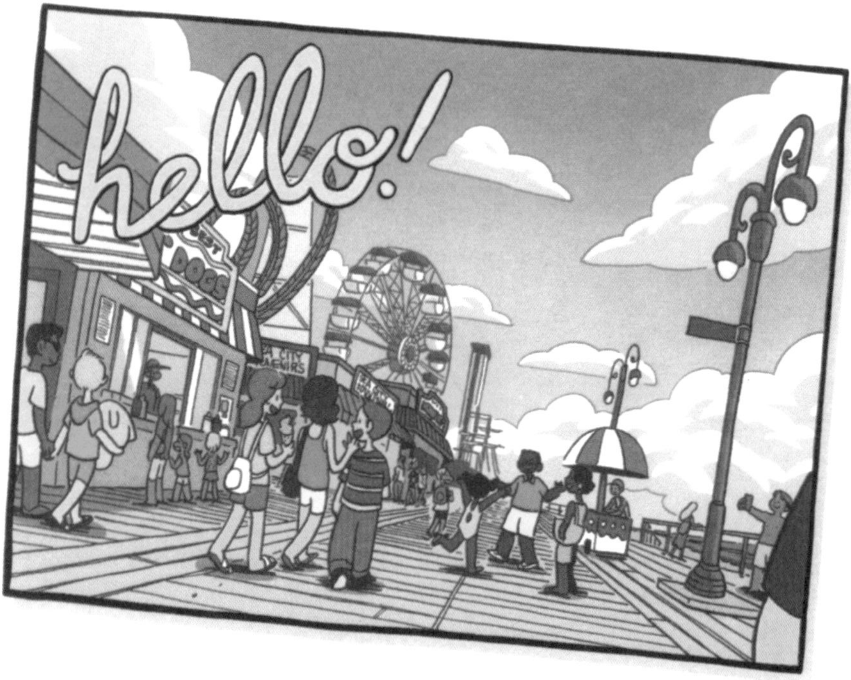
hello!
BEST
DOGS

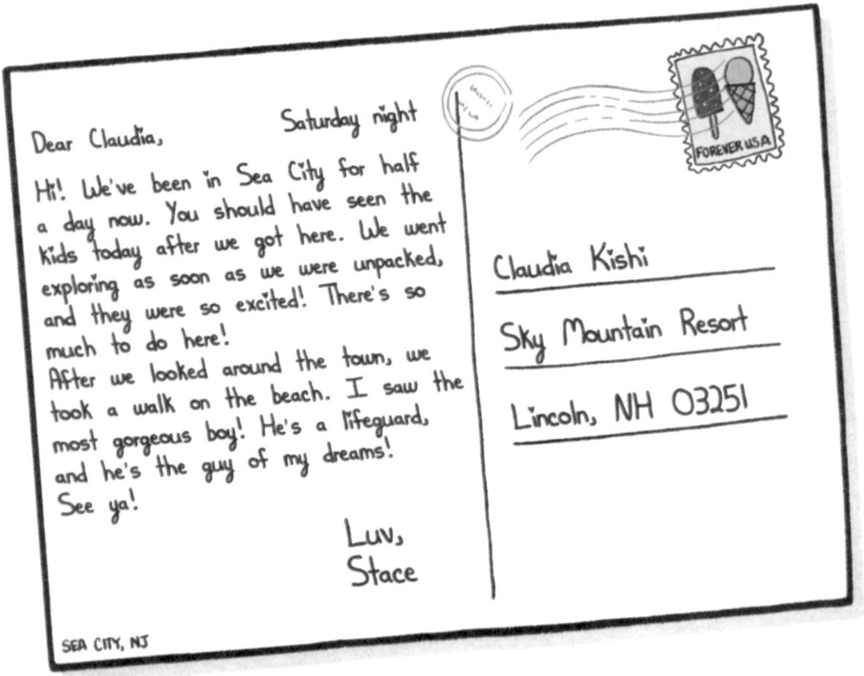

Dear Claudia,   Saturday night

Hi! We've been in Sea City for half
a day now. You should have seen the
kids today after we got here. We went
exploring as soon as we were unpacked,
and they were so excited! There's so
much to do here!
After we looked around the town, we
took a walk on the beach. I saw the
most gorgeous boy! He's a lifeguard,
and he's the guy of my dreams!
See ya!

                            Luv,
                            Stace

SEA CITY, NJ

Claudia Kishi

Sky Mountain Resort

Lincoln, NH 03251

FOREVER USA

CHAPTER 4

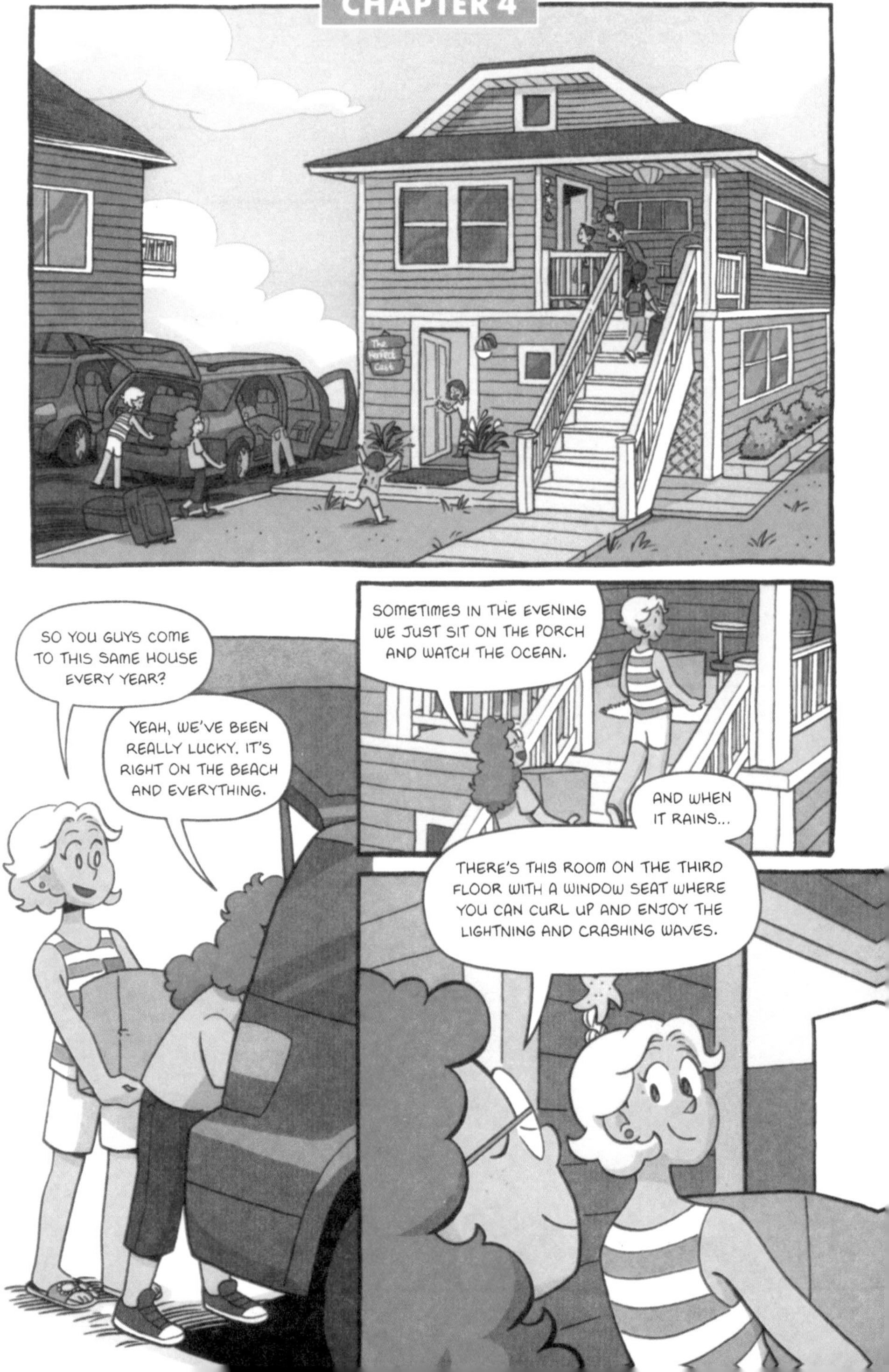
SO YOU GUYS COME TO THIS SAME HOUSE EVERY YEAR?
YEAH, WE'VE BEEN REALLY LUCKY. IT'S RIGHT ON THE BEACH AND EVERYTHING.
SOMETIMES IN THE EVENING WE JUST SIT ON THE PORCH AND WATCH THE OCEAN.
AND WHEN IT RAINS...
THERE'S THIS ROOM ON THE THIRD FLOOR WITH A WINDOW SEAT WHERE YOU CAN CURL UP AND ENJOY THE LIGHTNING AND CRASHING WAVES.

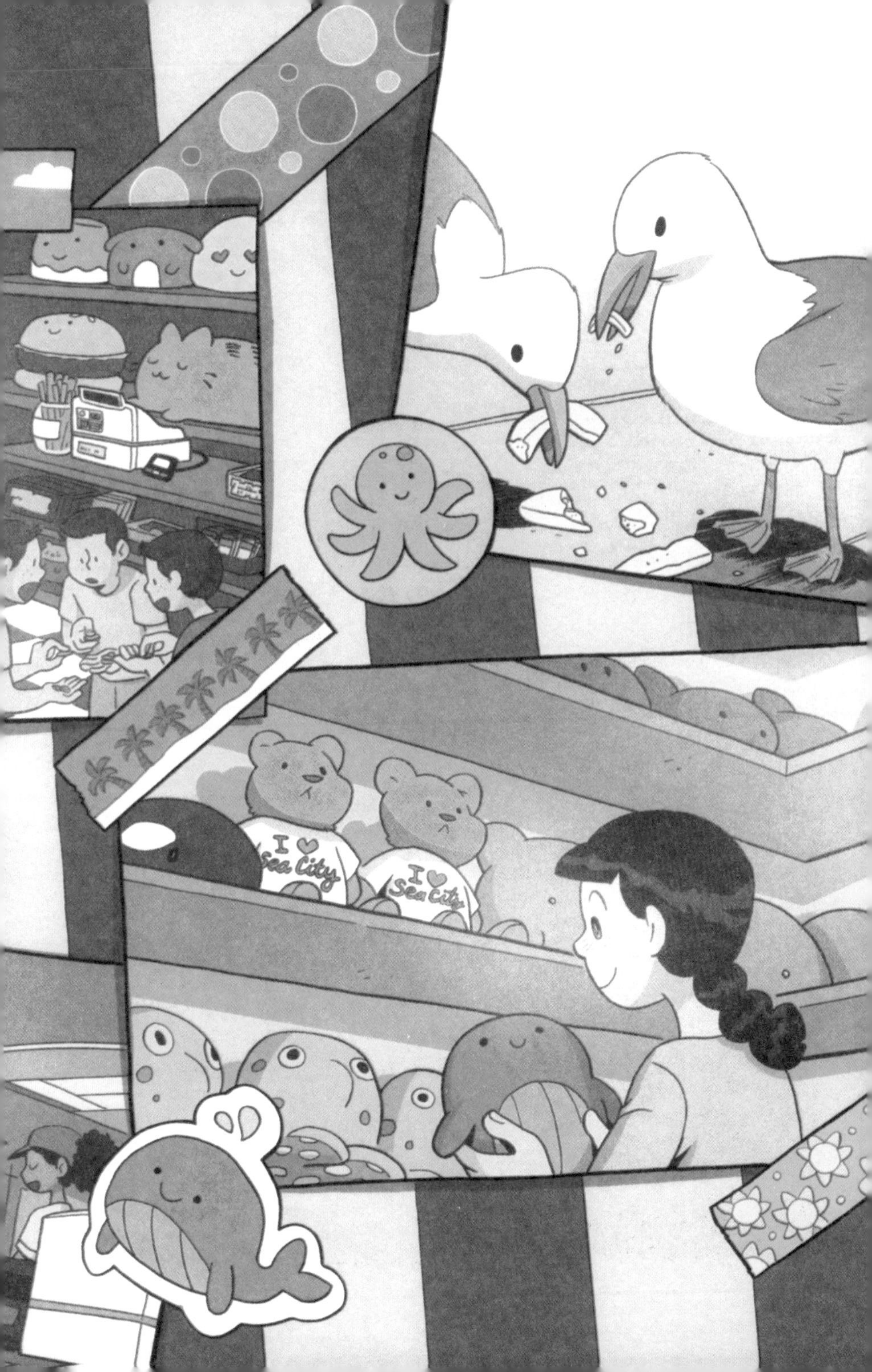
I ♥ Sea City
I ♥ Sea City

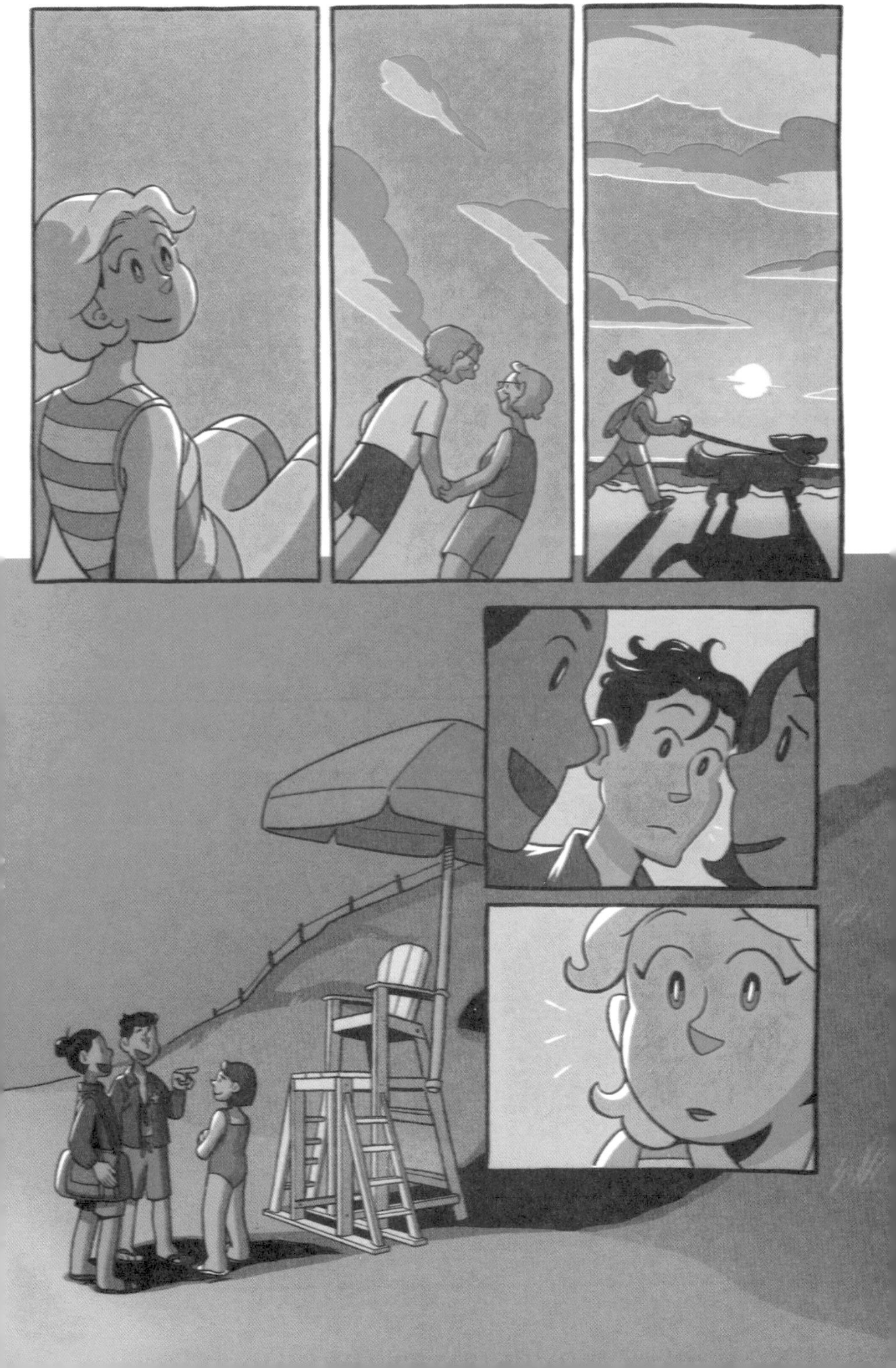

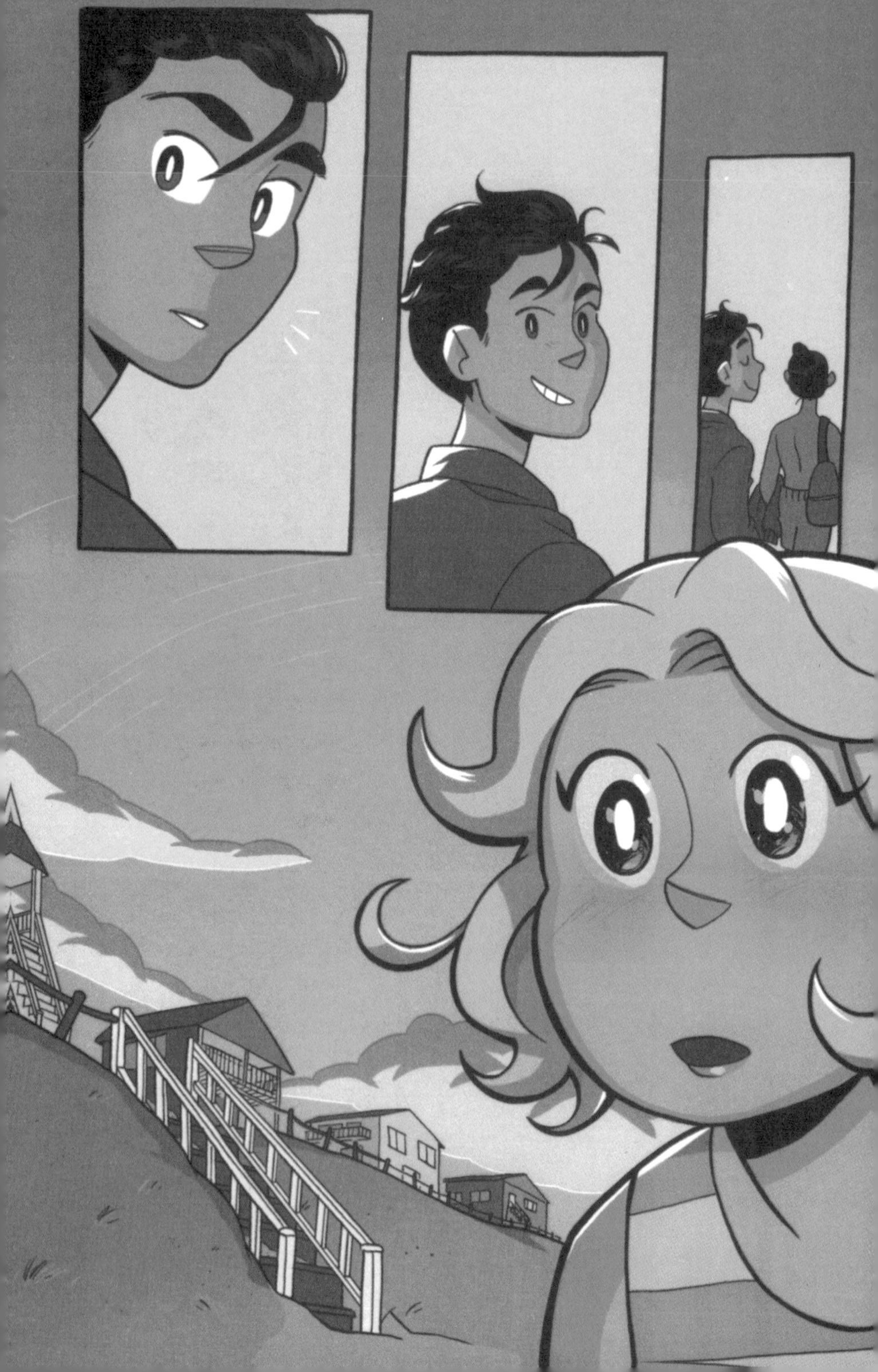

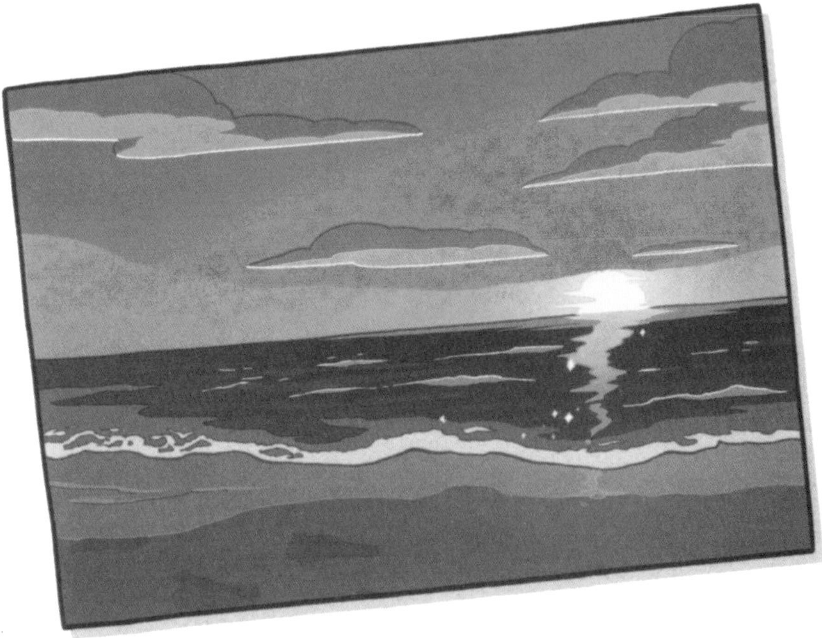

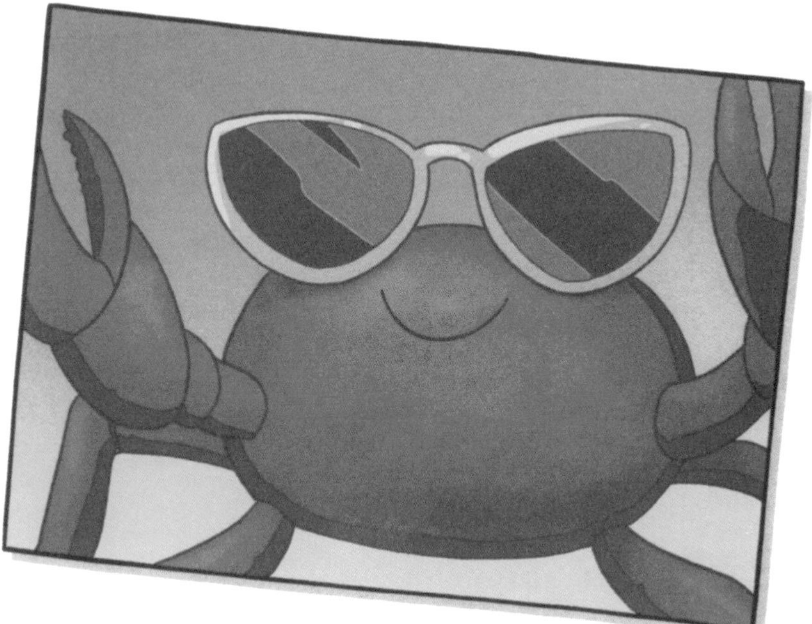

POSTCARD

Dear Kristy,

Sunday

Here's something for the notebook:
Pikes get up early. See ya!

Stacey

Kristy Thomas

1210 McLelland Rd.

Stoneybrook, CT 06800

Dear Claudia,

Sunday

Today I found out that gooorgeous lifeguard's name. It's SCOTT!! I can't wait to see him again.

Luv,
Stace

P.S. I can't let Mary Anne see this card. She doesn't understand about Scott at all. She thinks I've lost it.

Claudia Kishi

Sky Mountain Resort

Lincoln, NH 03251

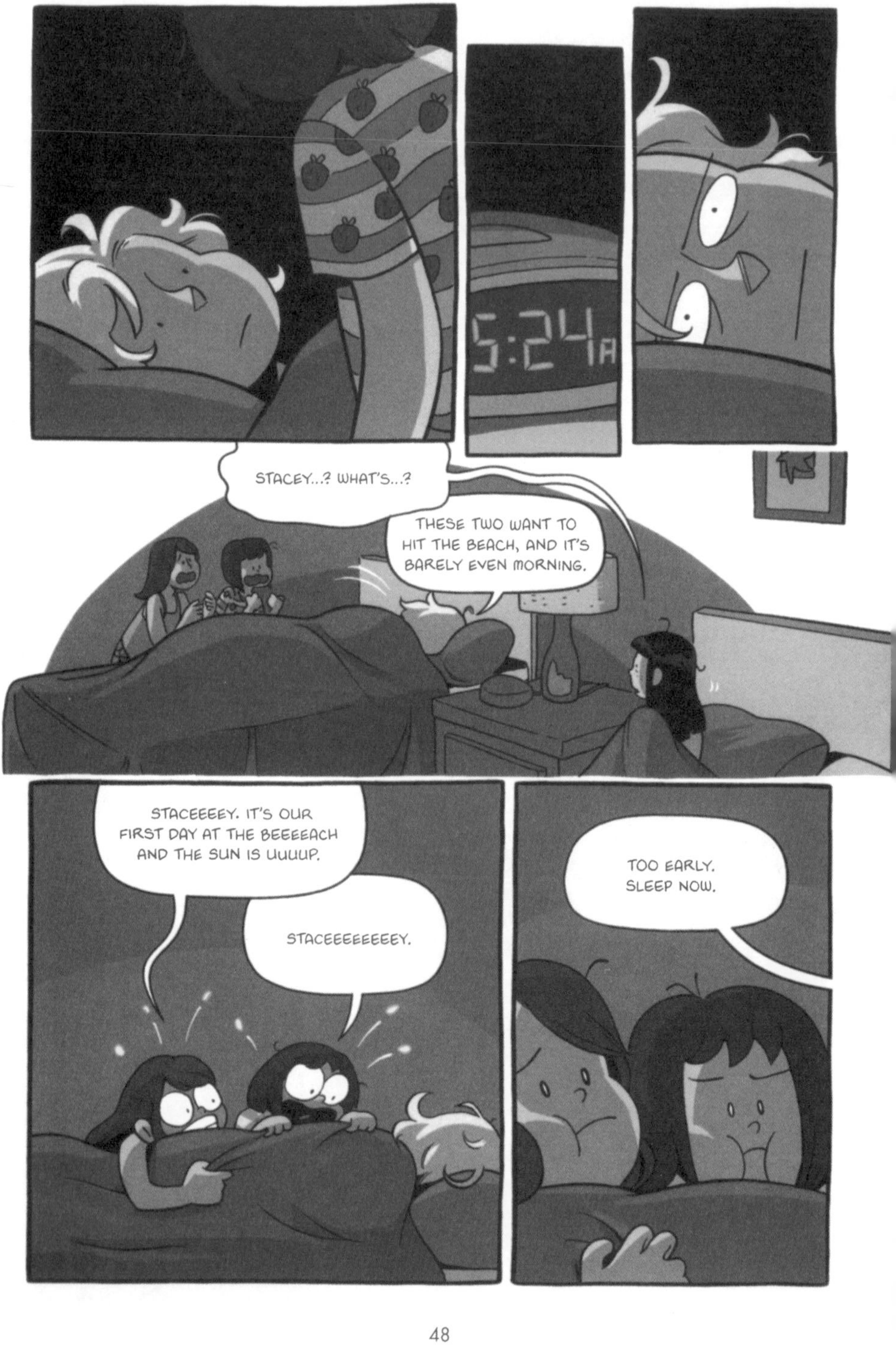
5:24 A
STACEY...? WHAT'S...?
THESE TWO WANT TO HIT THE BEACH, AND IT'S BARELY EVEN MORNING.
STACEEEEY. IT'S OUR FIRST DAY AT THE BEEEEACH AND THE SUN IS UUUUP.
STACEEEEEEEEY.
TOO EARLY. SLEEP NOW.

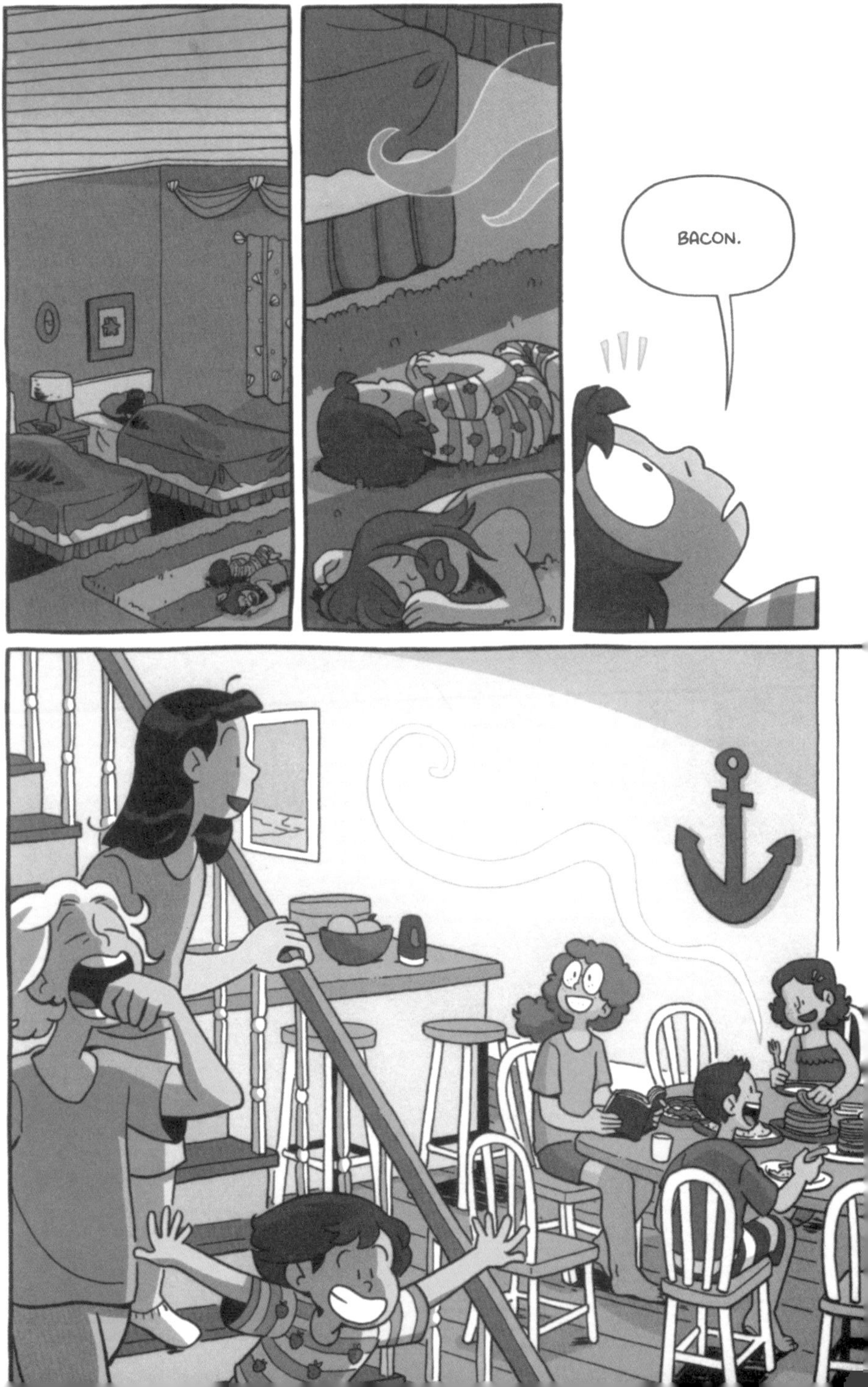
BACON.

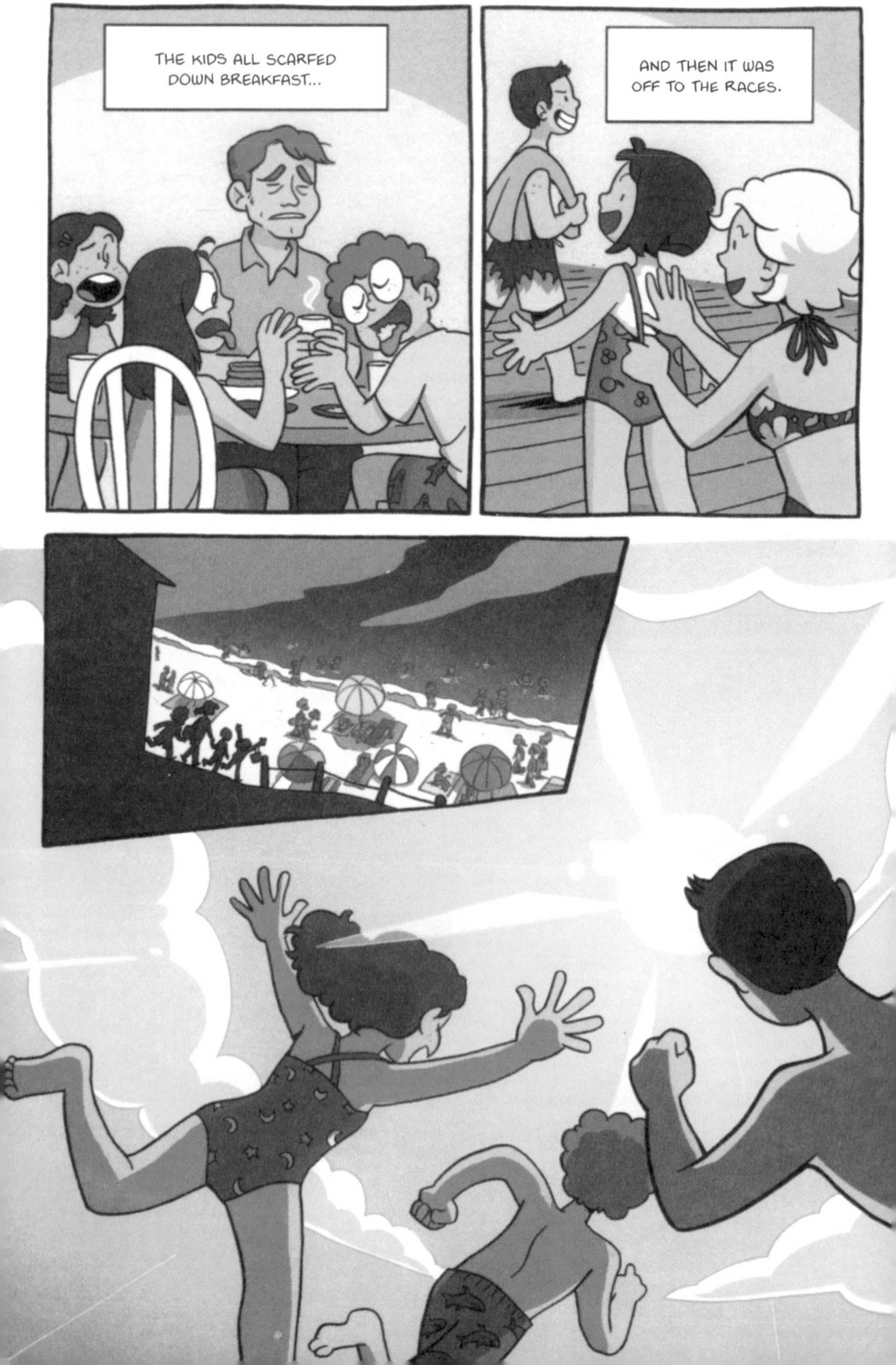
THE KIDS ALL SCARFED DOWN BREAKFAST...
AND THEN IT WAS OFF TO THE RACES.

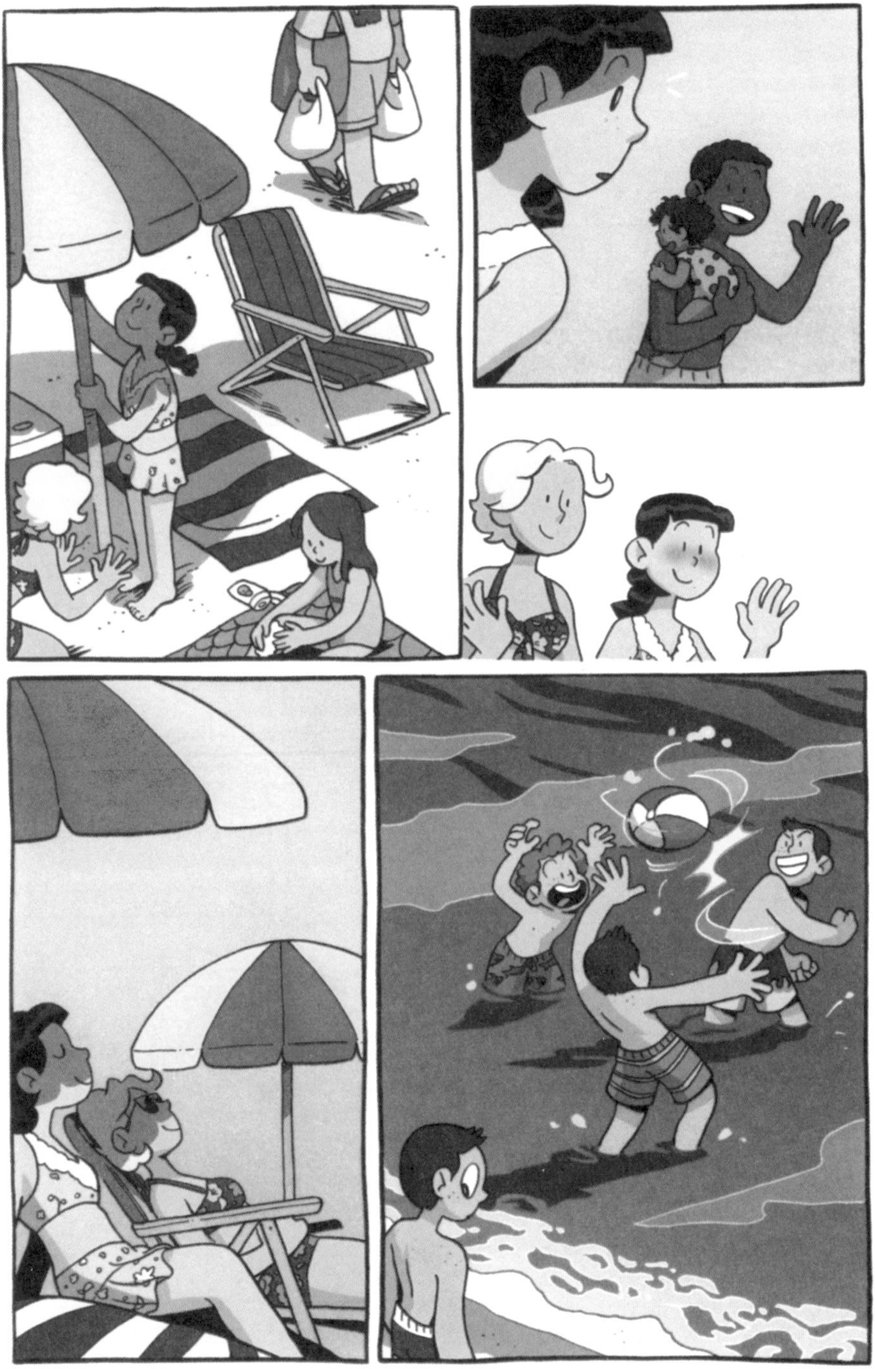

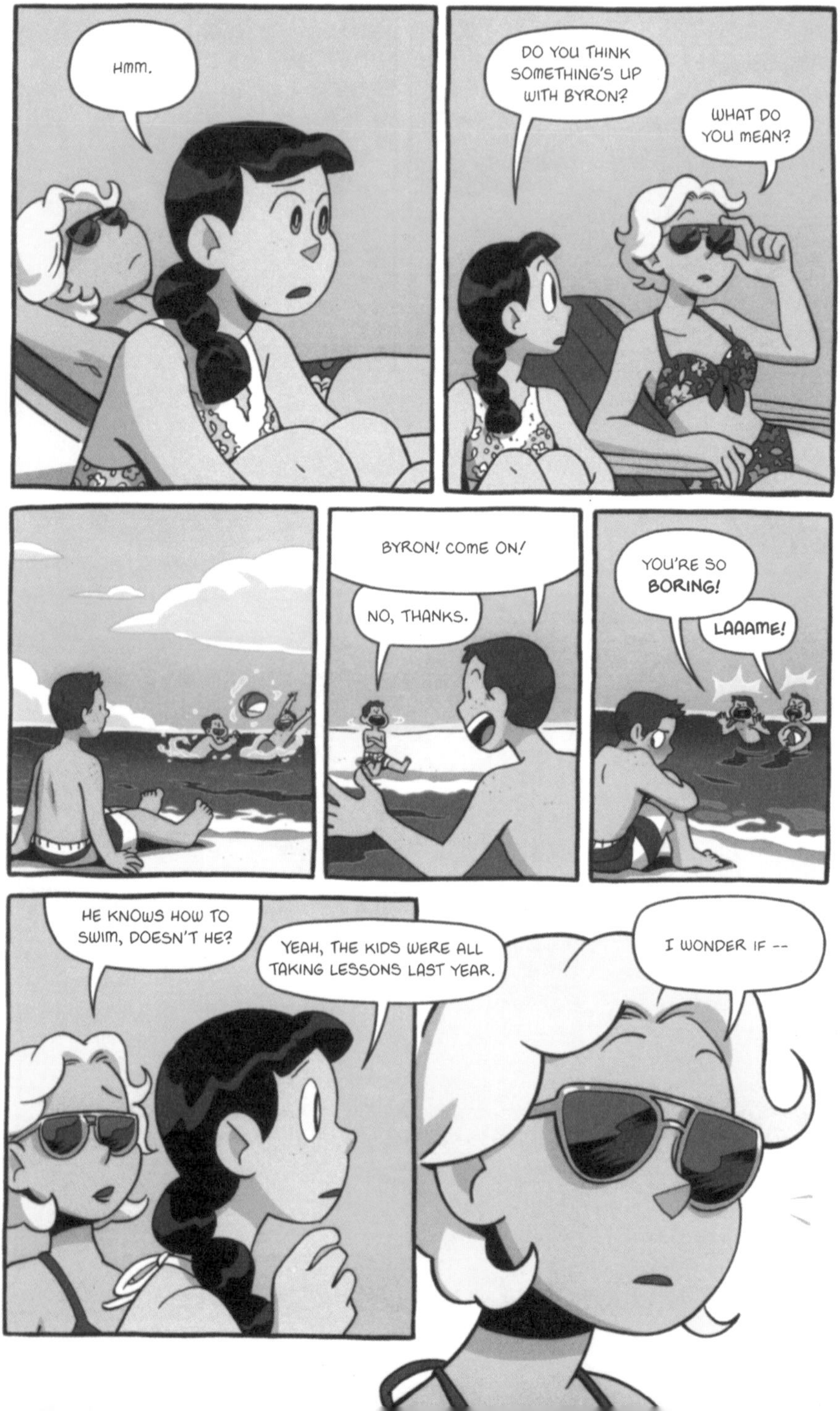
HMM.
DO YOU THINK SOMETHING'S UP WITH BYRON?
WHAT DO YOU MEAN?
BYRON! COME ON!
NO, THANKS.
YOU'RE SO **BORING!**
LAAAME!
HE KNOWS HOW TO SWIM, DOESN'T HE?
YEAH, THE KIDS WERE ALL TAKING LESSONS LAST YEAR.
I WONDER IF --

WHO DECIDED THAT YOU TRIPLETS **HAD** TO GO INTO THE WATER?

WHAT ABOUT WHAT BYRON WANTS TO DO?

WELL...I MEAN... IT'S THE **BEACH!**

AND IS THE BEACH MADE OF JUST WAT...

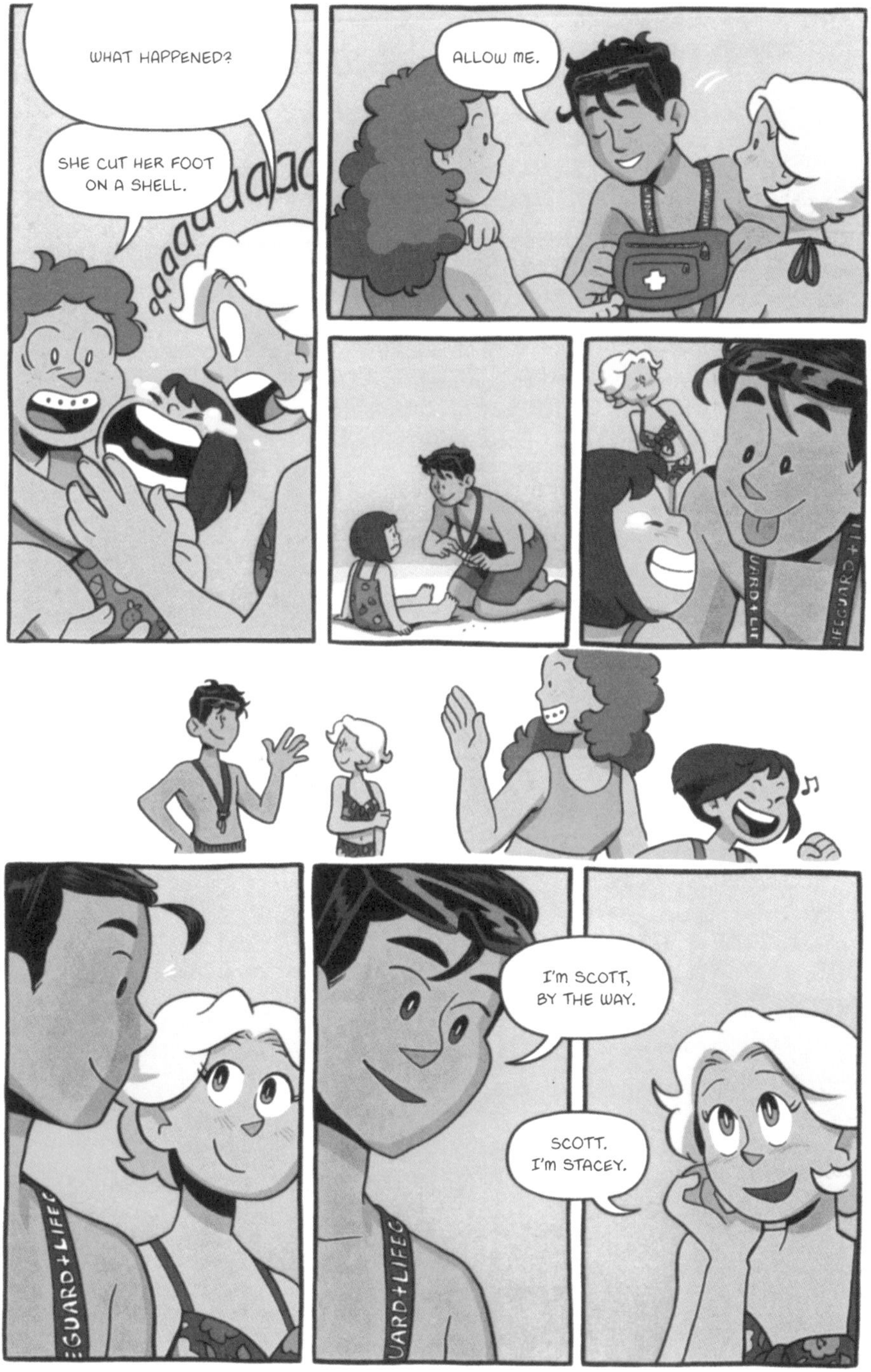
WHAT HAPPENED?
SHE CUT HER FOOT ON A SHELL.
ALLOW ME.
I'M SCOTT, BY THE WAY.
SCOTT. I'M STACEY.

IT LOOKED LIKE ADAM WAS GOING TO SPIKE THE BALL RIGHT AT ME, BUT THEN --

I BACKED INTO THIS BIG THING OF SEAWEED!

I'M GOING FOR A QUICK WALK.

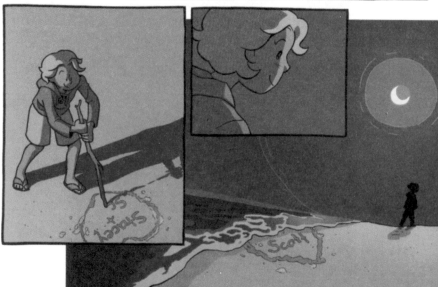

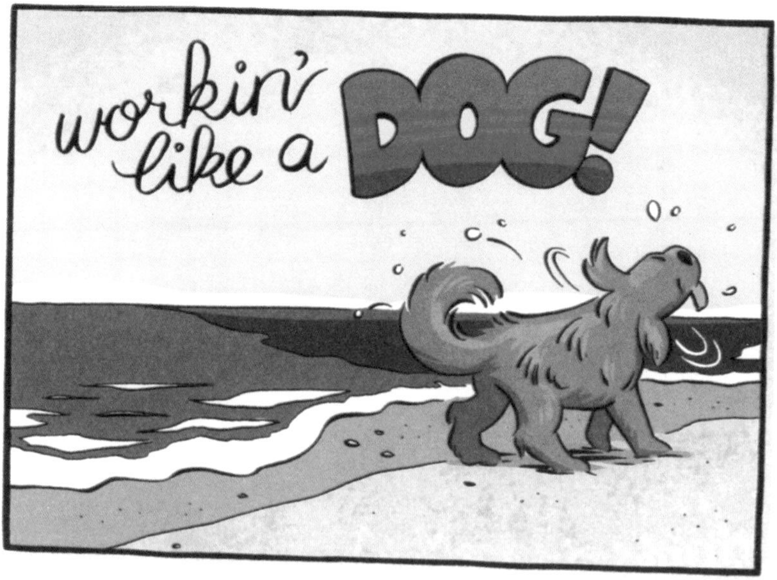
workin' like a DOG!

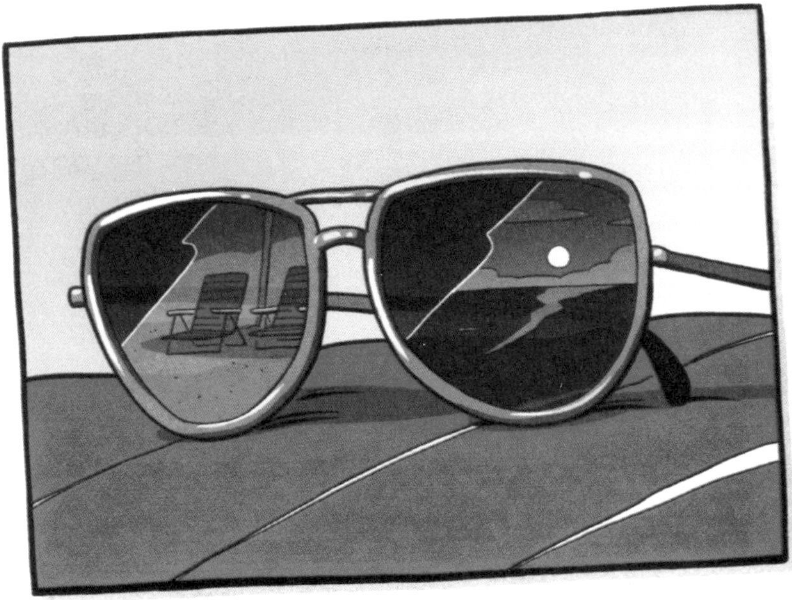

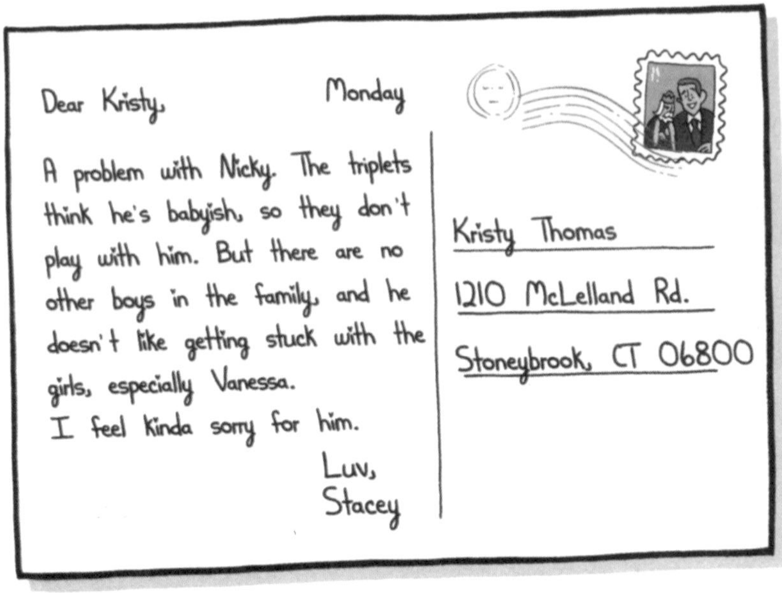

Dear Kristy, Monday

A problem with Nicky. The triplets think he's babyish, so they don't play with him. But there are no other boys in the family, and he doesn't like getting stuck with the girls, especially Vanessa.
I feel kinda sorry for him.

Luv,
Stacey

Kristy Thomas
1210 McLelland Rd.
Stoneybrook, CT 06800

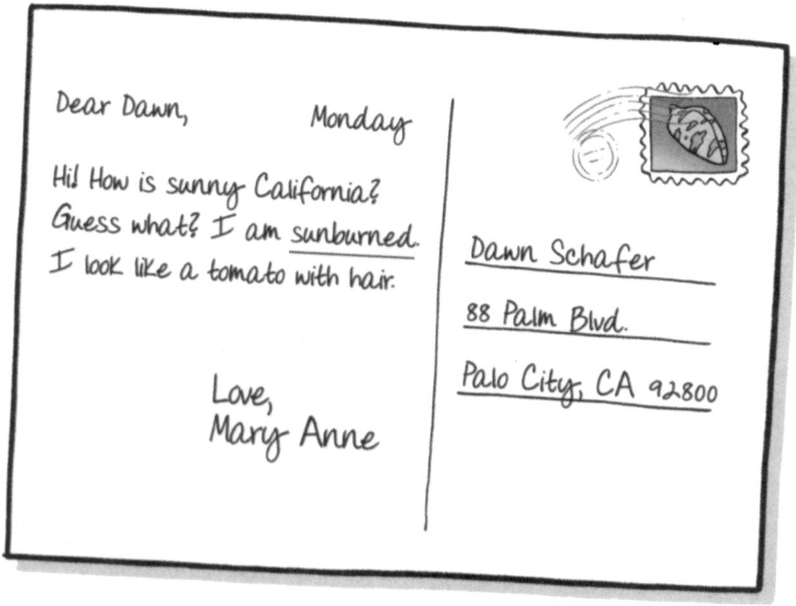

Dear Dawn, Monday

Hi! How is sunny California? Guess what? I am sunburned. I look like a tomato with hair.

Love,
Mary Anne

Dawn Schafer
88 Palm Blvd.
Palo City, CA 92800

CHAPTER 6

SCOTT WAS OFF DUTY THE NEXT DAY, BUT I COULDN'T STOP THINKING ABOUT HIM.

sigh

HE SEEMED HAPPY WHENEVER I CAME BY TO TALK TO HIM. DID THAT MEAN HE LIKED ME?

sigh

OR WAS I TOO OBVIOUS? WHAT IF SCOTT THOUGHT I WAS TRYING TOO HARD??

sighhh

THE WHOLE DAY WENT BY IN A HAZE, BUT THEN...

STACEY? MARY ANNE?

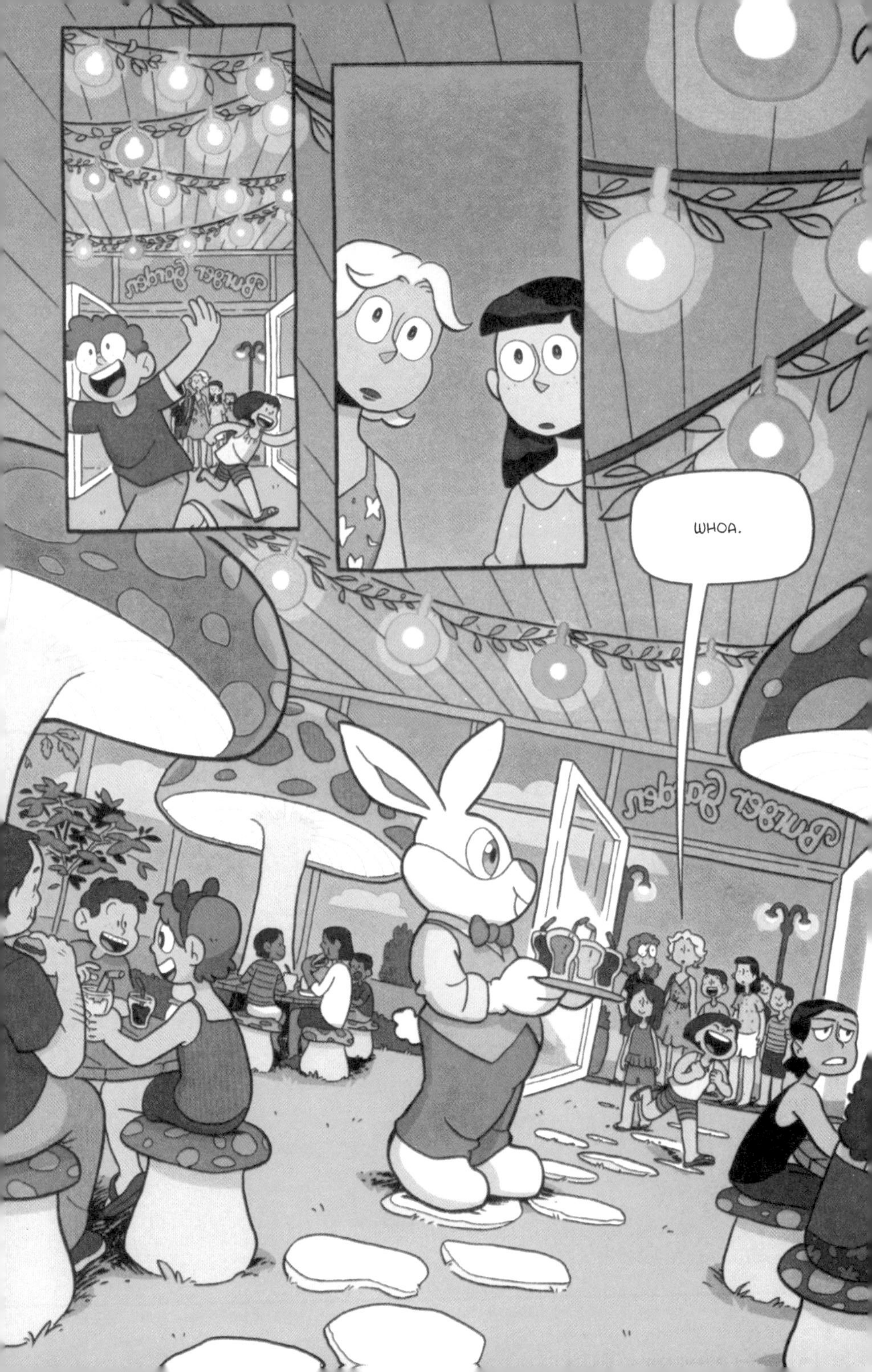
WHOA.

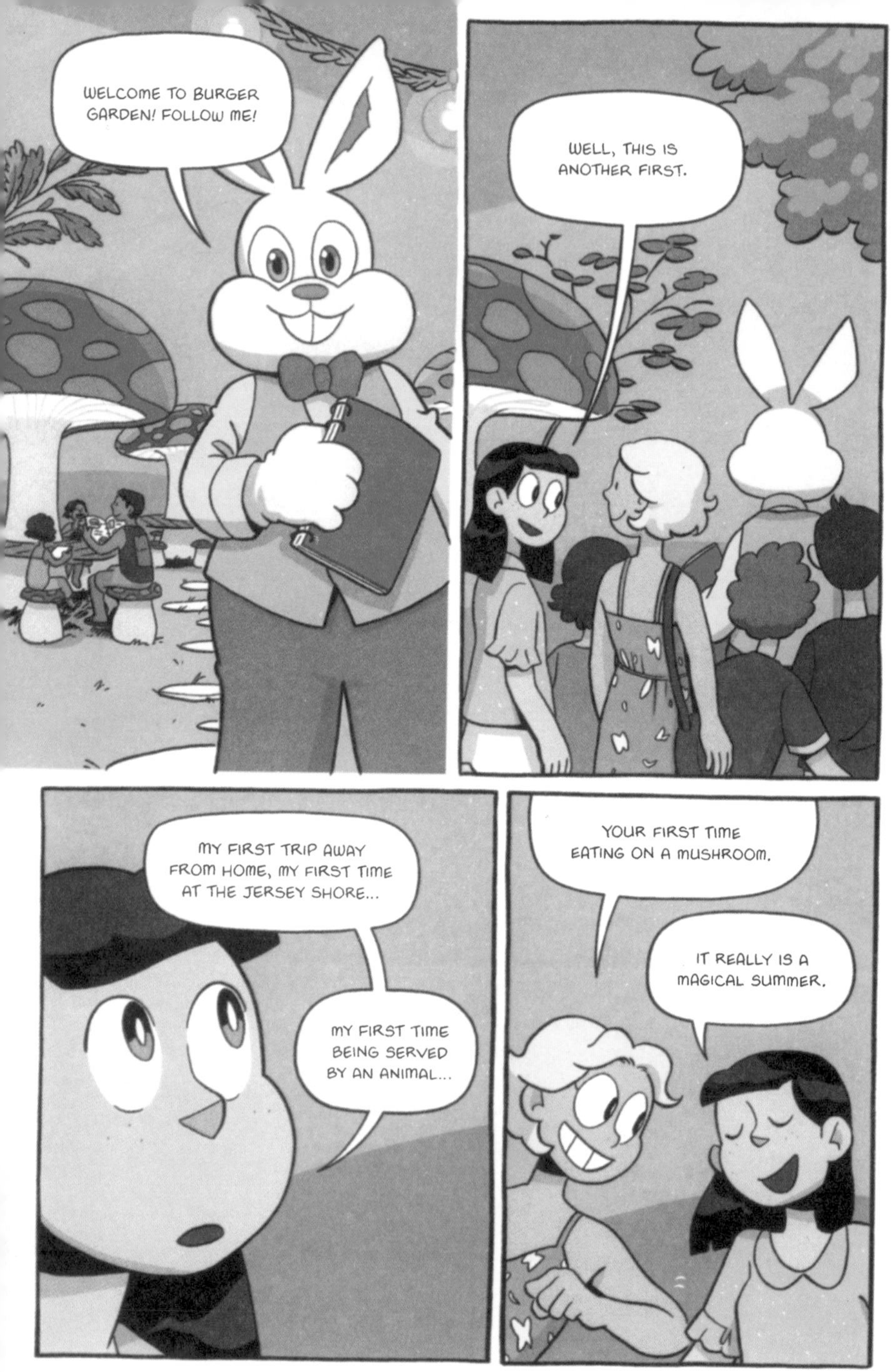
WELCOME TO BURGER GARDEN! FOLLOW ME!
WELL, THIS IS ANOTHER FIRST.
MY FIRST TRIP AWAY FROM HOME, MY FIRST TIME AT THE JERSEY SHORE...
MY FIRST TIME BEING SERVED BY AN ANIMAL...
YOUR FIRST TIME EATING ON A MUSHROOM.
IT REALLY IS A MAGICAL SUMMER.

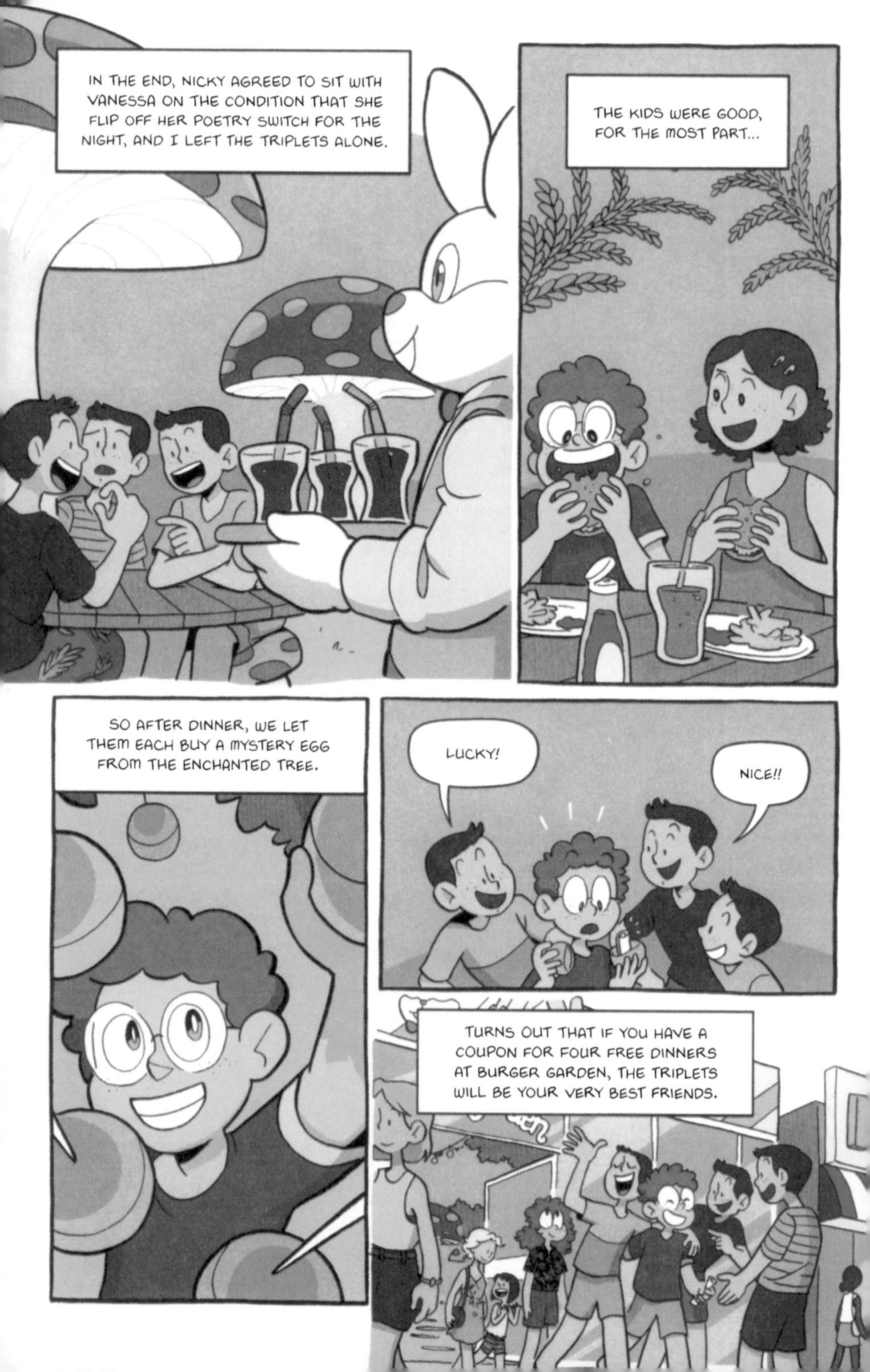
IN THE END, NICKY AGREED TO SIT WITH VANESSA ON THE CONDITION THAT SHE FLIP OFF HER POETRY SWITCH FOR THE NIGHT, AND I LEFT THE TRIPLETS ALONE.
THE KIDS WERE GOOD, FOR THE MOST PART...
SO AFTER DINNER, WE LET THEM EACH BUY A MYSTERY EGG FROM THE ENCHANTED TREE.
LUCKY!
NICE!!
TURNS OUT THAT IF YOU HAVE A COUPON FOR FOUR FREE DINNERS AT BURGER GARDEN, THE TRIPLETS WILL BE YOUR VERY BEST FRIENDS.

ONE HOUR LATER, WE ALL MET BACK UP AT ICE CREAM PALACE.

OKAY. I'M NOT GOING TO HAVE ANY ICE CREAM, SO THAT MEANS THERE'S ENOUGH FOR ONE SCOOP FOR EACH OF YOU.

AND SPRINKLES.

I'M NOT GOING TO HAVE ANY, EITHER, SO THERE'S A LITTLE EXTRA.

OH. WAIT, ARE YOU FEELING OKAY? YOU LOOK KIND OF FUNNY.

I DON'T KNOW. I FEEL HOT ON THE OUTSIDE, BUT...CHILLY?

OH MY GOSH.

YOU'RE SUNBURNED!!

NOOOOOOOOO.

WE GOT MARY ANNE SOME ICE CREAM TO COOL HER DOWN...

AND THEN OUR SECOND BEACH DAY CAME TO A CLOSE.

WHAT DID I DO TO DESERVE THISSSSS.

MARY ANNE?

I BROUGHT YOU SOMETHING.

WE ALL DID.

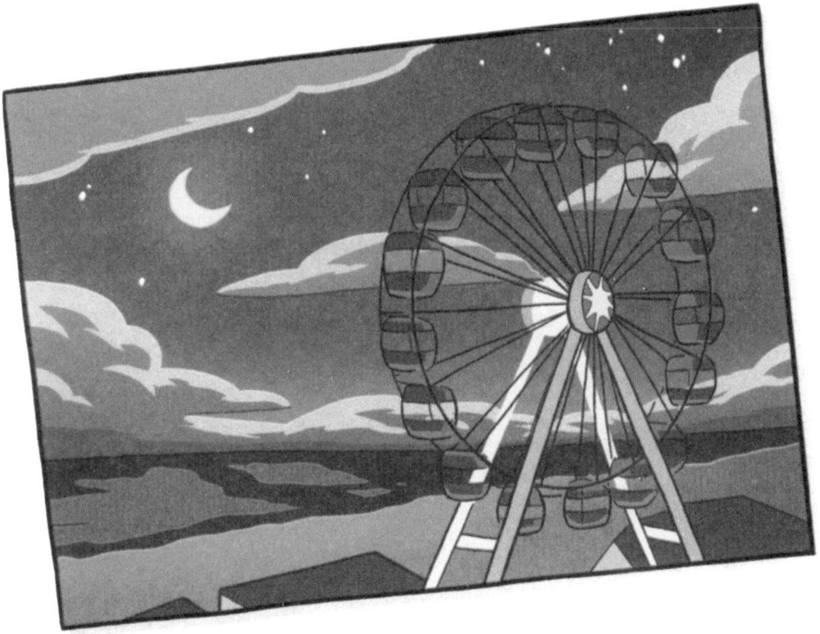

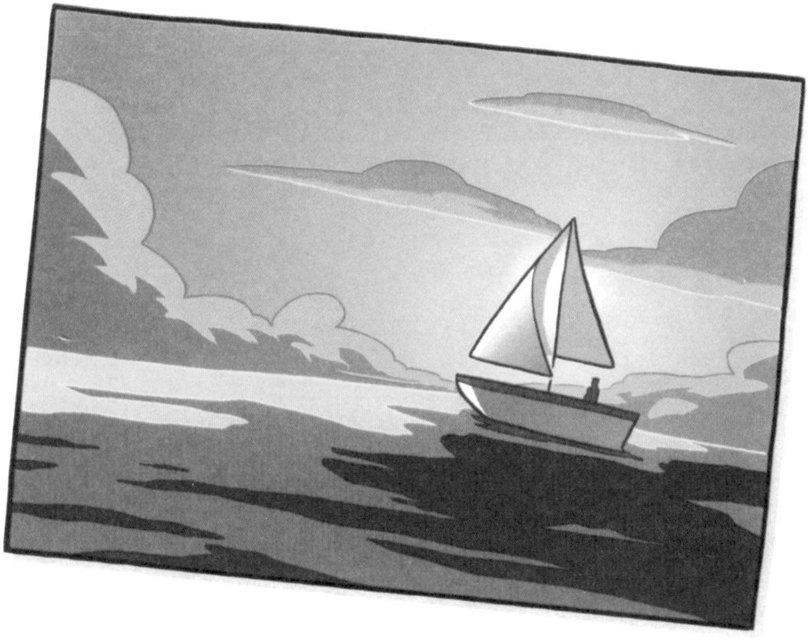

Dear Claudia,   Tuesday

I know I'm supposed to be
baby-sitting, but Scott was on
duty today and he's all I can
think of. He said the sweetest
thing when I went to say
good-bye for the day... I can't
wait to tell you all about it. Say
hi to Mimi!

                    Luv,
                    Stace

P.S. Mary Anne thinks I'm
overthinking it. She doesn't understand.

Claudia Kishi

Sky Mountain Resort

Lincoln, NH 03251

Dear Kristy,   Tuesday

I'd never have suspected it, but
Byron has a lot of fears. He's
afraid to go in the ocean (even
though he can swim), and last
night when we went to the
amusement park on the boardwalk,
he wouldn't go through the
haunted house. We'll have to talk
about this.

                    Luv,
                    Stacey

Kristy Thomas

1210 McLelland Rd.

Stoneybrook, CT 06800

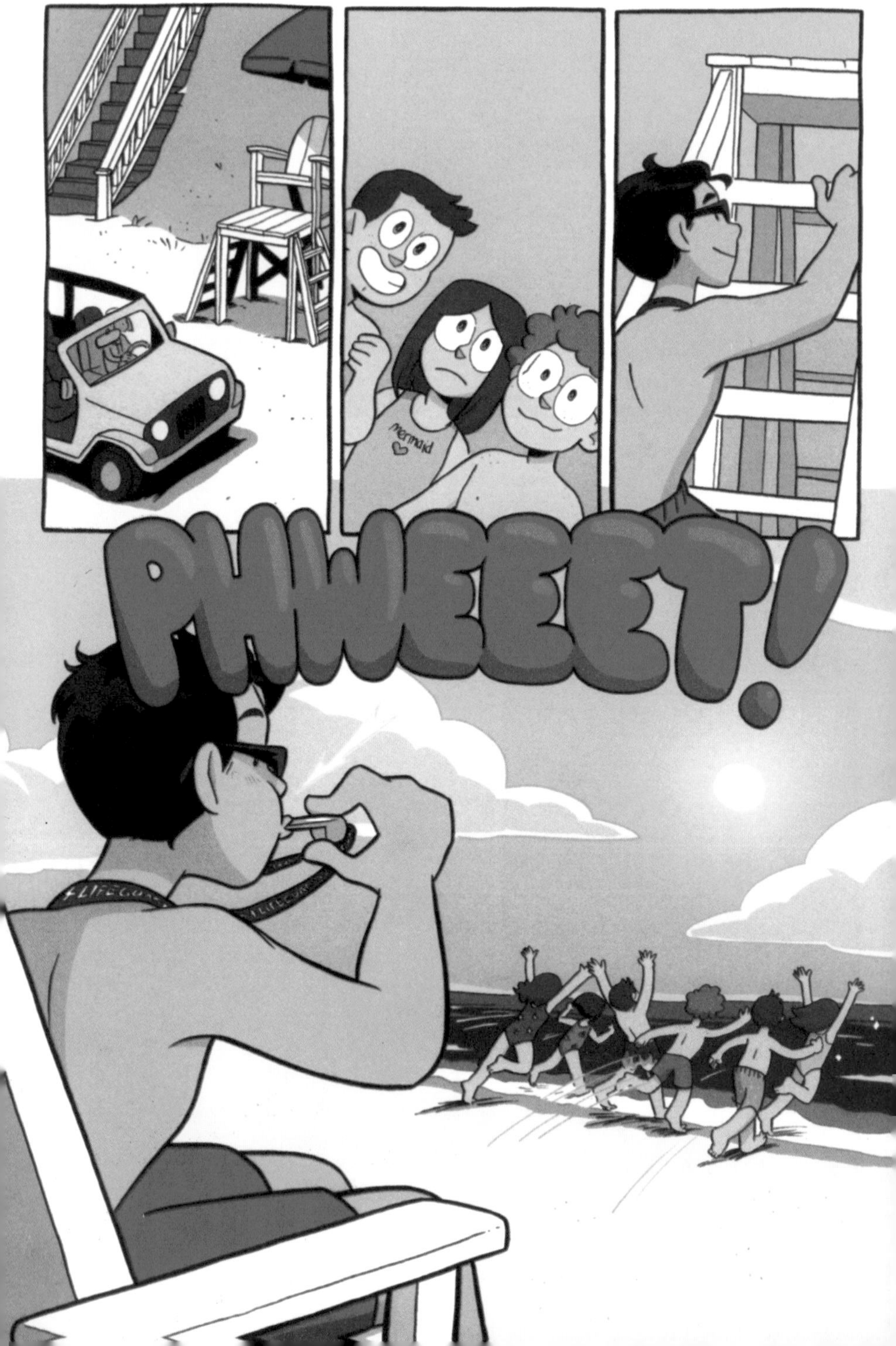
mermaid
PHWEEET!

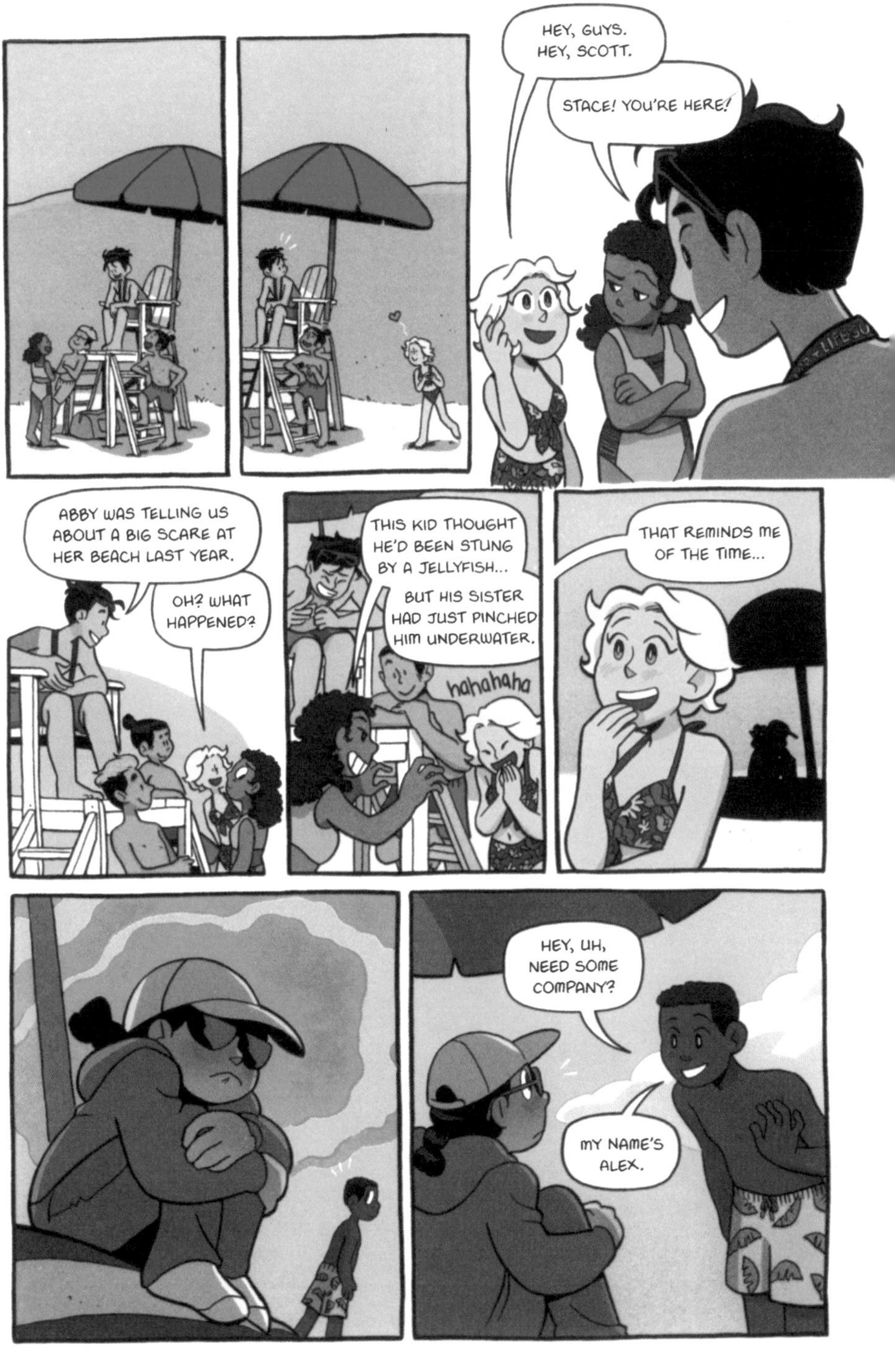
HEY, GUYS.
HEY, SCOTT.
STACE! YOU'RE HERE!
ABBY WAS TELLING US ABOUT A BIG SCARE AT HER BEACH LAST YEAR.
OH? WHAT HAPPENED?
THIS KID THOUGHT HE'D BEEN STUNG BY A JELLYFISH...
BUT HIS SISTER HAD JUST PINCHED HIM UNDERWATER.
hahahaha
THAT REMINDS ME OF THE TIME...
HEY, UH, NEED SOME COMPANY?
MY NAME'S ALEX.

78

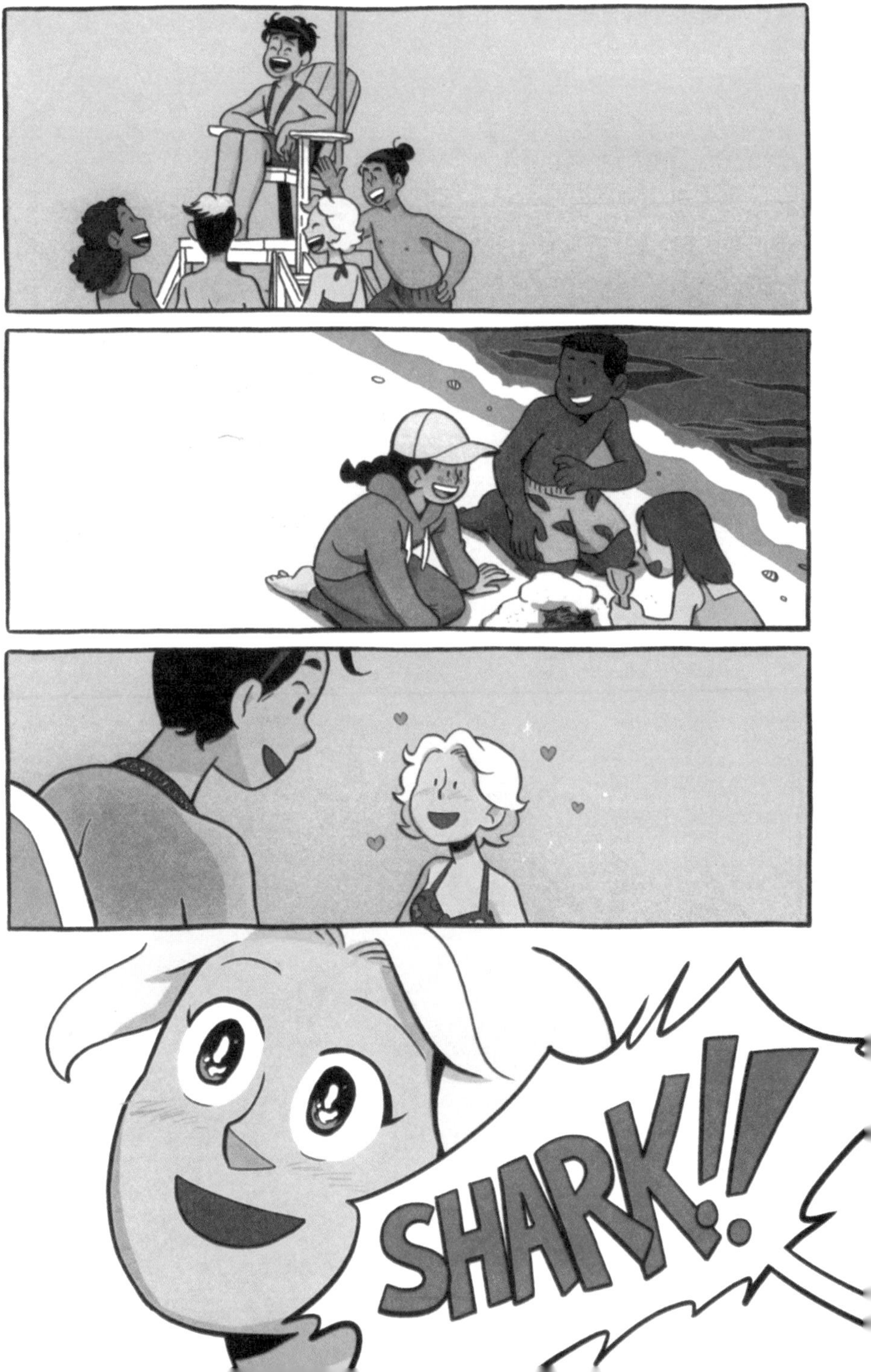
SHARK!!

80

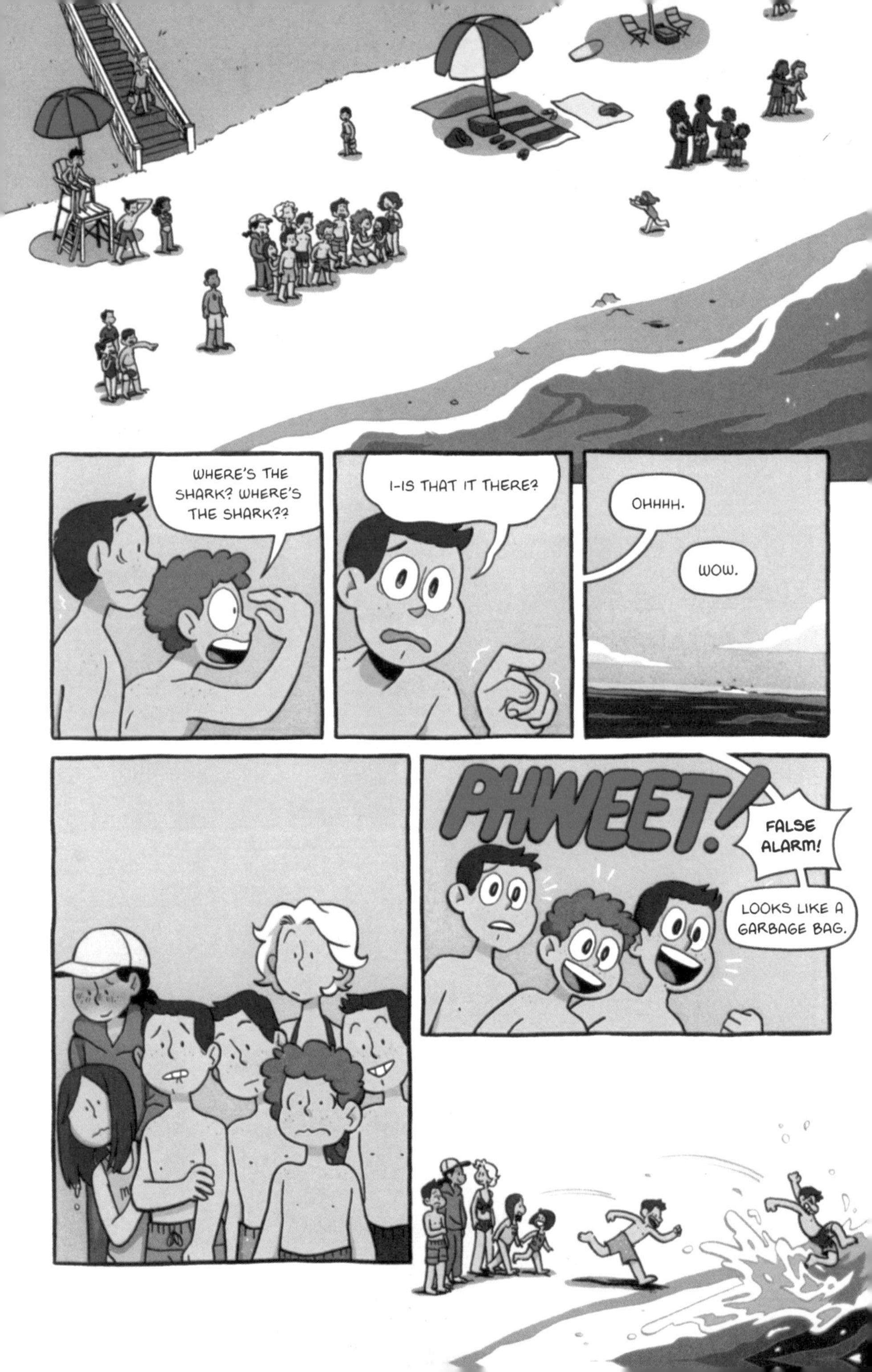
WHERE'S THE SHARK? WHERE'S THE SHARK??
I-IS THAT IT THERE?
OHHHH.
WOW.
PHWEET!
FALSE ALARM!
LOOKS LIKE A GARBAGE BAG.

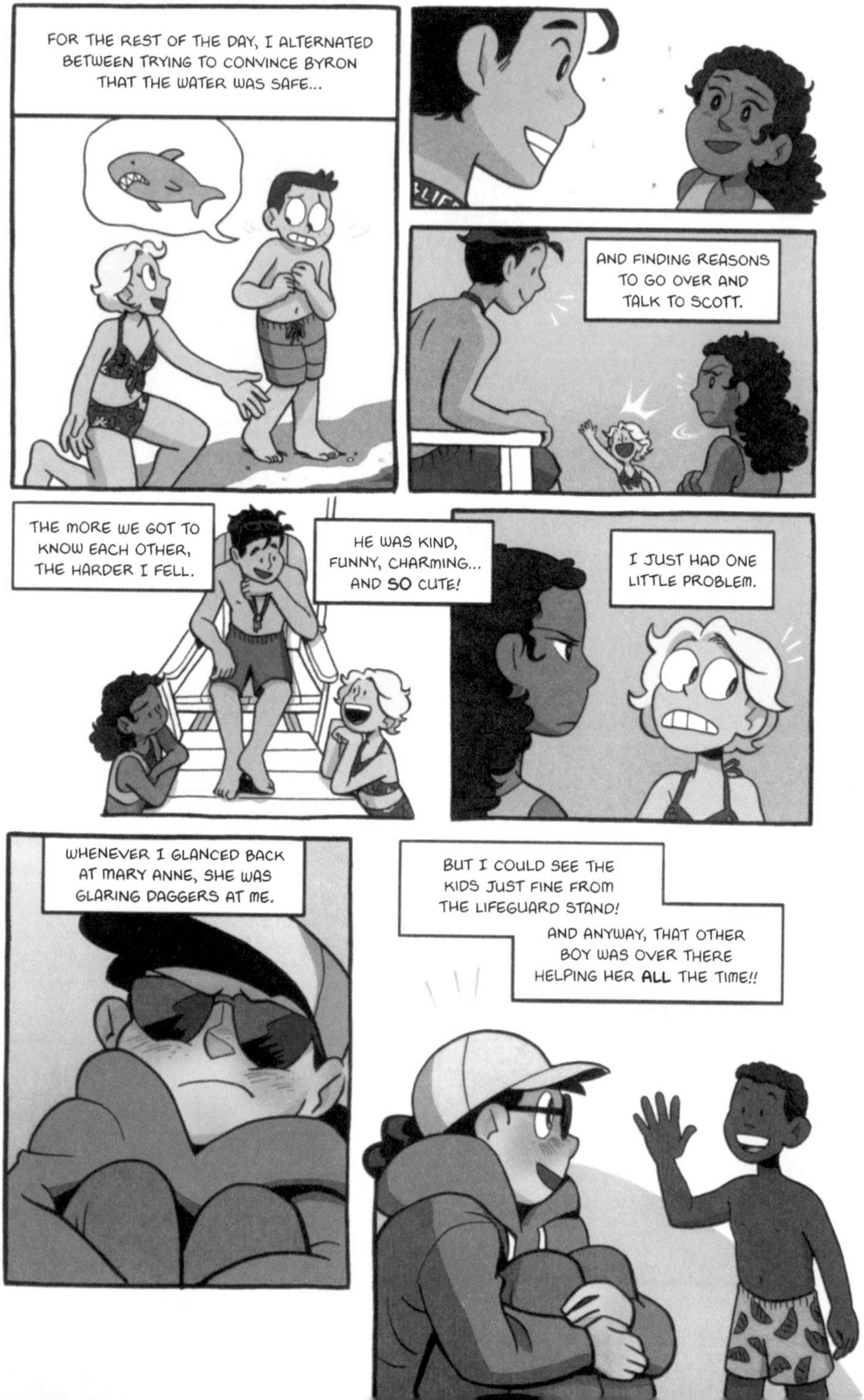

FOR THE REST OF THE DAY, I ALTERNATED BETWEEN TRYING TO CONVINCE BYRON THAT THE WATER WAS SAFE...
AND FINDING REASONS TO GO OVER AND TALK TO SCOTT.
THE MORE WE GOT TO KNOW EACH OTHER, THE HARDER I FELL.
HE WAS KIND, FUNNY, CHARMING... AND SO CUTE!
I JUST HAD ONE LITTLE PROBLEM.
WHENEVER I GLANCED BACK AT MARY ANNE, SHE WAS GLARING DAGGERS AT ME.
BUT I COULD SEE THE KIDS JUST FINE FROM THE LIFEGUARD STAND!
AND ANYWAY, THAT OTHER BOY WAS OVER THERE HELPING HER ALL THE TIME!!

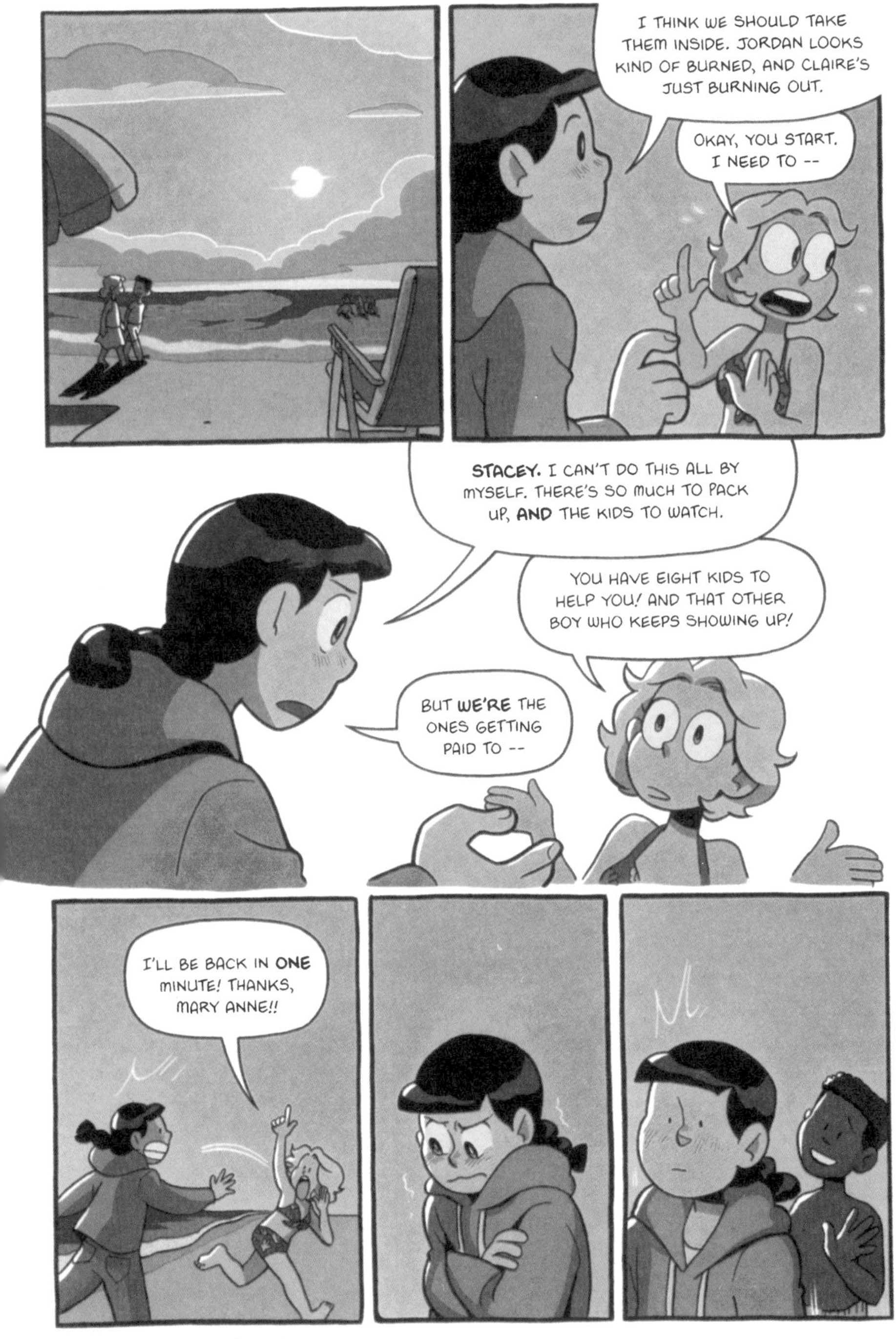

I THINK WE SHOULD TAKE THEM INSIDE. JORDAN LOOKS KIND OF BURNED, AND CLAIRE'S JUST BURNING OUT.
OKAY, YOU START. I NEED TO --
STACEY. I CAN'T DO THIS ALL BY MYSELF. THERE'S SO MUCH TO PACK UP, AND THE KIDS TO WATCH.
YOU HAVE EIGHT KIDS TO HELP YOU! AND THAT OTHER BOY WHO KEEPS SHOWING UP!
BUT WE'RE THE ONES GETTING PAID TO --
I'LL BE BACK IN ONE MINUTE! THANKS, MARY ANNE!!

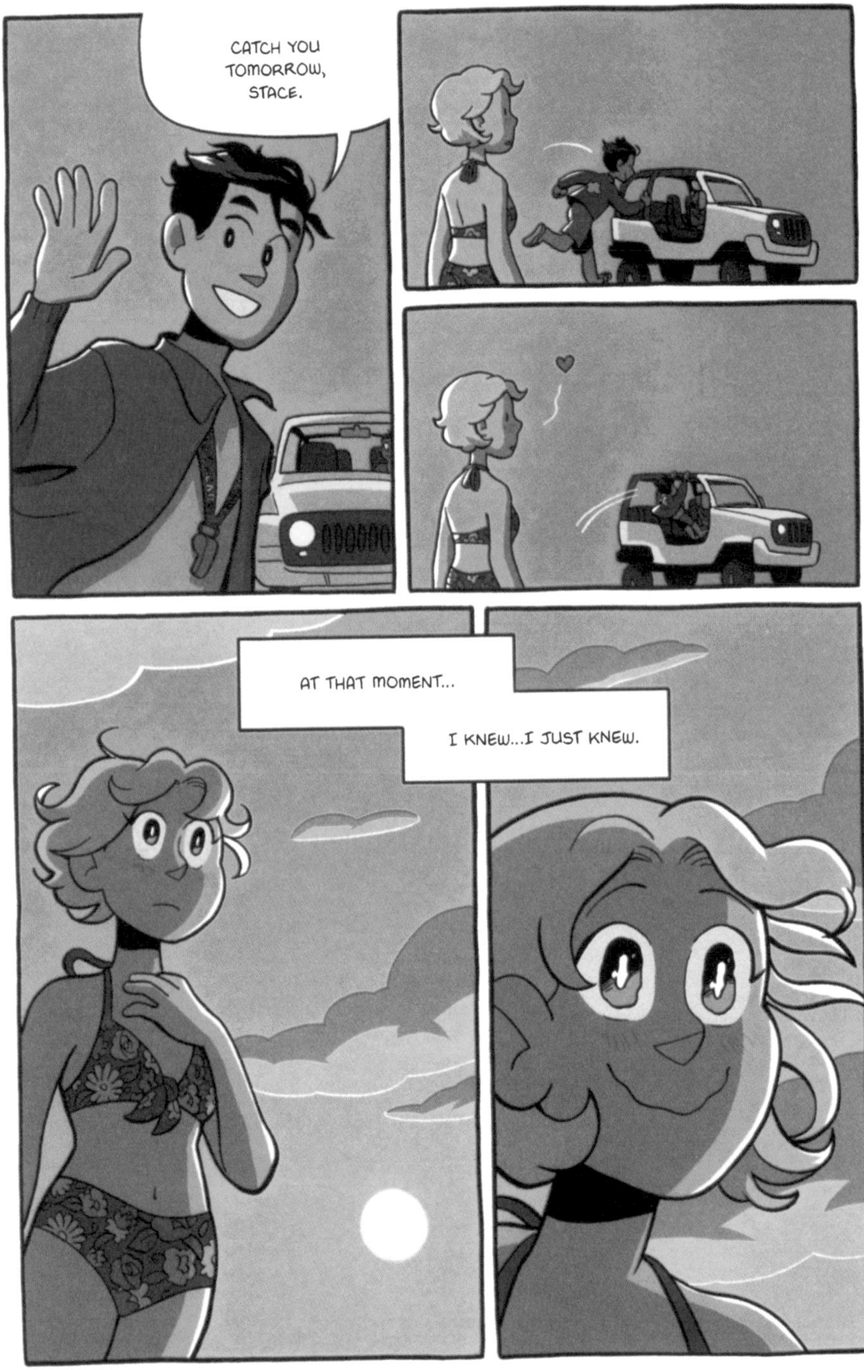
CATCH YOU TOMORROW, STACE.
AT THAT MOMENT...
I KNEW...I JUST KNEW.

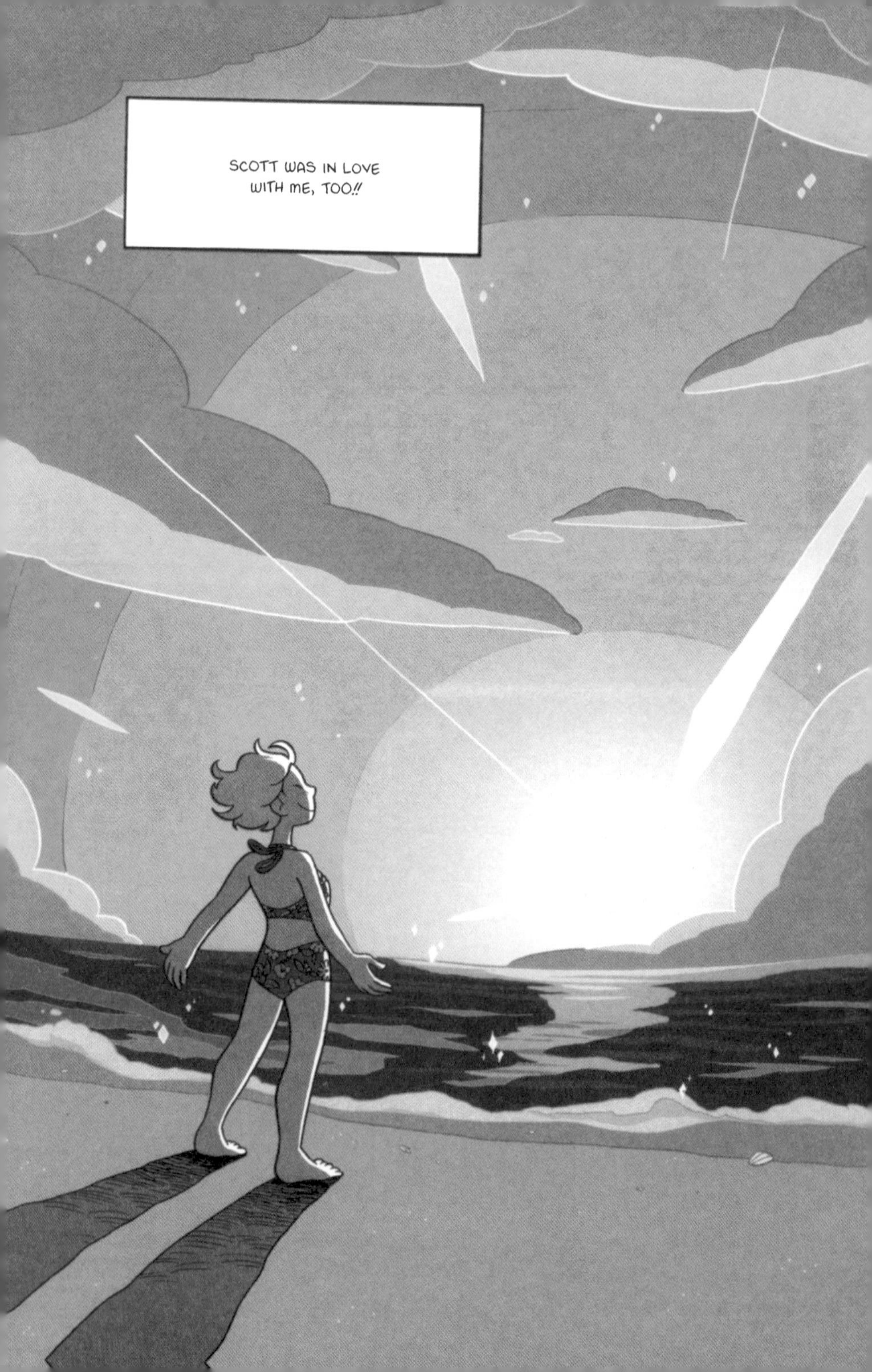
SCOTT WAS IN LOVE
WITH ME, TOO!!

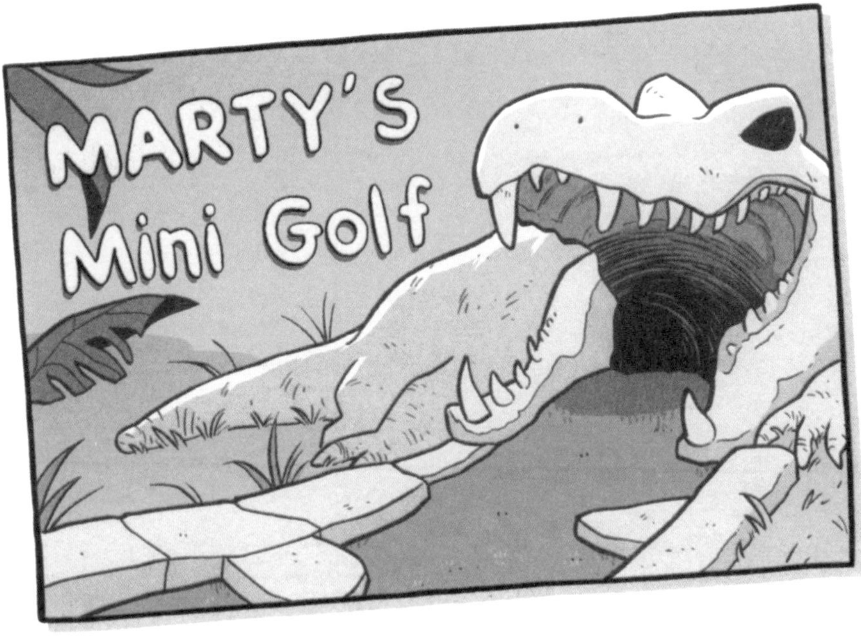
MARTY'S
Mini Golf

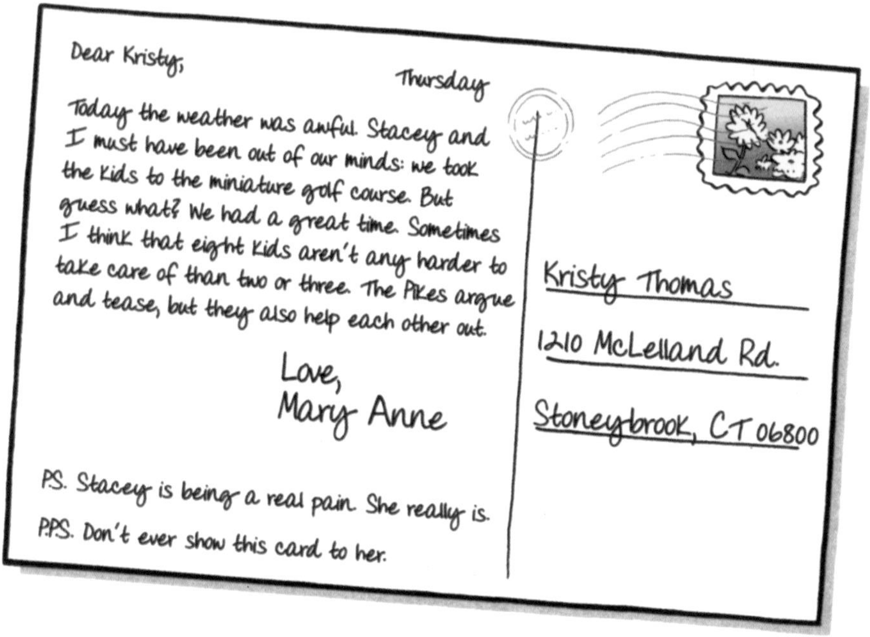

Dear Kristy,

Thursday

Today the weather was awful. Stacey and I must have been out of our minds: we took the kids to the miniature golf course. But guess what? We had a great time. Sometimes I think that eight kids aren't any harder to take care of than two or three. The Pikes argue and tease, but they also help each other out.

Love,
Mary Anne

P.S. Stacey is being a real pain. She really is.

P.P.S. Don't ever show this card to her.

Kristy Thomas
1210 McLelland Rd.
Stoneybrook, CT 06800

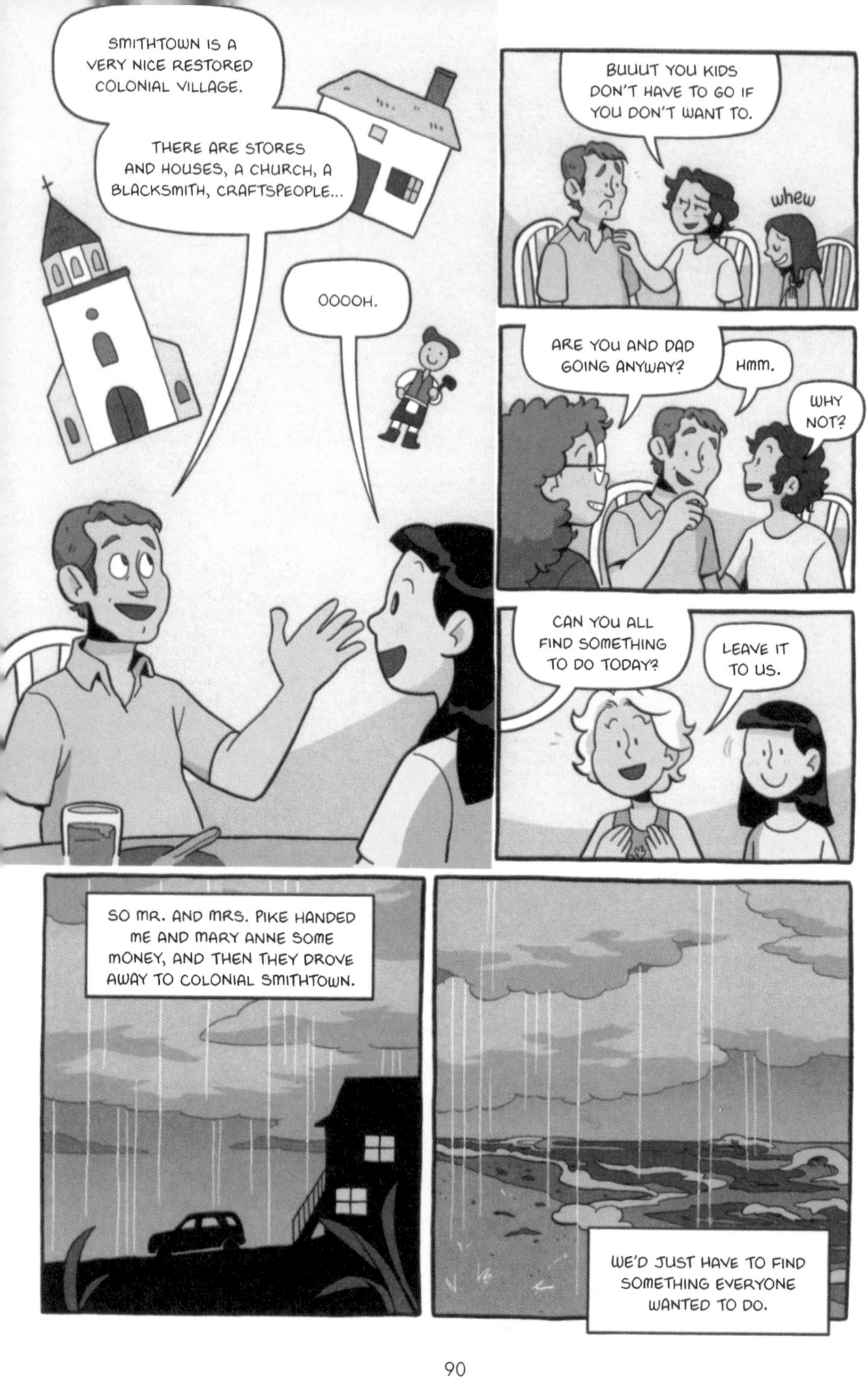
SMITHTOWN IS A VERY NICE RESTORED COLONIAL VILLAGE.
THERE ARE STORES AND HOUSES, A CHURCH, A BLACKSMITH, CRAFTSPEOPLE...
OOOOH.
BUUUT YOU KIDS DON'T HAVE TO GO IF YOU DON'T WANT TO.
whew
ARE YOU AND DAD GOING ANYWAY?
Hmm.
WHY NOT?
CAN YOU ALL FIND SOMETHING TO DO TODAY?
LEAVE IT TO US.
SO MR. AND MRS. PIKE HANDED ME AND MARY ANNE SOME MONEY, AND THEN THEY DROVE AWAY TO COLONIAL SMITHTOWN.
WE'D JUST HAVE TO FIND SOMETHING EVERYONE WANTED TO DO.

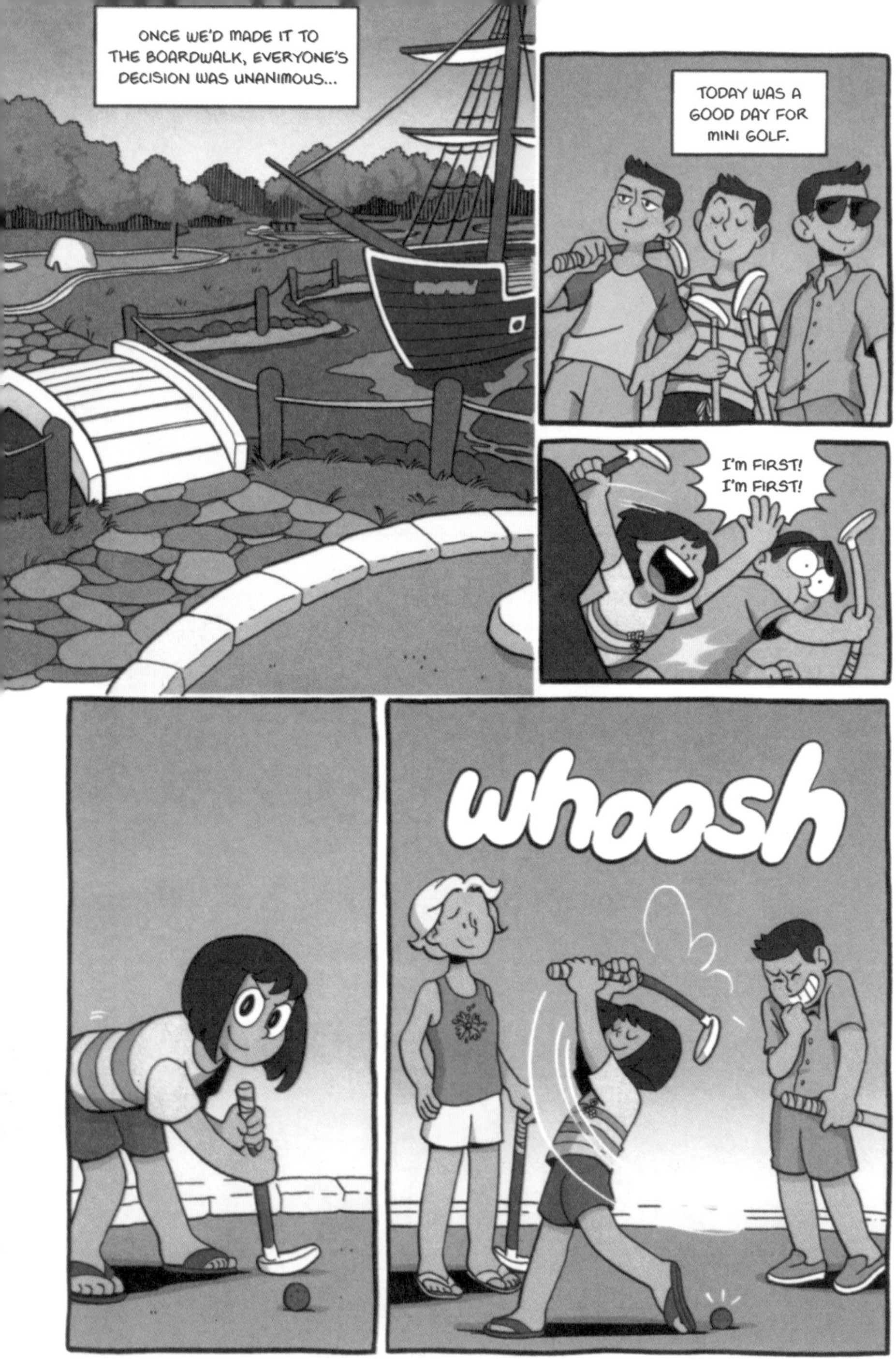
ONCE WE'D MADE IT TO THE BOARDWALK, EVERYONE'S DECISION WAS UNANIMOUS...
TODAY WAS A GOOD DAY FOR MINI GOLF.
I'M FIRST! I'M FIRST!
whoosh

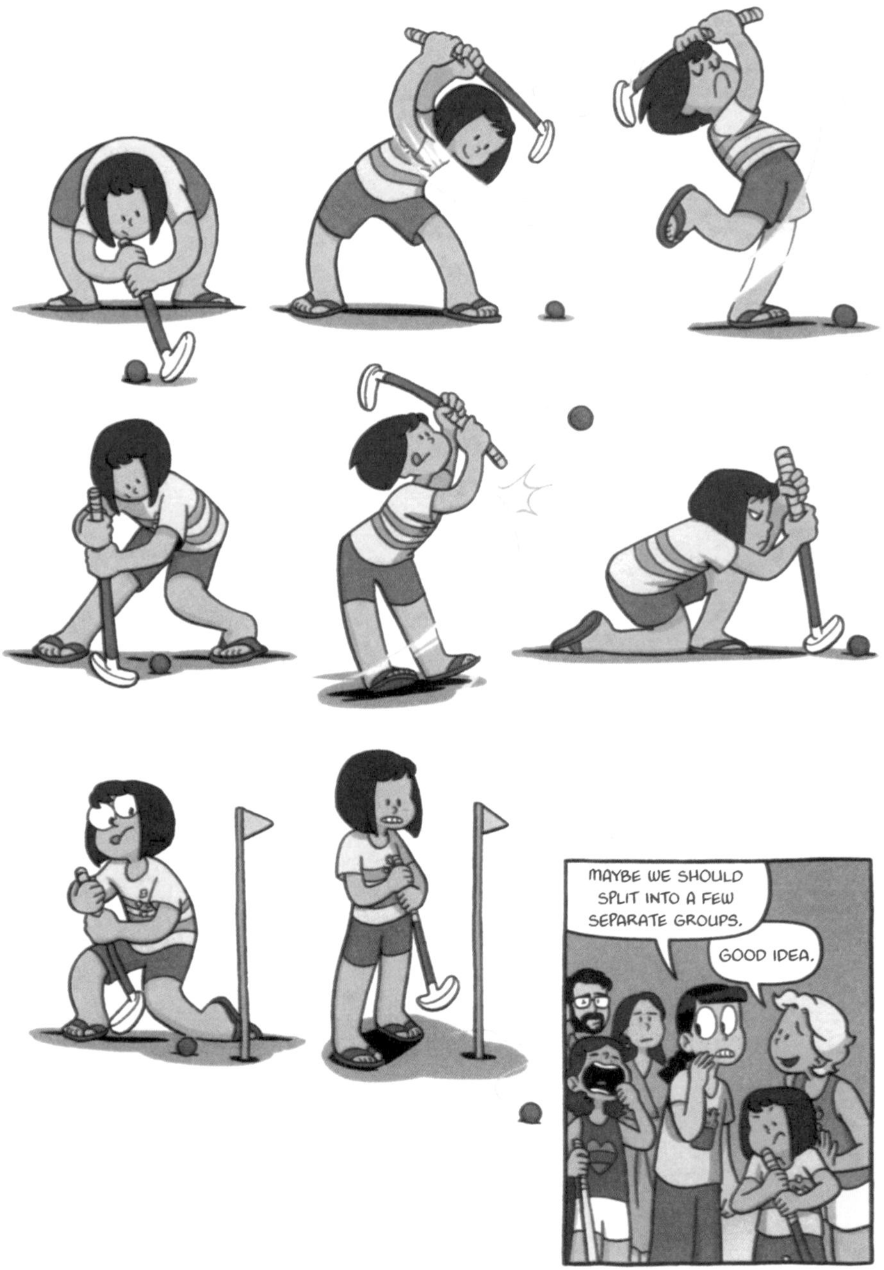
MAYBE WE SHOULD SPLIT INTO A FEW SEPARATE GROUPS.
GOOD IDEA.

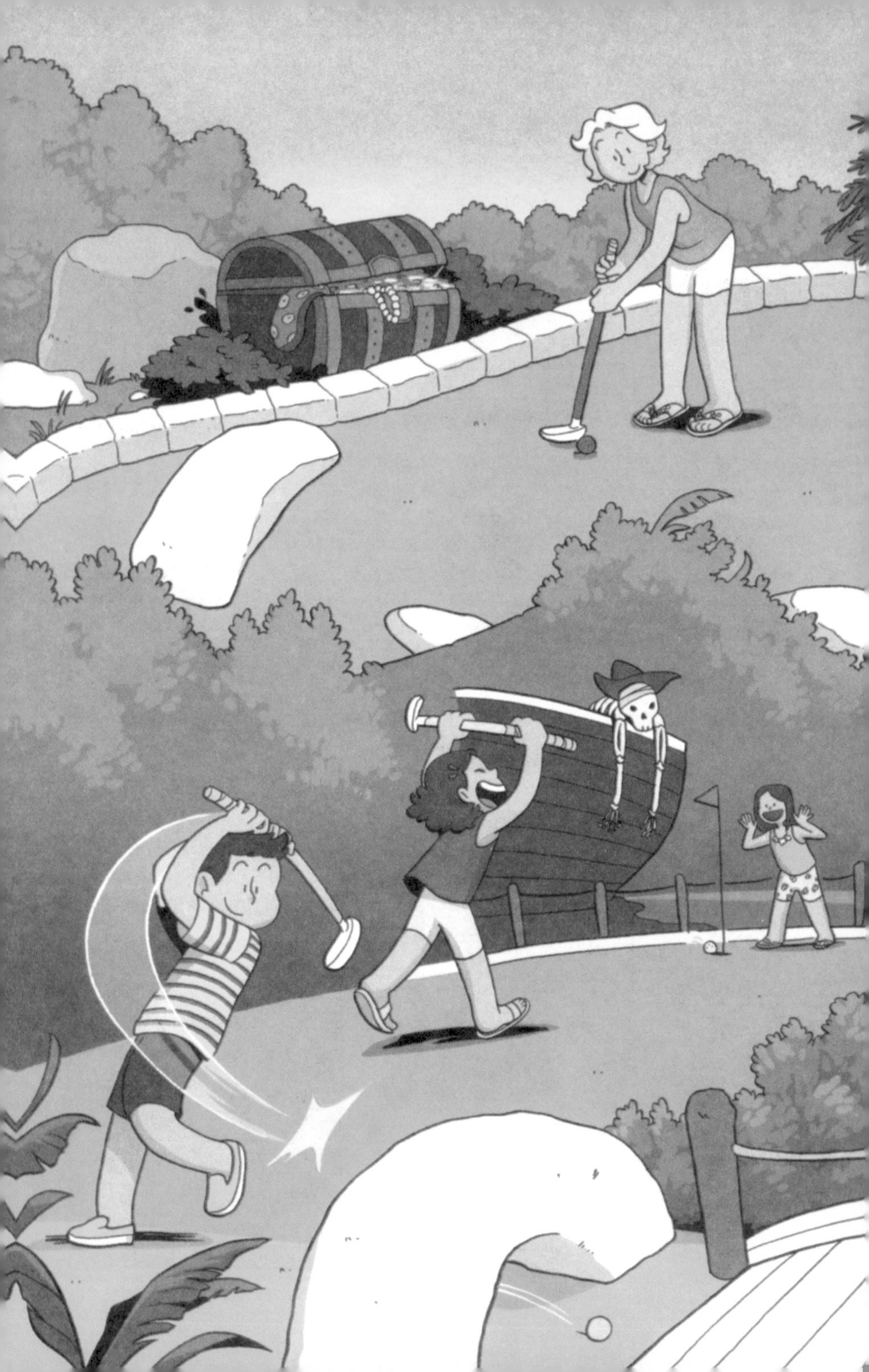

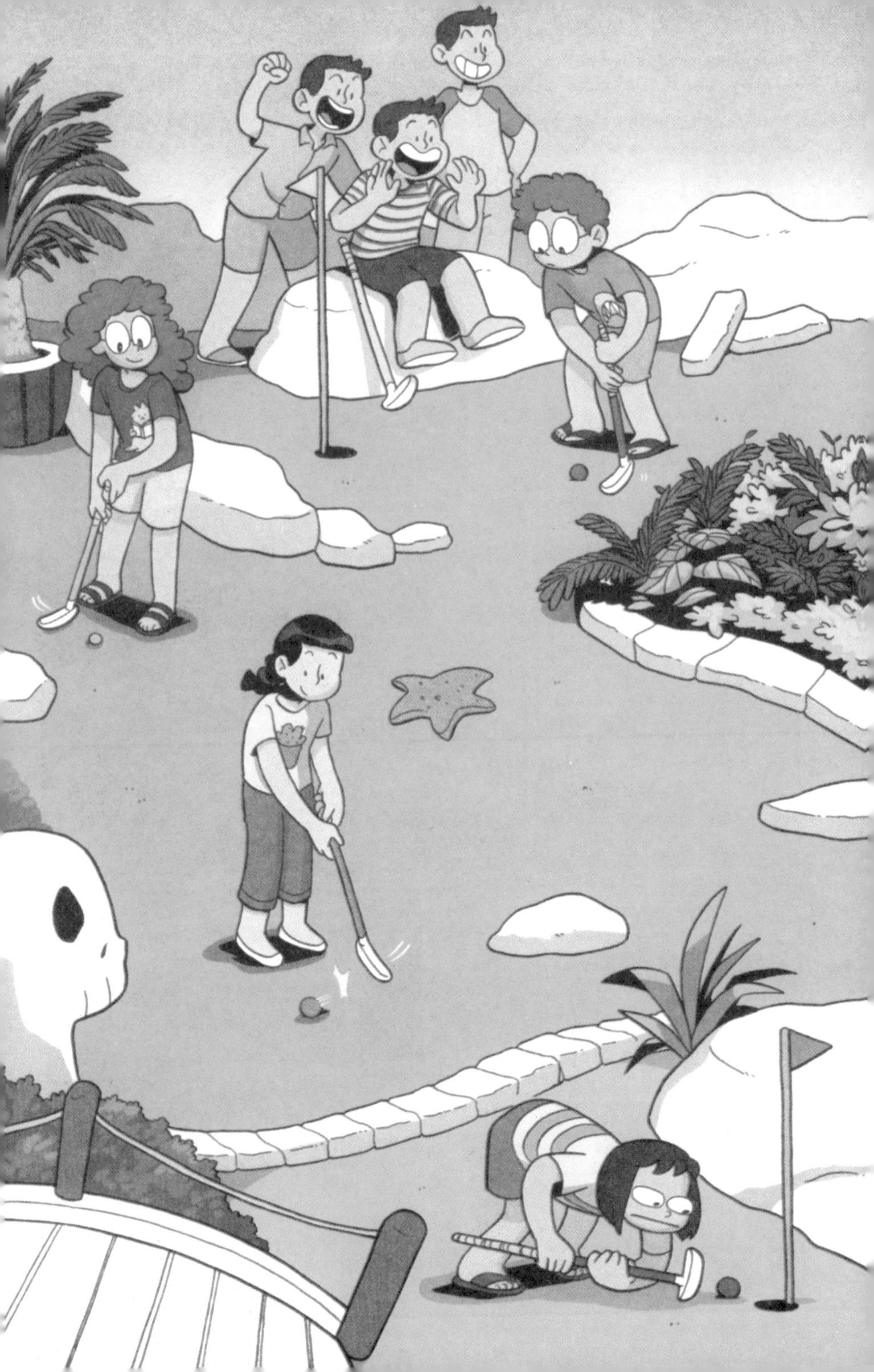

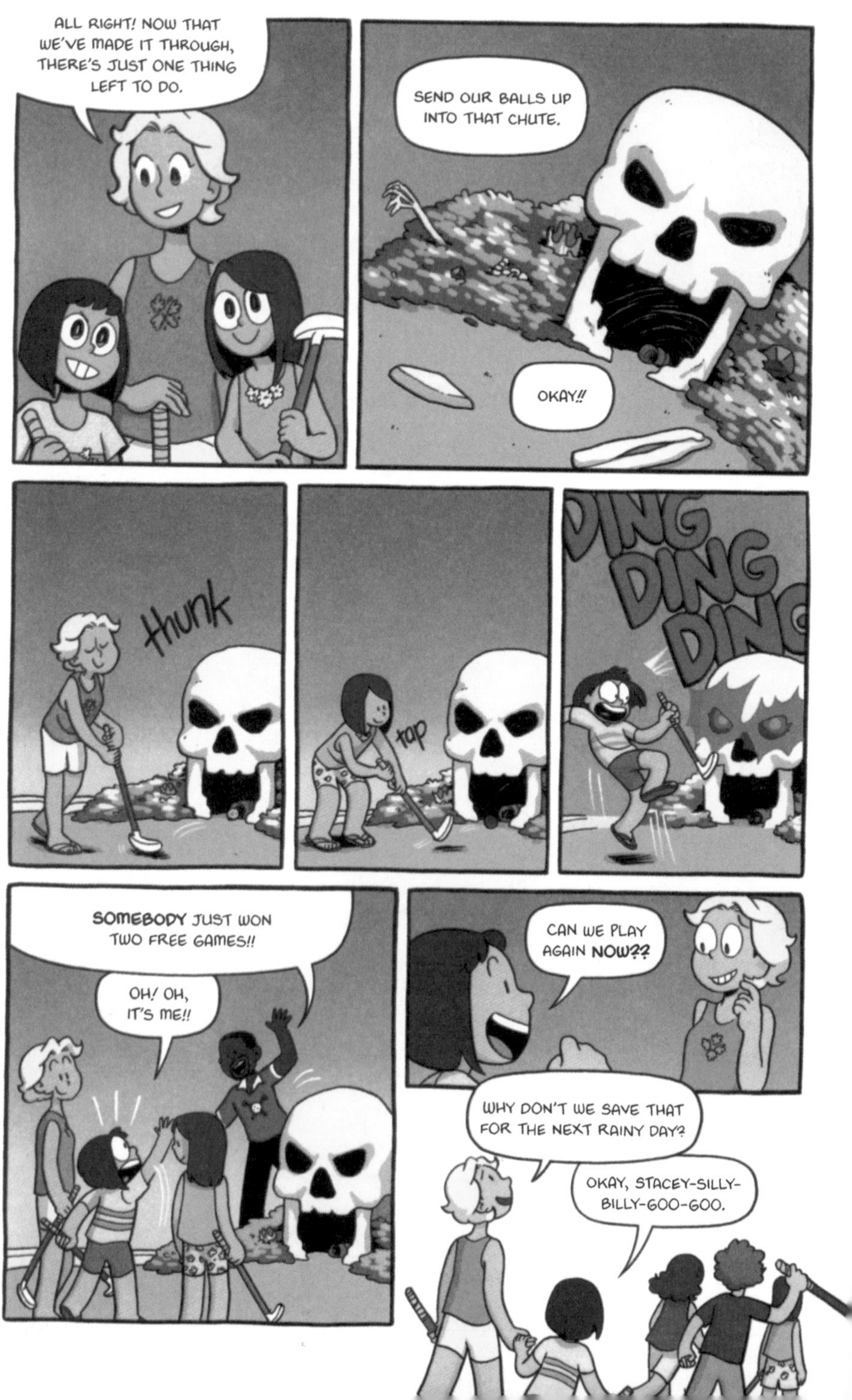
ALL RIGHT! NOW THAT WE'VE MADE IT THROUGH, THERE'S JUST ONE THING LEFT TO DO.
SEND OUR BALLS UP INTO THAT CHUTE.
OKAY!!
thunk
tap
DING DING DING
SOMEBODY JUST WON TWO FREE GAMES!!
OH! OH, IT'S ME!!
CAN WE PLAY AGAIN NOW??
WHY DON'T WE SAVE THAT FOR THE NEXT RAINY DAY?
OKAY, STACEY-SILLY-BILLY-GOO-GOO.

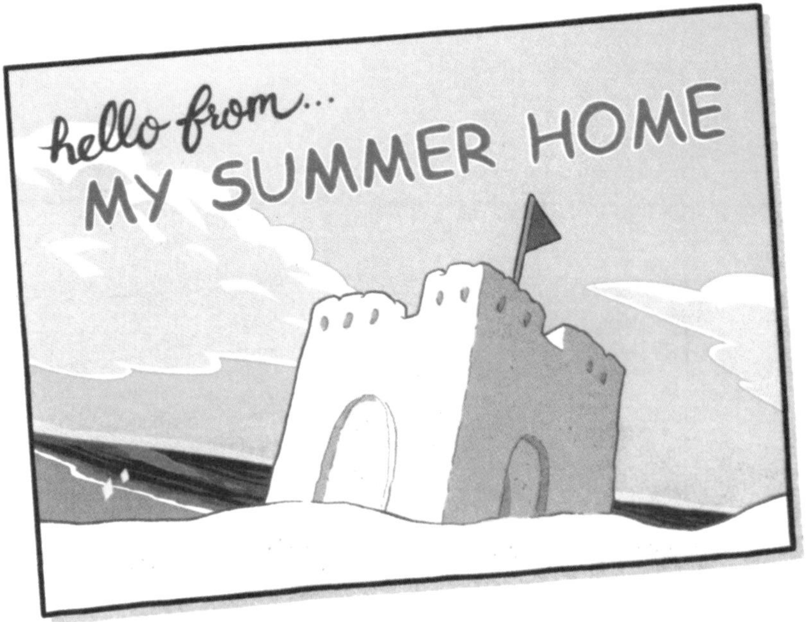
hello from...
MY SUMMER HOME

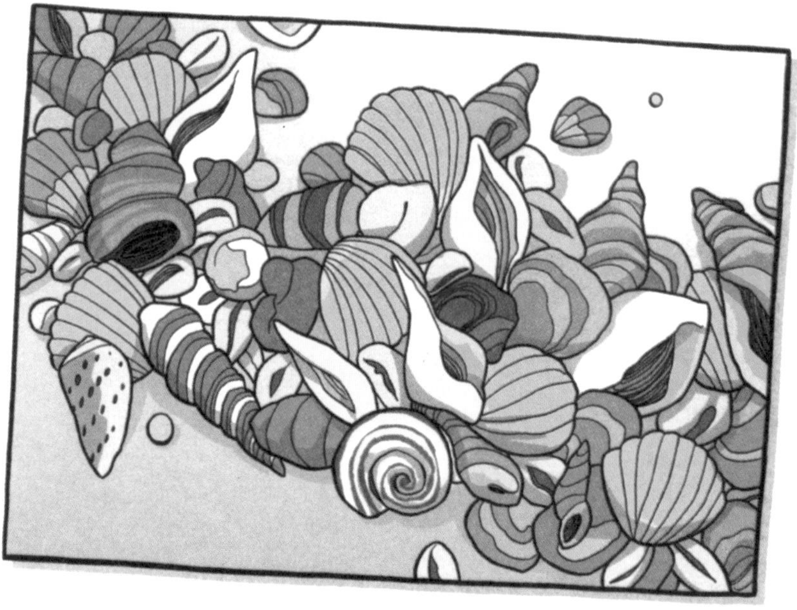

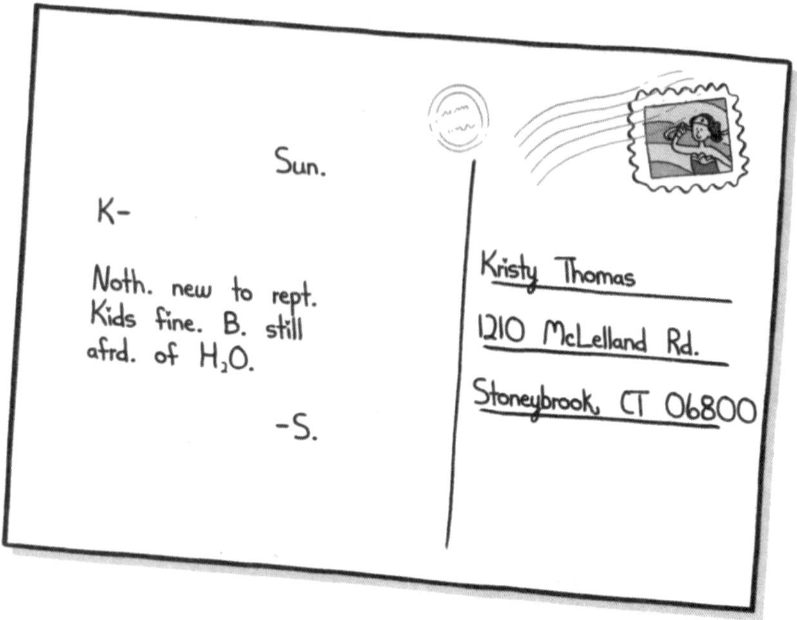

Sun.

K-

Noth. new to rept. Kids fine. B. still afrd. of H_2O.

-S.

Kristy Thomas
1210 McLelland Rd.
Stoneybrook, CT 06800

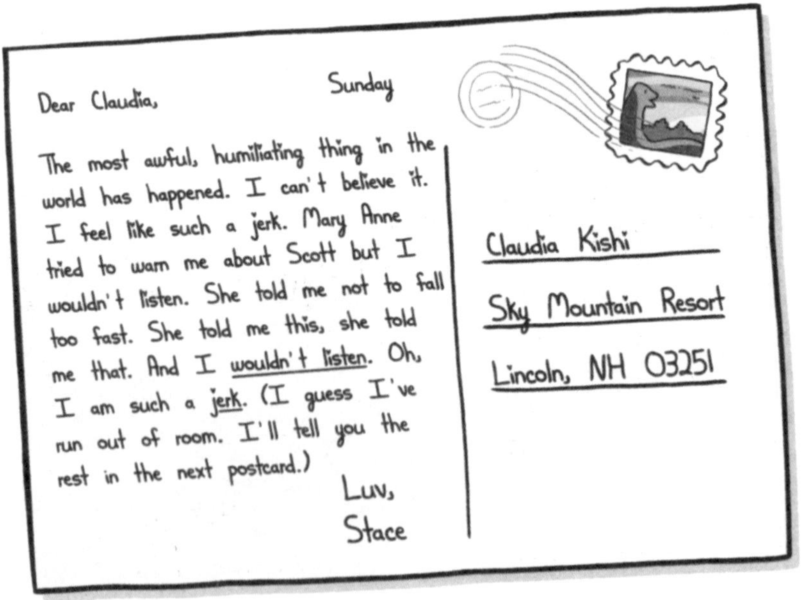

Sunday

Dear Claudia,

The most awful, humiliating thing in the world has happened. I can't believe it. I feel like such a jerk. Mary Anne tried to warn me about Scott but I wouldn't listen. She told me not to fall too fast. She told me this, she told me that. And I <u>wouldn't listen</u>. Oh, I am such a <u>jerk</u>. (I guess I've run out of room. I'll tell you the rest in the next postcard.)

Luv,
Stace

Claudia Kishi
Sky Mountain Resort
Lincoln, NH 03251

CHAPTER 9

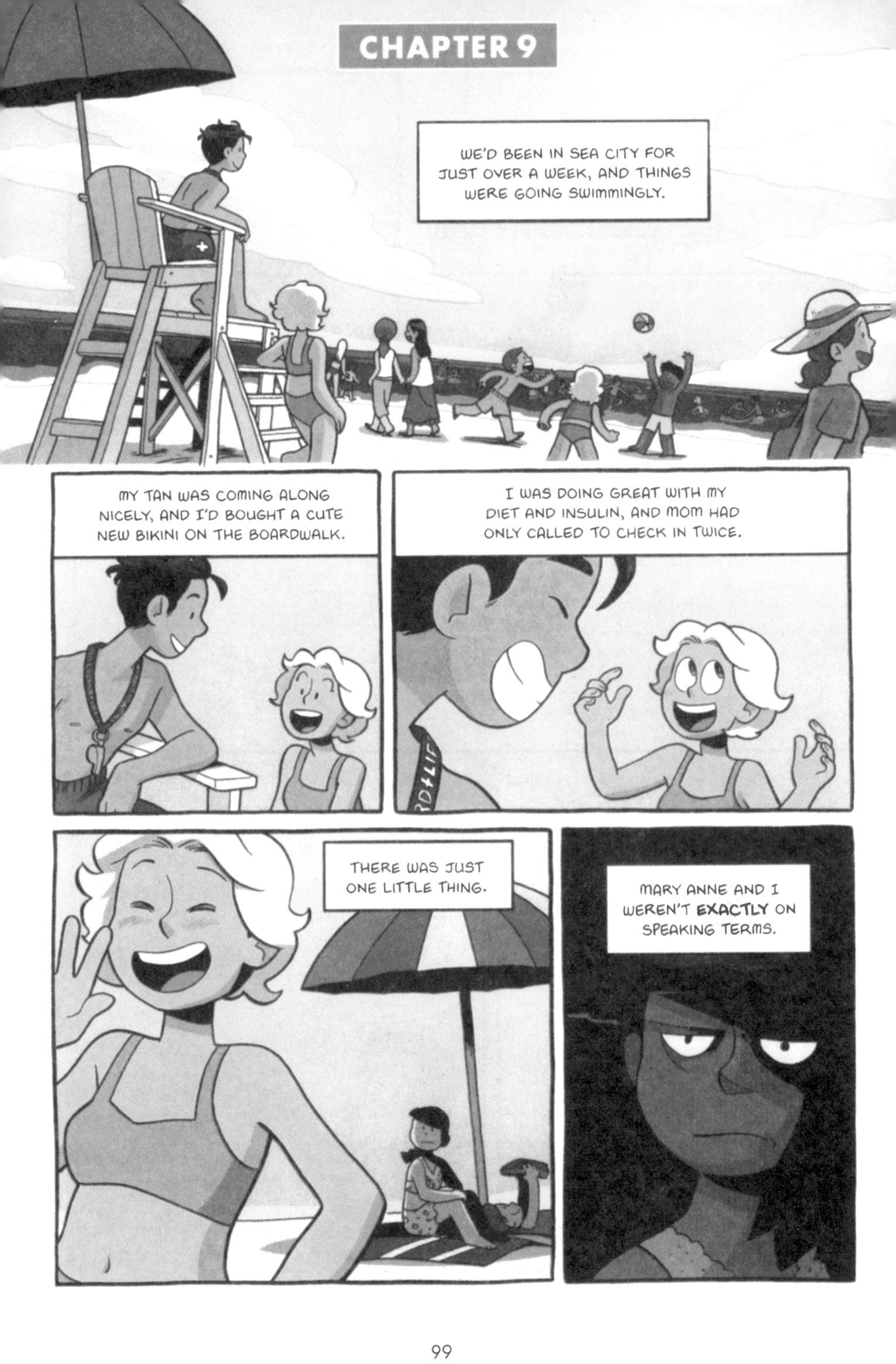
WE'D BEEN IN SEA CITY FOR JUST OVER A WEEK, AND THINGS WERE GOING SWIMMINGLY.
MY TAN WAS COMING ALONG NICELY, AND I'D BOUGHT A CUTE NEW BIKINI ON THE BOARDWALK.
I WAS DOING GREAT WITH MY DIET AND INSULIN, AND MOM HAD ONLY CALLED TO CHECK IN TWICE.
THERE WAS JUST ONE LITTLE THING.
MARY ANNE AND I WEREN'T **EXACTLY** ON SPEAKING TERMS.

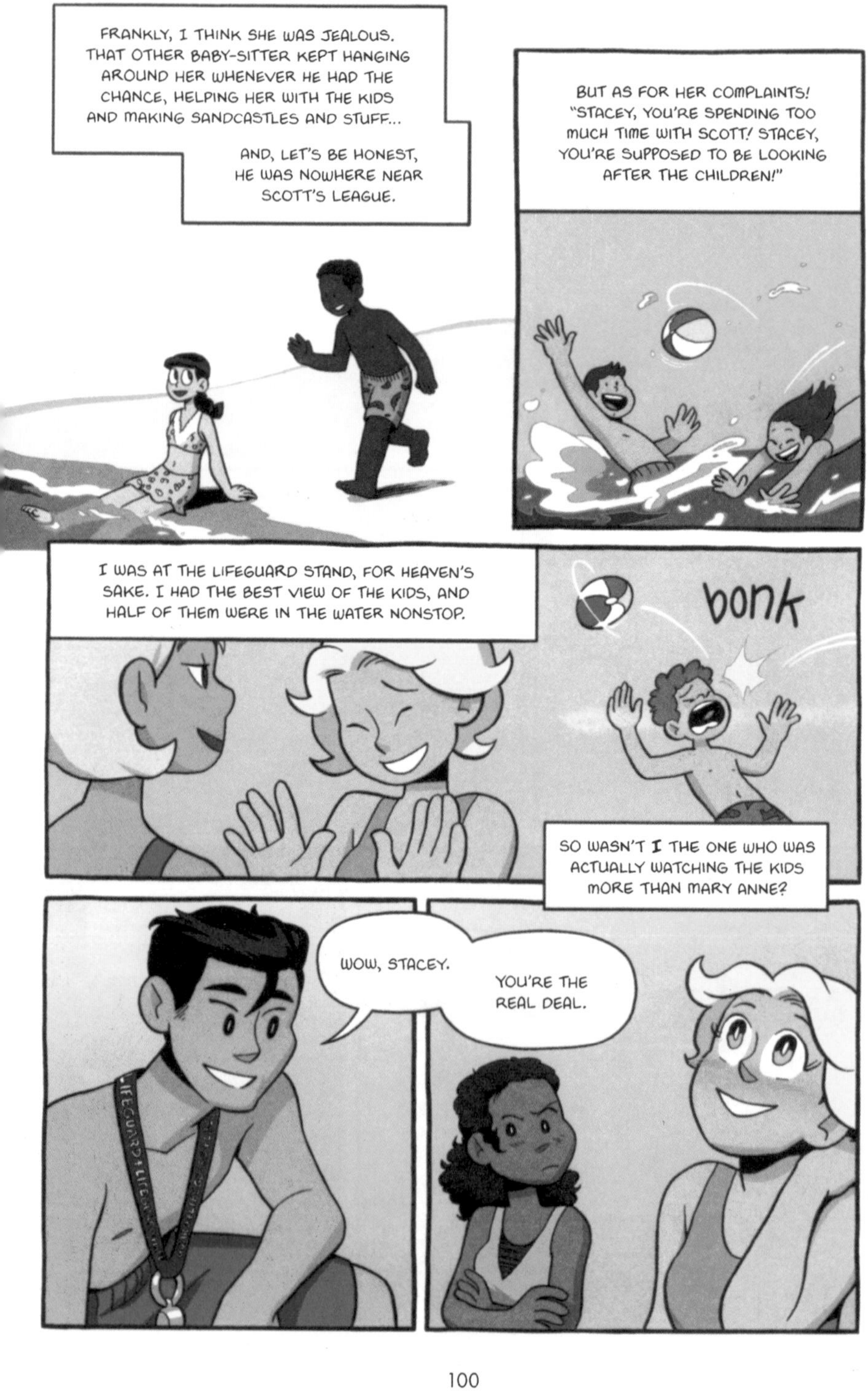
FRANKLY, I THINK SHE WAS JEALOUS. THAT OTHER BABY-SITTER KEPT HANGING AROUND HER WHENEVER HE HAD THE CHANCE, HELPING HER WITH THE KIDS AND MAKING SANDCASTLES AND STUFF...
AND, LET'S BE HONEST, HE WAS NOWHERE NEAR SCOTT'S LEAGUE.
BUT AS FOR HER COMPLAINTS! "STACEY, YOU'RE SPENDING TOO MUCH TIME WITH SCOTT! STACEY, YOU'RE SUPPOSED TO BE LOOKING AFTER THE CHILDREN!"
I WAS AT THE LIFEGUARD STAND, FOR HEAVEN'S SAKE. I HAD THE BEST VIEW OF THE KIDS, AND HALF OF THEM WERE IN THE WATER NONSTOP.
bonk
SO WASN'T I THE ONE WHO WAS ACTUALLY WATCHING THE KIDS MORE THAN MARY ANNE?
WOW, STACEY.
YOU'RE THE REAL DEAL.

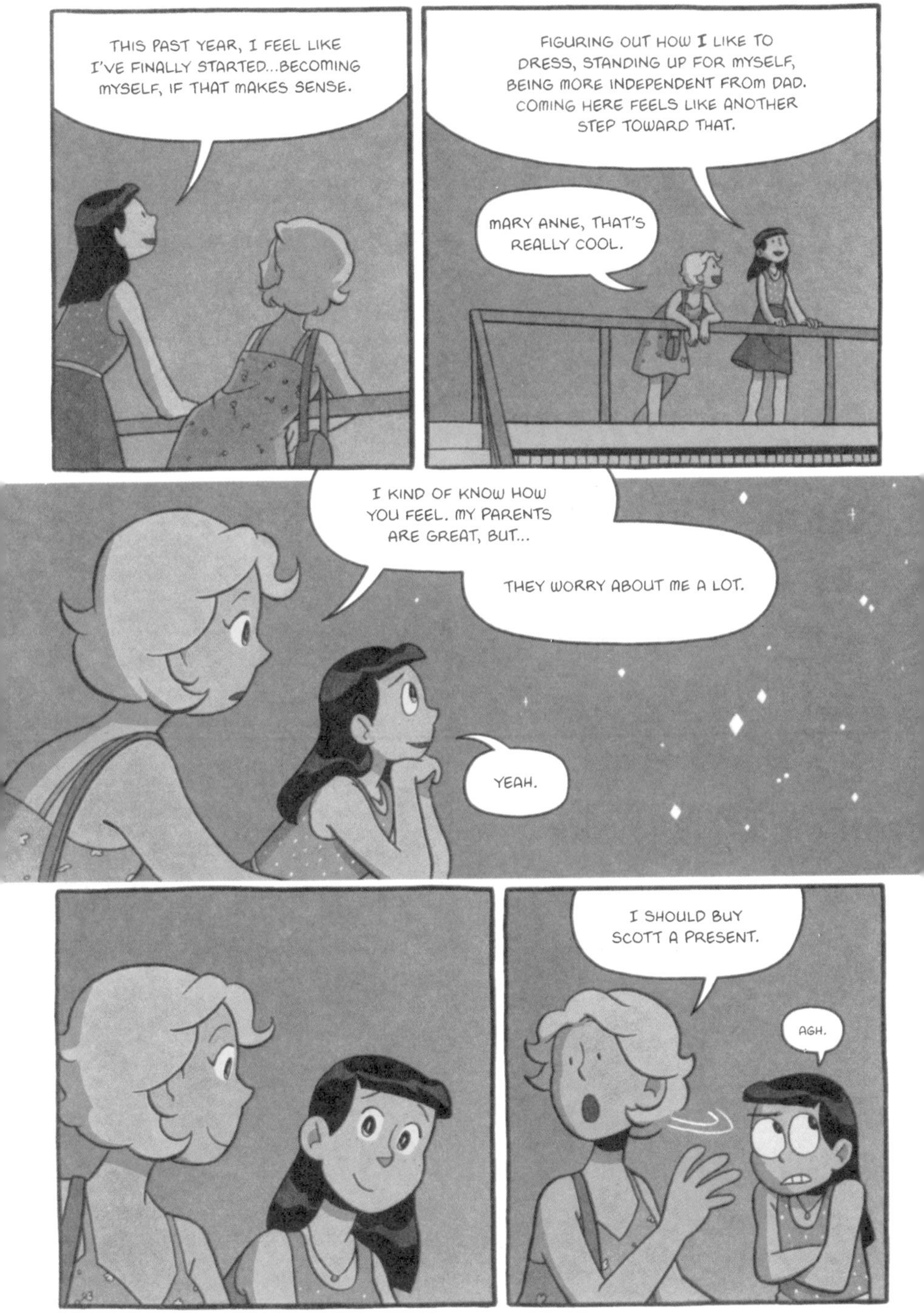
THIS PAST YEAR, I FEEL LIKE I'VE FINALLY STARTED...BECOMING MYSELF, IF THAT MAKES SENSE.
FIGURING OUT HOW I LIKE TO DRESS, STANDING UP FOR MYSELF, BEING MORE INDEPENDENT FROM DAD. COMING HERE FEELS LIKE ANOTHER STEP TOWARD THAT.
MARY ANNE, THAT'S REALLY COOL.
I KIND OF KNOW HOW YOU FEEL. MY PARENTS ARE GREAT, BUT...
THEY WORRY ABOUT ME A LOT.
YEAH.
I SHOULD BUY SCOTT A PRESENT.
AGH.

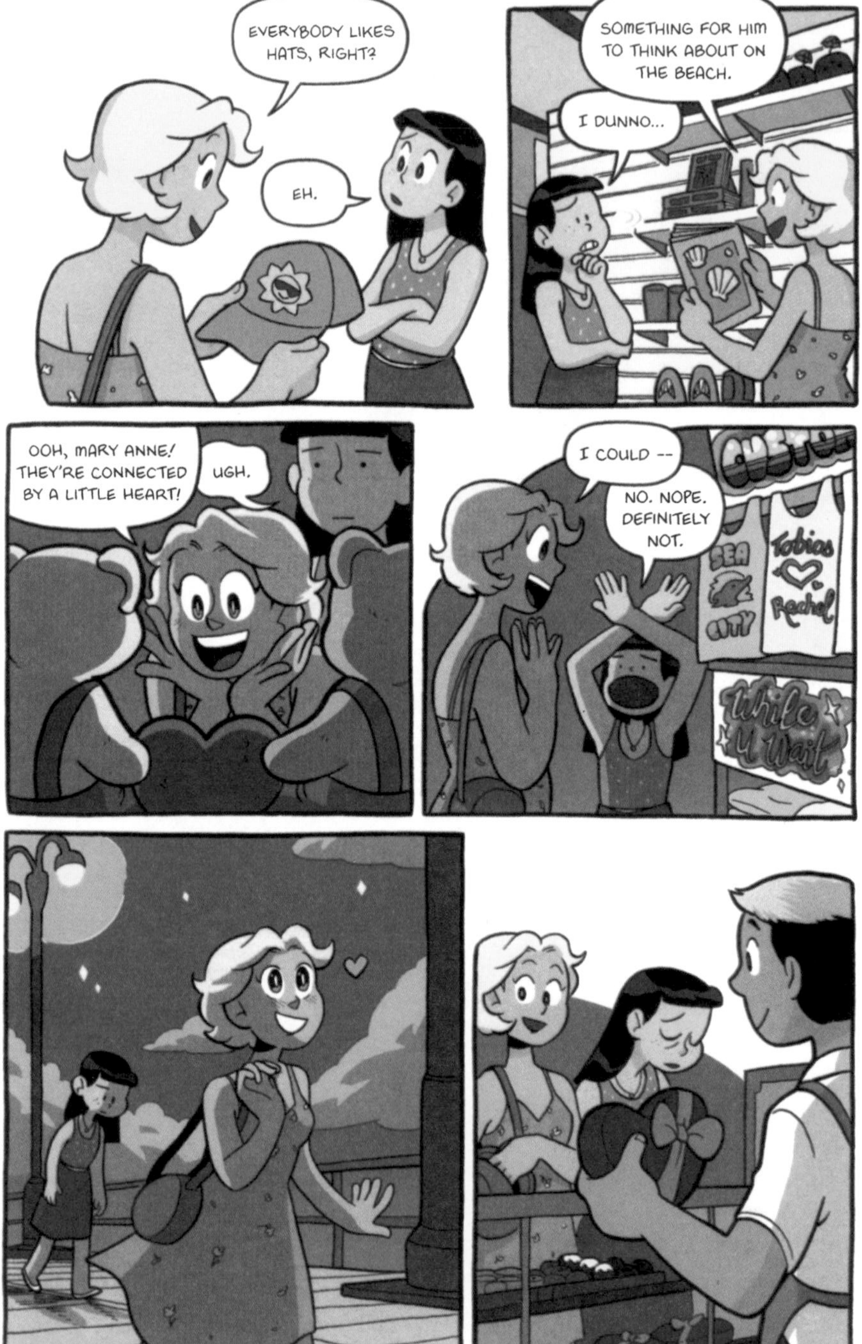
EVERYBODY LIKES HATS, RIGHT?
EH.
SOMETHING FOR HIM TO THINK ABOUT ON THE BEACH.
I DUNNO...
OOH, MARY ANNE! THEY'RE CONNECTED BY A LITTLE HEART!
UGH.
I COULD --
NO. NOPE. DEFINITELY NOT.
SEA CITY
Tobias Rachel
While U Wait

105

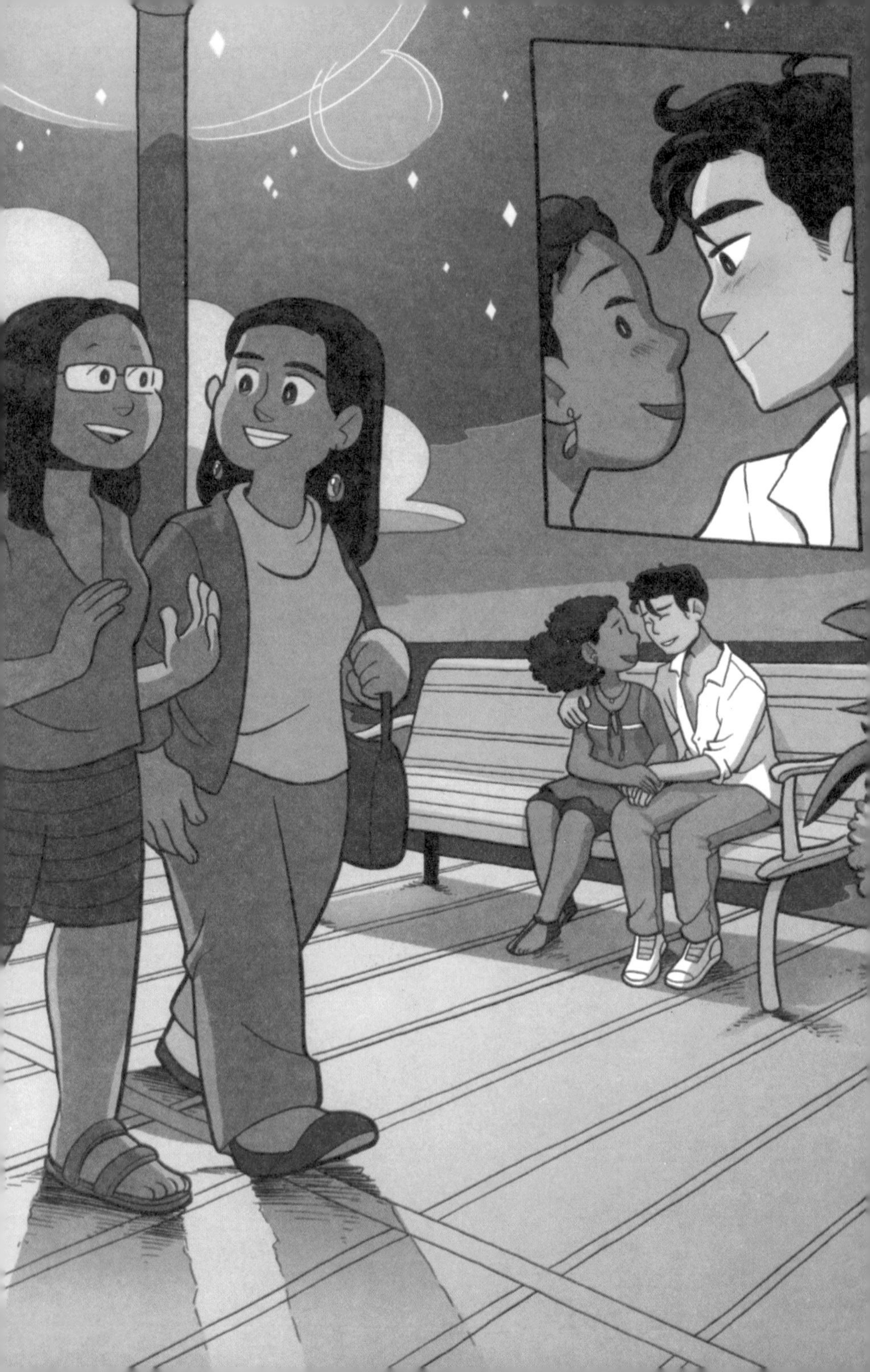

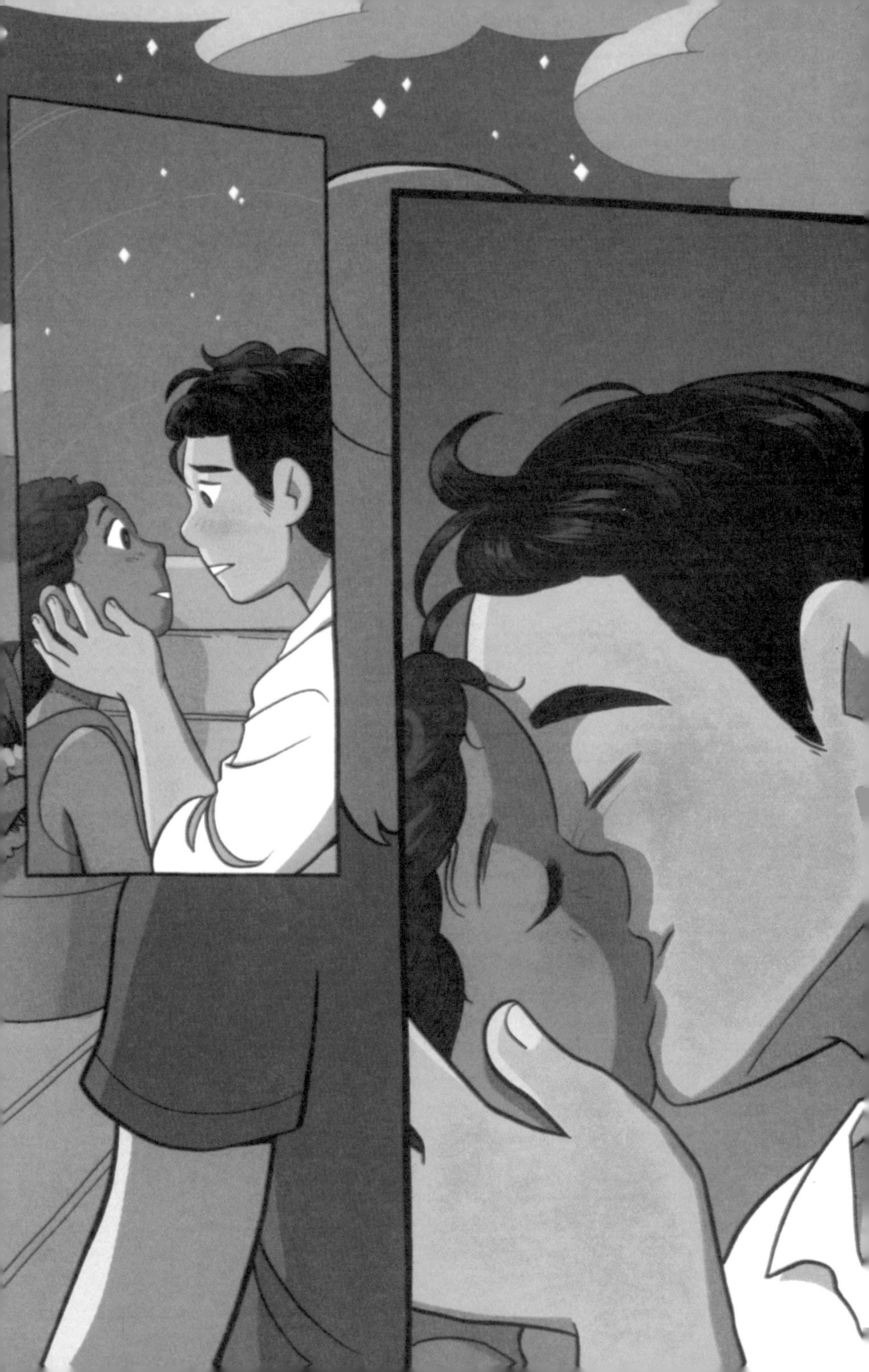

STACEY --

C-CONGRATULATIONS. YOU WERE **RIGHT.**

I WON'T BE NEEDING TH-THIS --

ANYM--

SOB

SOB SOB SOB

C'MON, STACE.

SNF

LET'S GO.

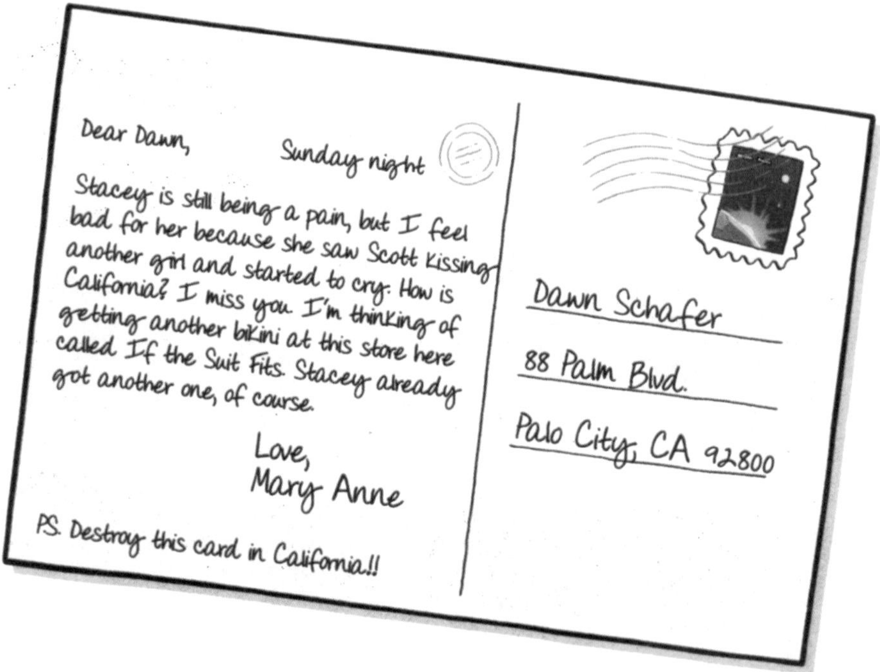

Dear Dawn,   Sunday night

Stacey is still being a pain, but I feel
bad for her because she saw Scott kissing
another girl and started to cry. How is
California? I miss you. I'm thinking of
getting another bikini at this store here
called If the Suit Fits. Stacey already
got another one, of course.

          Love,
          Mary Anne

P.S. Destroy this card in California.!!

Dawn Schafer

88 Palm Blvd.

Palo City, CA 92800

CHAPTER 10

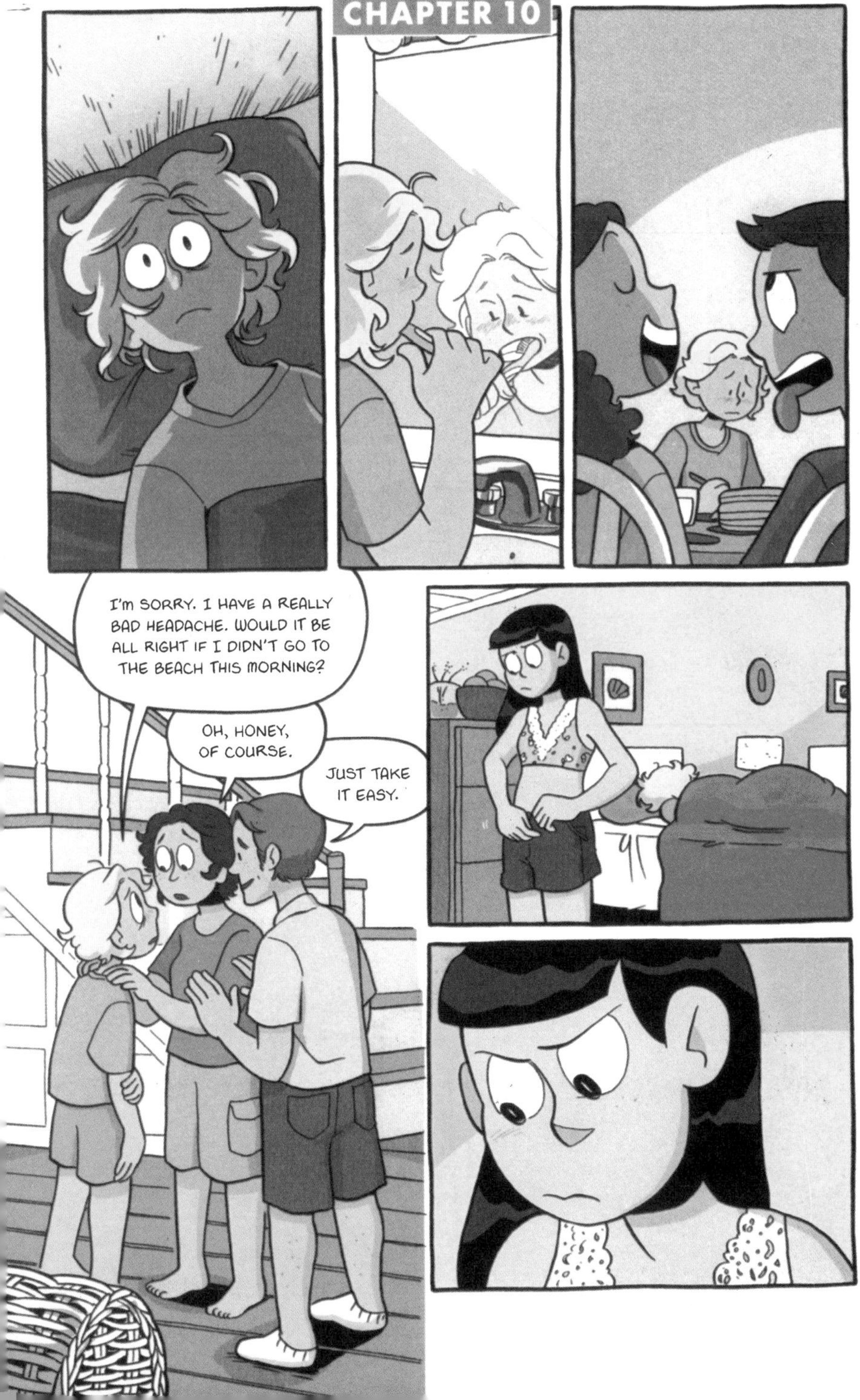
I'M SORRY. I HAVE A REALLY BAD HEADACHE. WOULD IT BE ALL RIGHT IF I DIDN'T GO TO THE BEACH THIS MORNING?
OH, HONEY, OF COURSE.
JUST TAKE IT EASY.

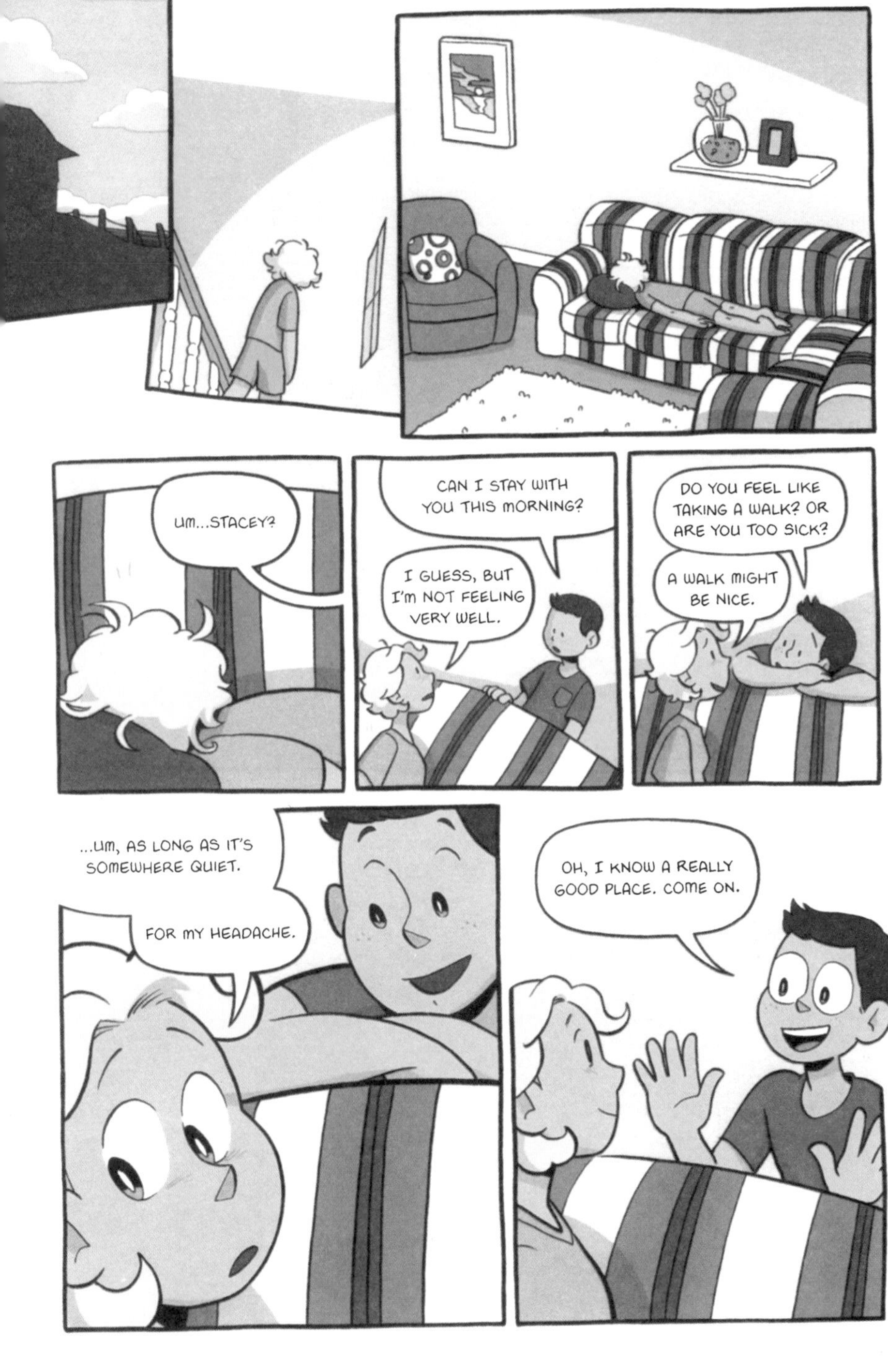
UM...STACEY?
CAN I STAY WITH YOU THIS MORNING?
I GUESS, BUT I'M NOT FEELING VERY WELL.
DO YOU FEEL LIKE TAKING A WALK? OR ARE YOU TOO SICK?
A WALK MIGHT BE NICE.
...UM, AS LONG AS IT'S SOMEWHERE QUIET.
FOR MY HEADACHE.
OH, I KNOW A REALLY GOOD PLACE. COME ON.

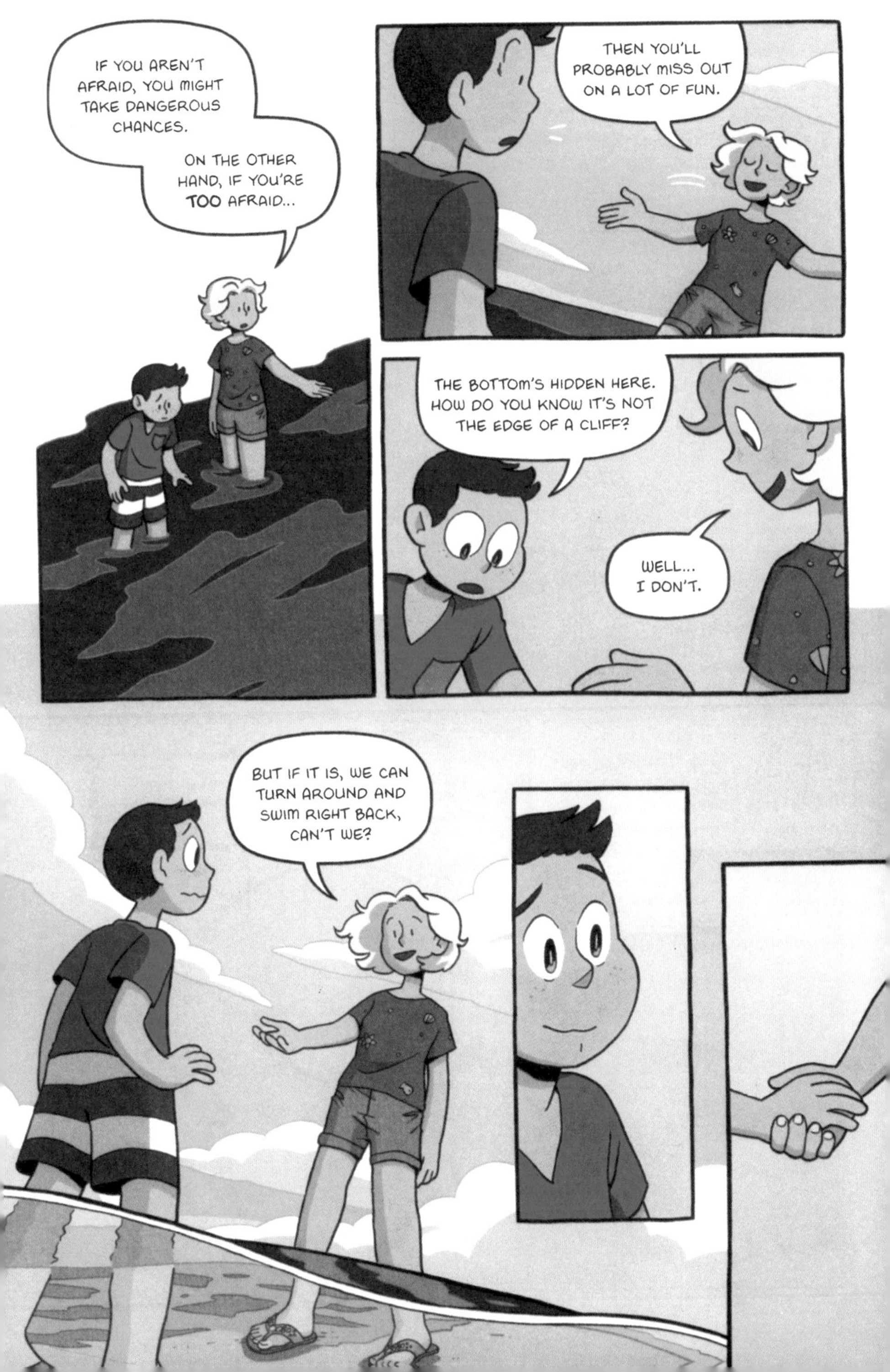
IF YOU AREN'T AFRAID, YOU MIGHT TAKE DANGEROUS CHANCES.
ON THE OTHER HAND, IF YOU'RE TOO AFRAID...
THEN YOU'LL PROBABLY MISS OUT ON A LOT OF FUN.
THE BOTTOM'S HIDDEN HERE. HOW DO YOU KNOW IT'S NOT THE EDGE OF A CLIFF?
WELL... I DON'T.
BUT IF IT IS, WE CAN TURN AROUND AND SWIM RIGHT BACK, CAN'T WE?

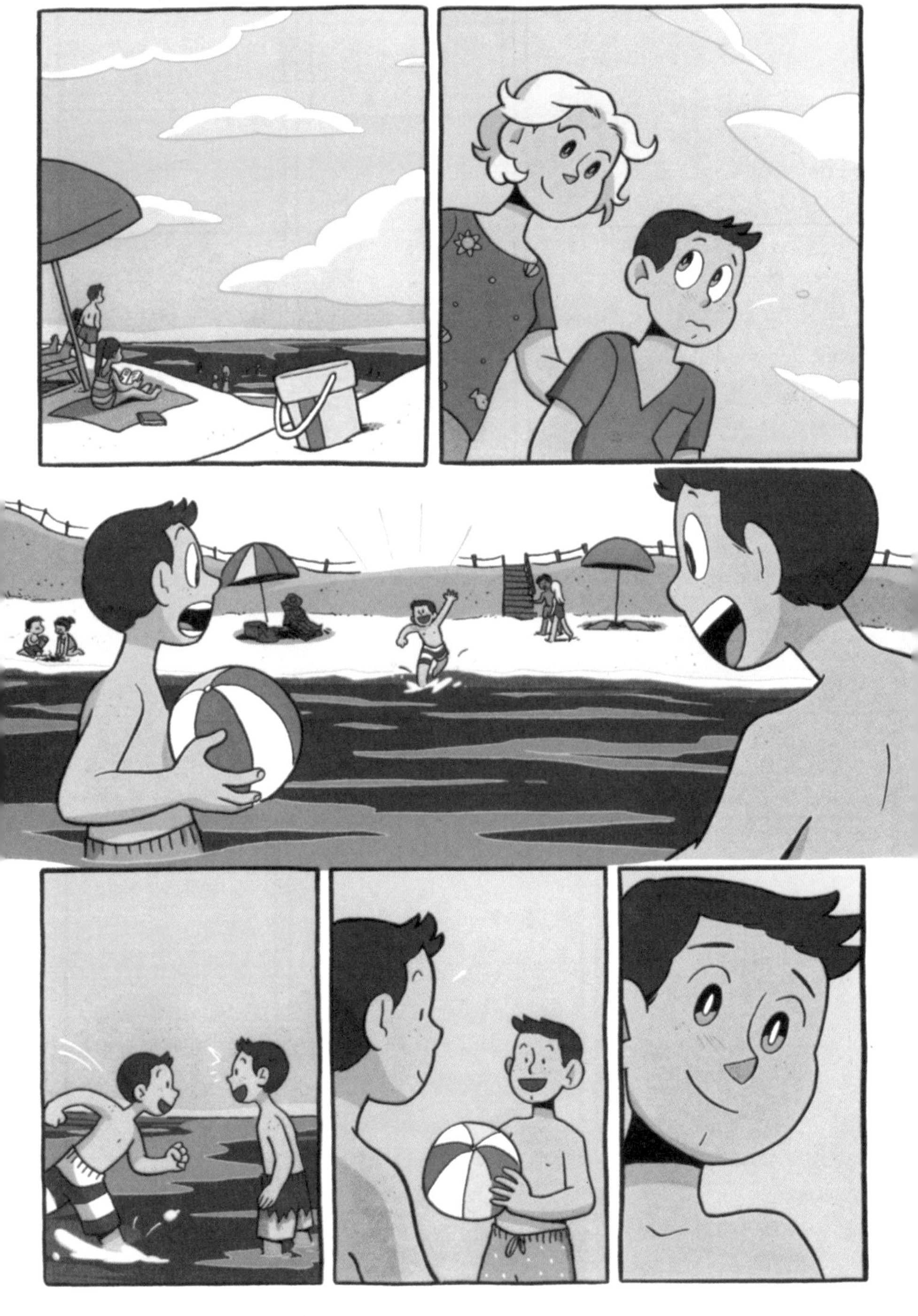

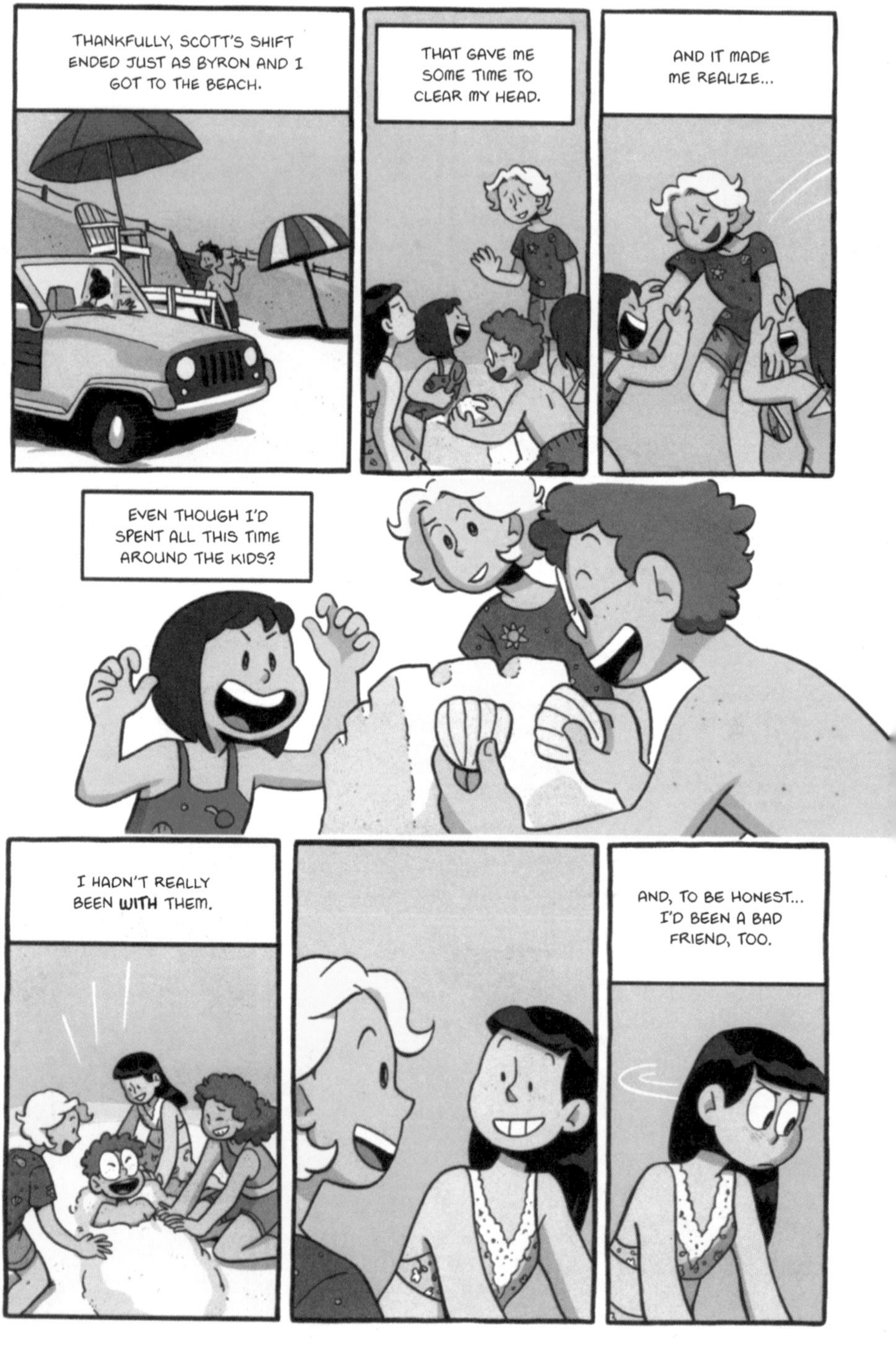
THANKFULLY, SCOTT'S SHIFT ENDED JUST AS BYRON AND I GOT TO THE BEACH.
THAT GAVE ME SOME TIME TO CLEAR MY HEAD.
AND IT MADE ME REALIZE...
EVEN THOUGH I'D SPENT ALL THIS TIME AROUND THE KIDS?
I HADN'T REALLY BEEN **WITH** THEM.
AND, TO BE HONEST... I'D BEEN A BAD FRIEND, TOO.

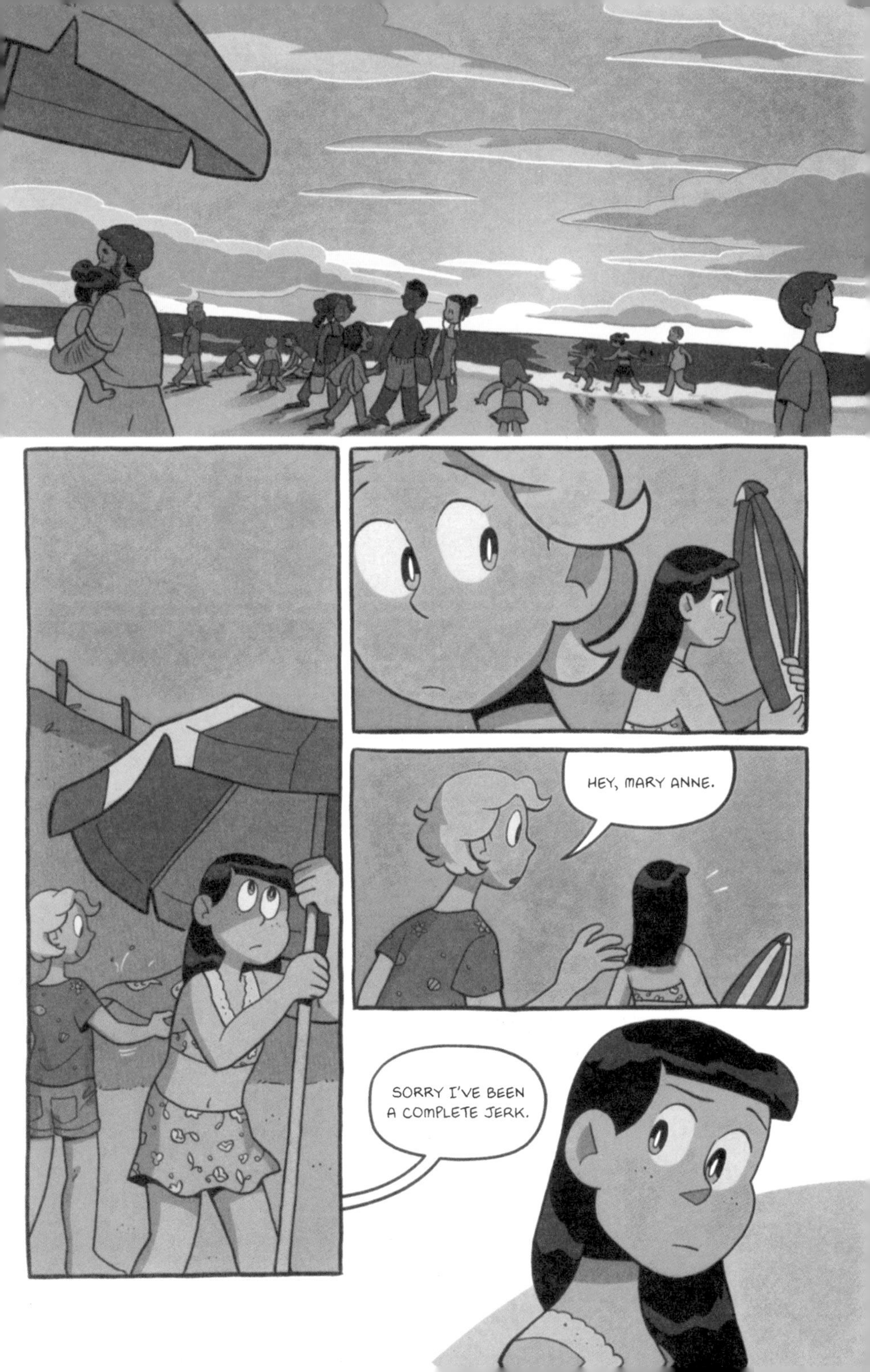
HEY, MARY ANNE.
SORRY I'VE BEEN A COMPLETE JERK.

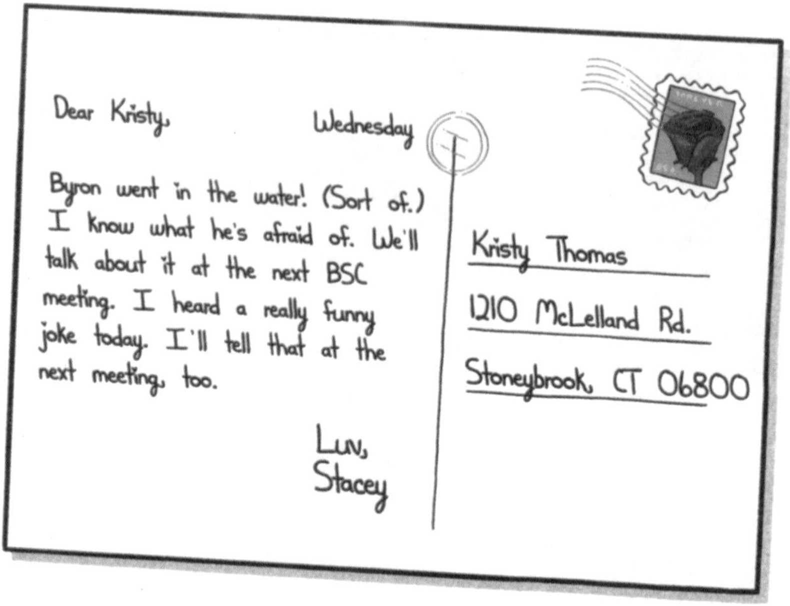

Dear Kristy,   Wednesday

Byron went in the water! (Sort of.)
I know what he's afraid of. We'll
talk about it at the next BSC
meeting. I heard a really funny
joke today. I'll tell that at the
next meeting, too.

                        Luv,
                        Stacey

Kristy Thomas

1210 McLelland Rd.

Stoneybrook, CT 06800

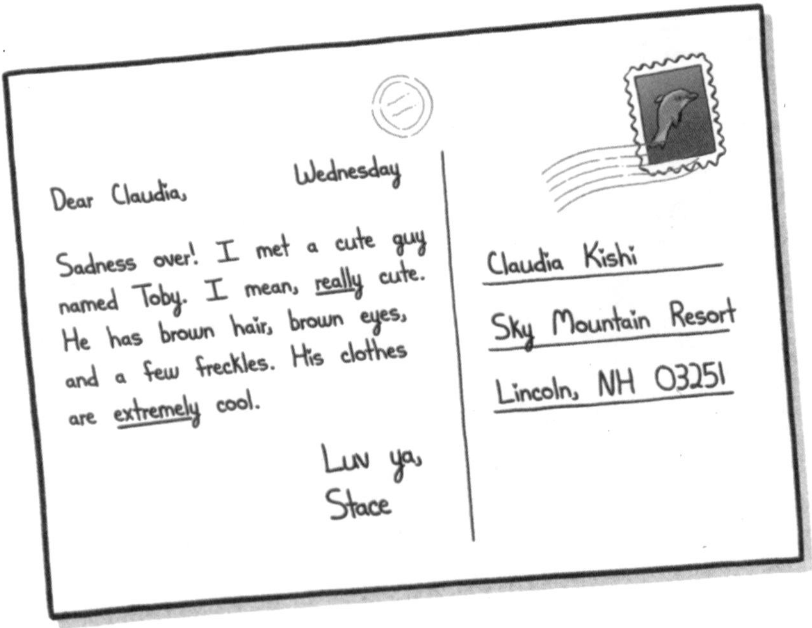

Dear Claudia,   Wednesday

Sadness over! I met a cute guy
named Toby. I mean, _really_ cute.
He has brown hair, brown eyes,
and a few freckles. His clothes
are _extremely_ cool.

                    Luv ya,
                    Stace

Claudia Kishi

Sky Mountain Resort

Lincoln, NH 03251

CHAPTER 11

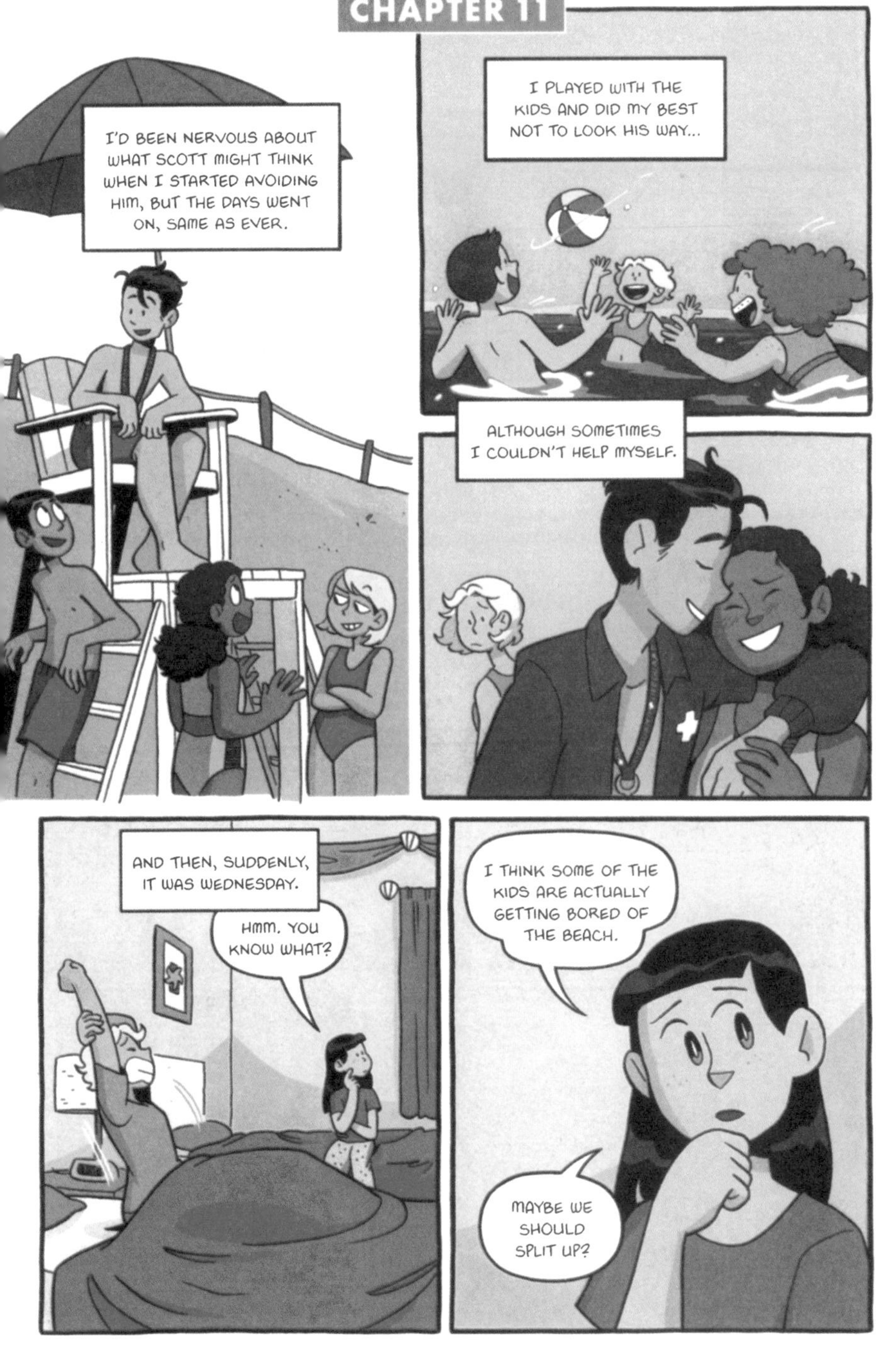
I'D BEEN NERVOUS ABOUT WHAT SCOTT MIGHT THINK WHEN I STARTED AVOIDING HIM, BUT THE DAYS WENT ON, SAME AS EVER.
I PLAYED WITH THE KIDS AND DID MY BEST NOT TO LOOK HIS WAY...
ALTHOUGH SOMETIMES I COULDN'T HELP MYSELF.
AND THEN, SUDDENLY, IT WAS WEDNESDAY.
HMM. YOU KNOW WHAT?
I THINK SOME OF THE KIDS ARE ACTUALLY GETTING BORED OF THE BEACH.
MAYBE WE SHOULD SPLIT UP?

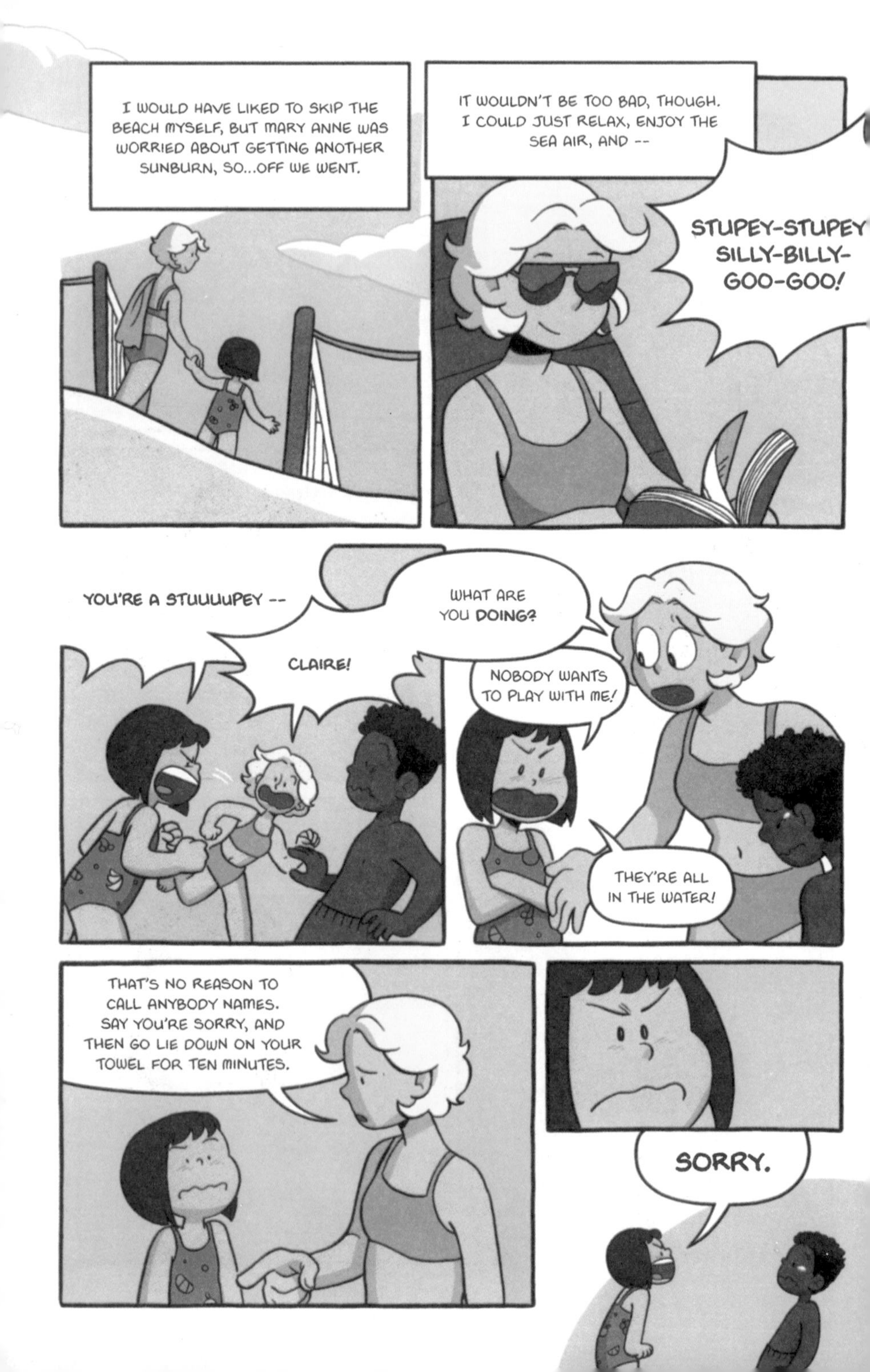
I WOULD HAVE LIKED TO SKIP THE BEACH MYSELF, BUT MARY ANNE WAS WORRIED ABOUT GETTING ANOTHER SUNBURN, SO...OFF WE WENT.
IT WOULDN'T BE TOO BAD, THOUGH. I COULD JUST RELAX, ENJOY THE SEA AIR, AND --
STUPEY-STUPEY SILLY-BILLY-GOO-GOO!
YOU'RE A STUUUUPEY --
CLAIRE!
WHAT ARE YOU DOING?
NOBODY WANTS TO PLAY WITH ME!
THEY'RE ALL IN THE WATER!
THAT'S NO REASON TO CALL ANYBODY NAMES. SAY YOU'RE SORRY, AND THEN GO LIE DOWN ON YOUR TOWEL FOR TEN MINUTES.
SORRY.

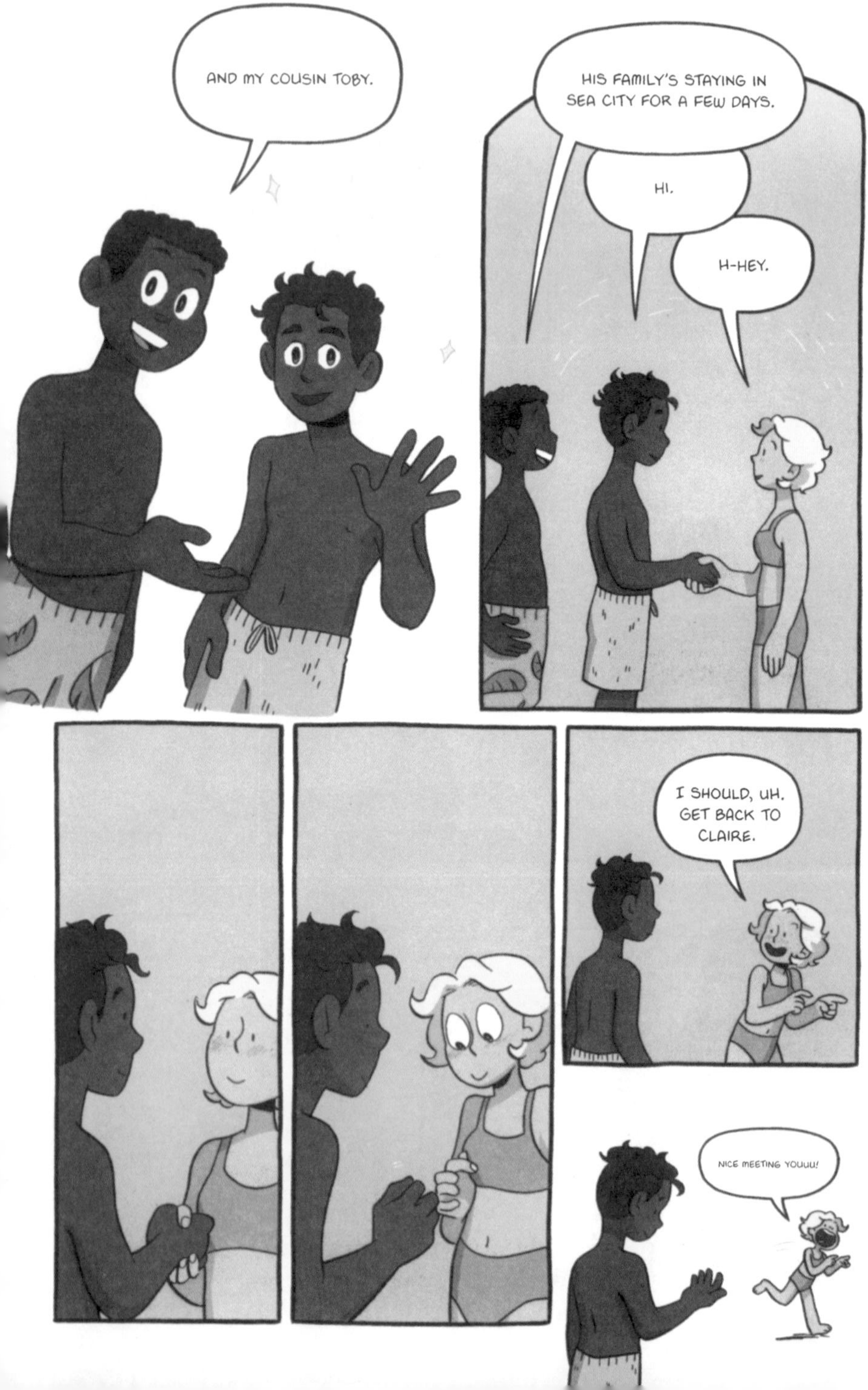
AND MY COUSIN TOBY.
HIS FAMILY'S STAYING IN SEA CITY FOR A FEW DAYS.
HI.
H-HEY.
I SHOULD, UH. GET BACK TO CLAIRE.
NICE MEETING YOUUU!

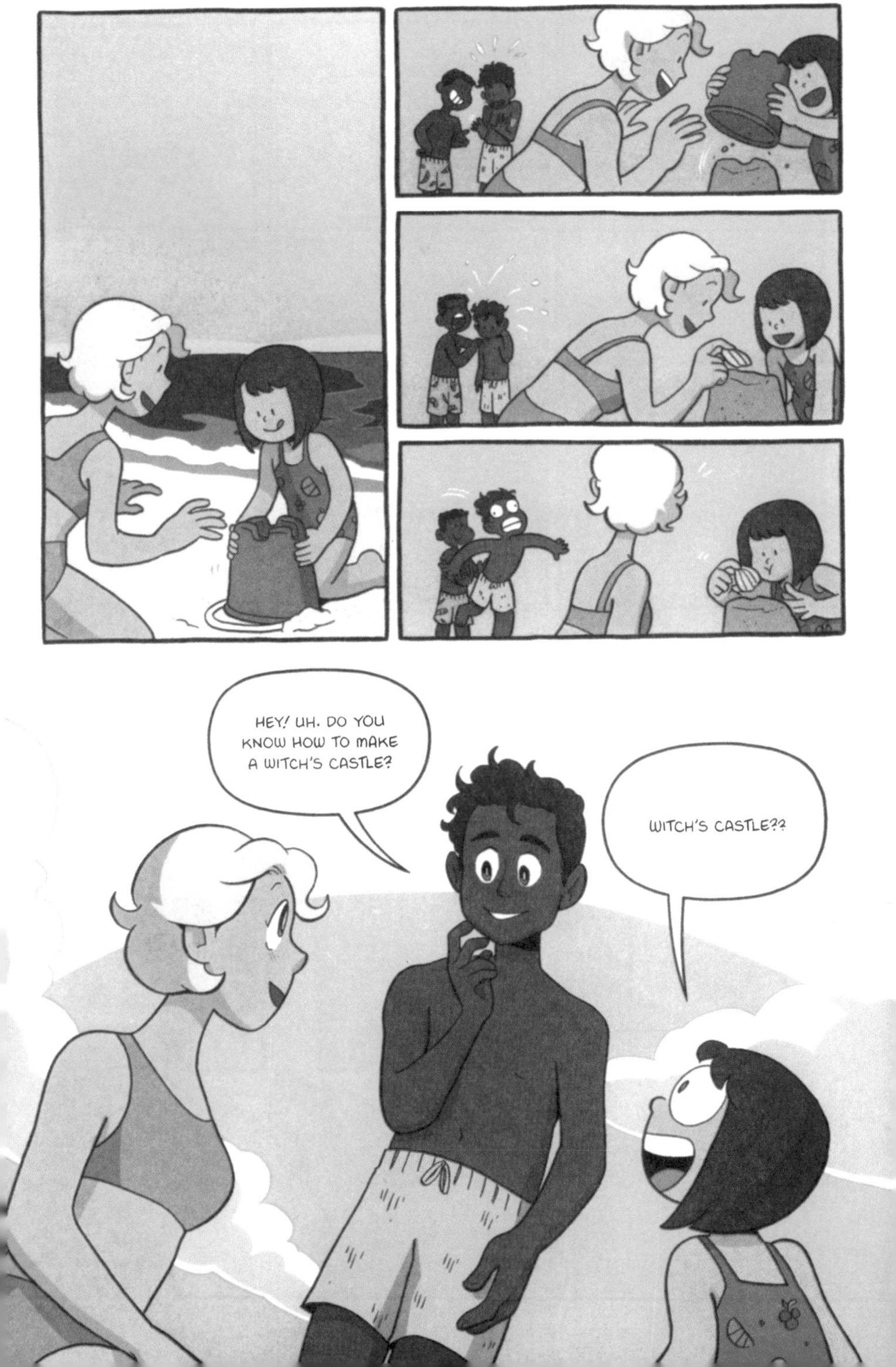
HEY! UH. DO YOU KNOW HOW TO MAKE A WITCH'S CASTLE?
WITCH'S CASTLE??

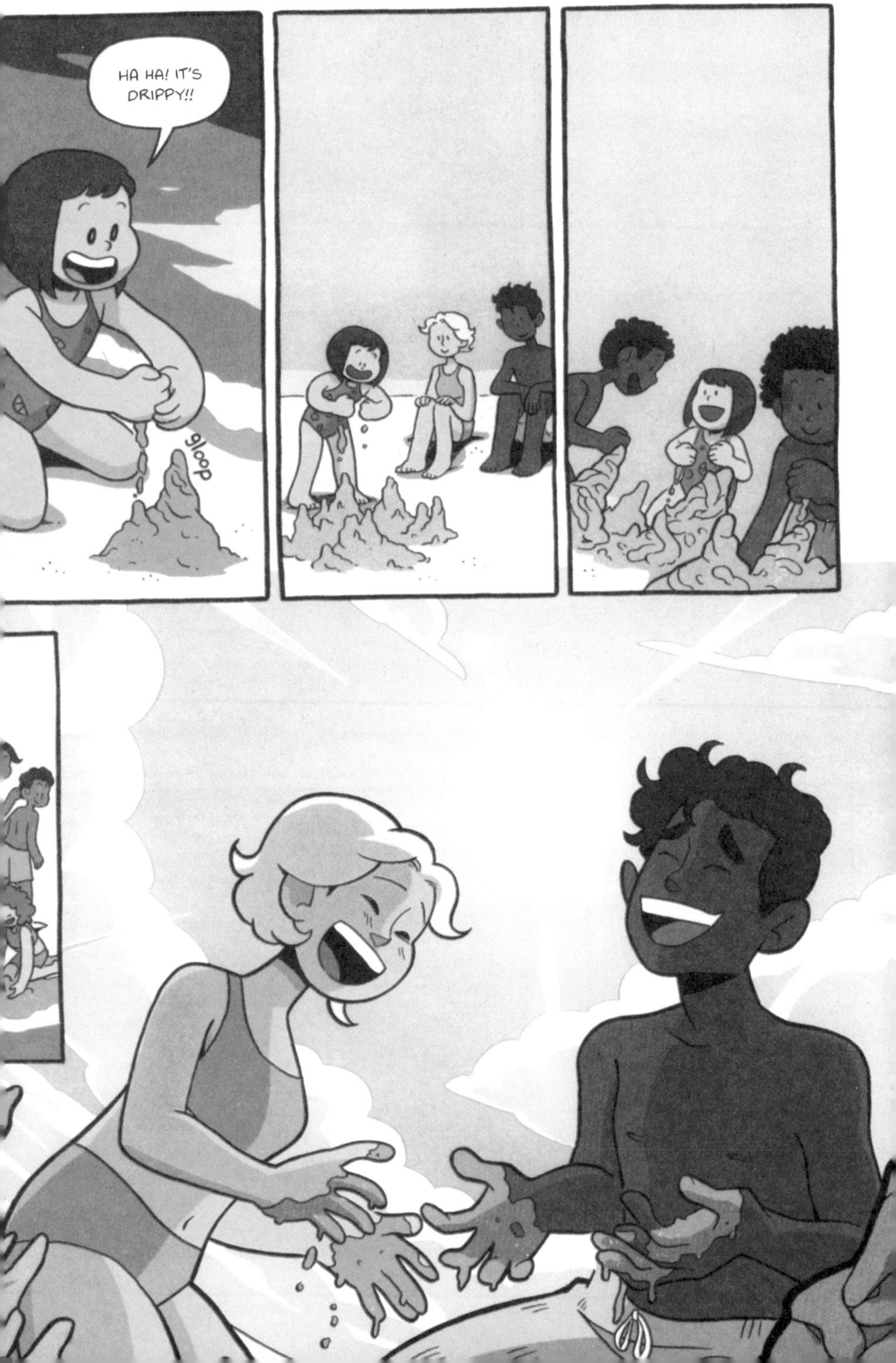
HA HA! IT'S DRIPPY!!
gloop

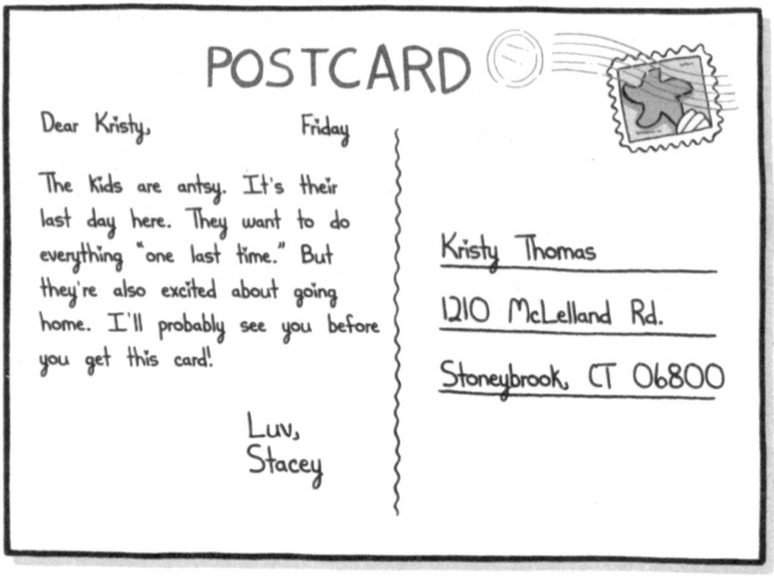
POSTCARD

Dear Kristy, Friday

The kids are antsy. It's their last day here. They want to do everything "one last time." But they're also excited about going home. I'll probably see you before you get this card!

Luv,
Stacey

Kristy Thomas
1210 McLelland Rd.
Stoneybrook, CT 06800

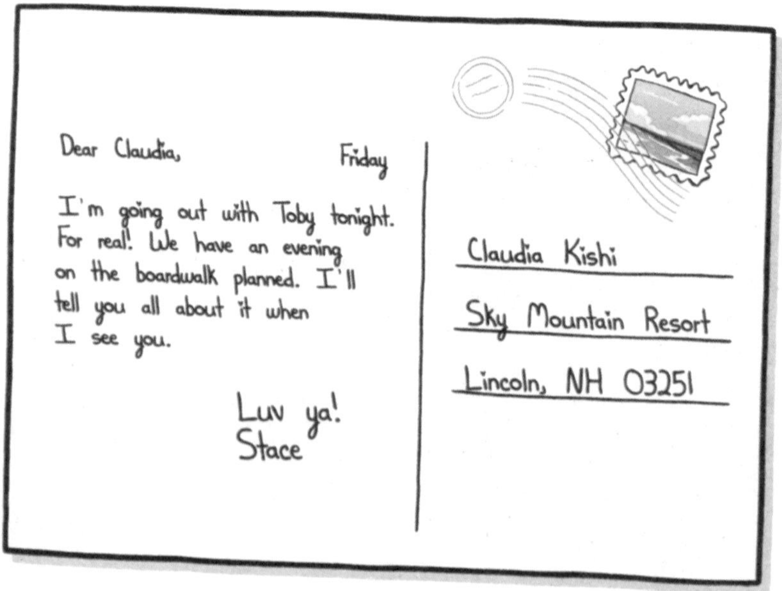
Dear Claudia, Friday

I'm going out with Toby tonight. For real! We have an evening on the boardwalk planned. I'll tell you all about it when I see you.

Luv ya!
Stace

Claudia Kishi
Sky Mountain Resort
Lincoln, NH 03251

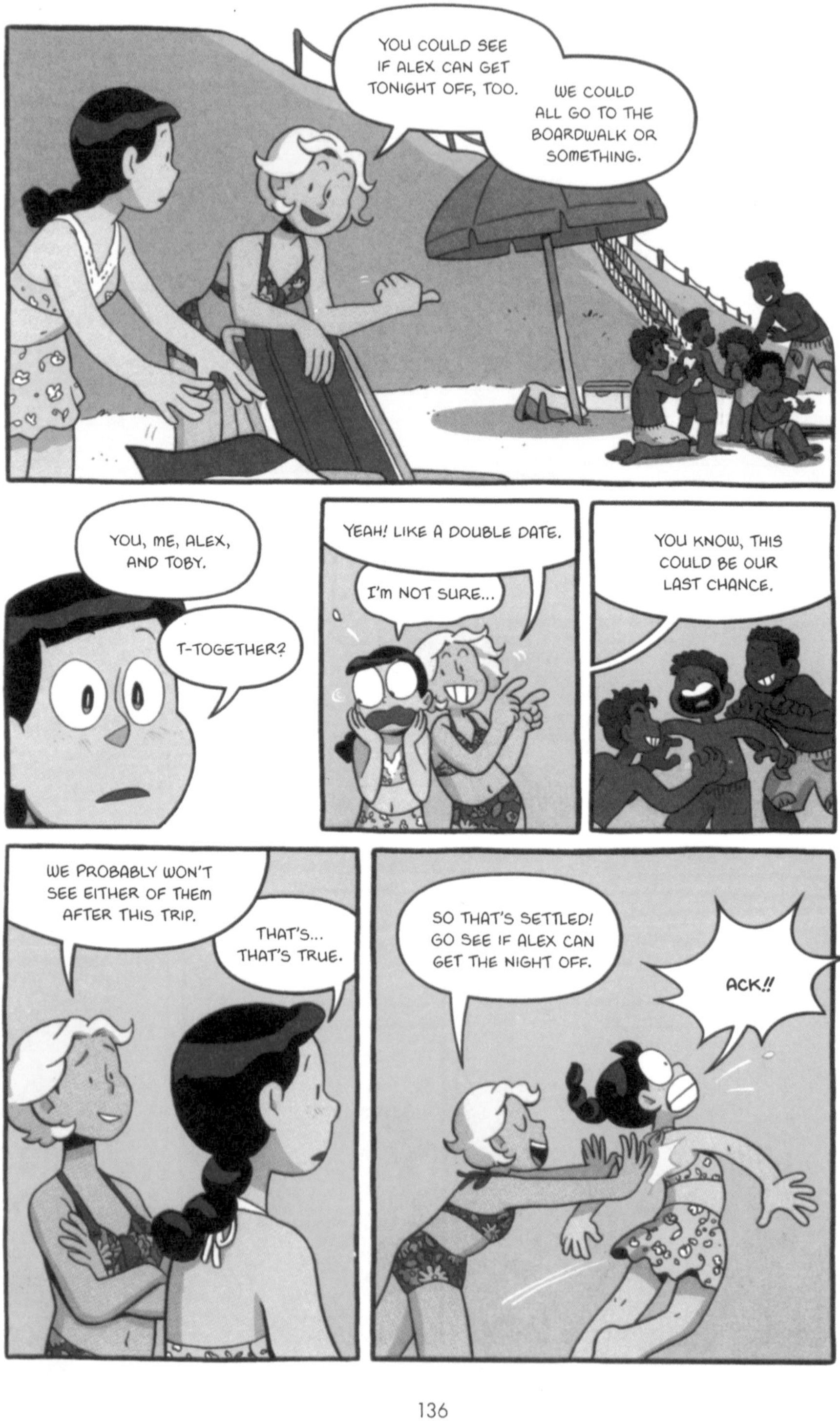
YOU COULD SEE IF ALEX CAN GET TONIGHT OFF, TOO.
WE COULD ALL GO TO THE BOARDWALK OR SOMETHING.
YOU, ME, ALEX, AND TOBY.
T-TOGETHER?
YEAH! LIKE A DOUBLE DATE.
I'M NOT SURE...
YOU KNOW, THIS COULD BE OUR LAST CHANCE.
WE PROBABLY WON'T SEE EITHER OF THEM AFTER THIS TRIP.
THAT'S... THAT'S TRUE.
SO THAT'S SETTLED! GO SEE IF ALEX CAN GET THE NIGHT OFF.
ACK!!

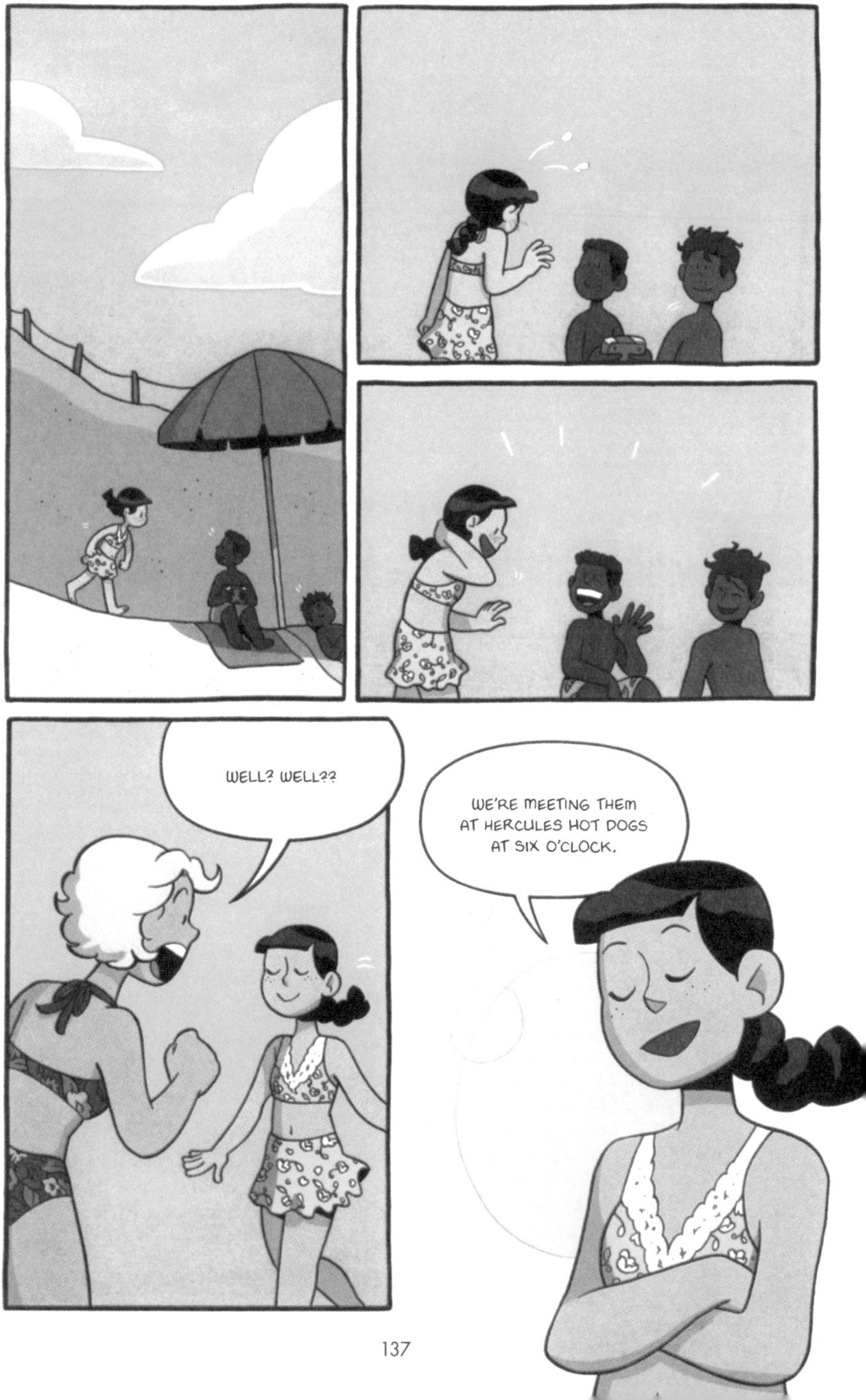
WELL? WELL??
WE'RE MEETING THEM AT HERCULES HOT DOGS AT SIX O'CLOCK.

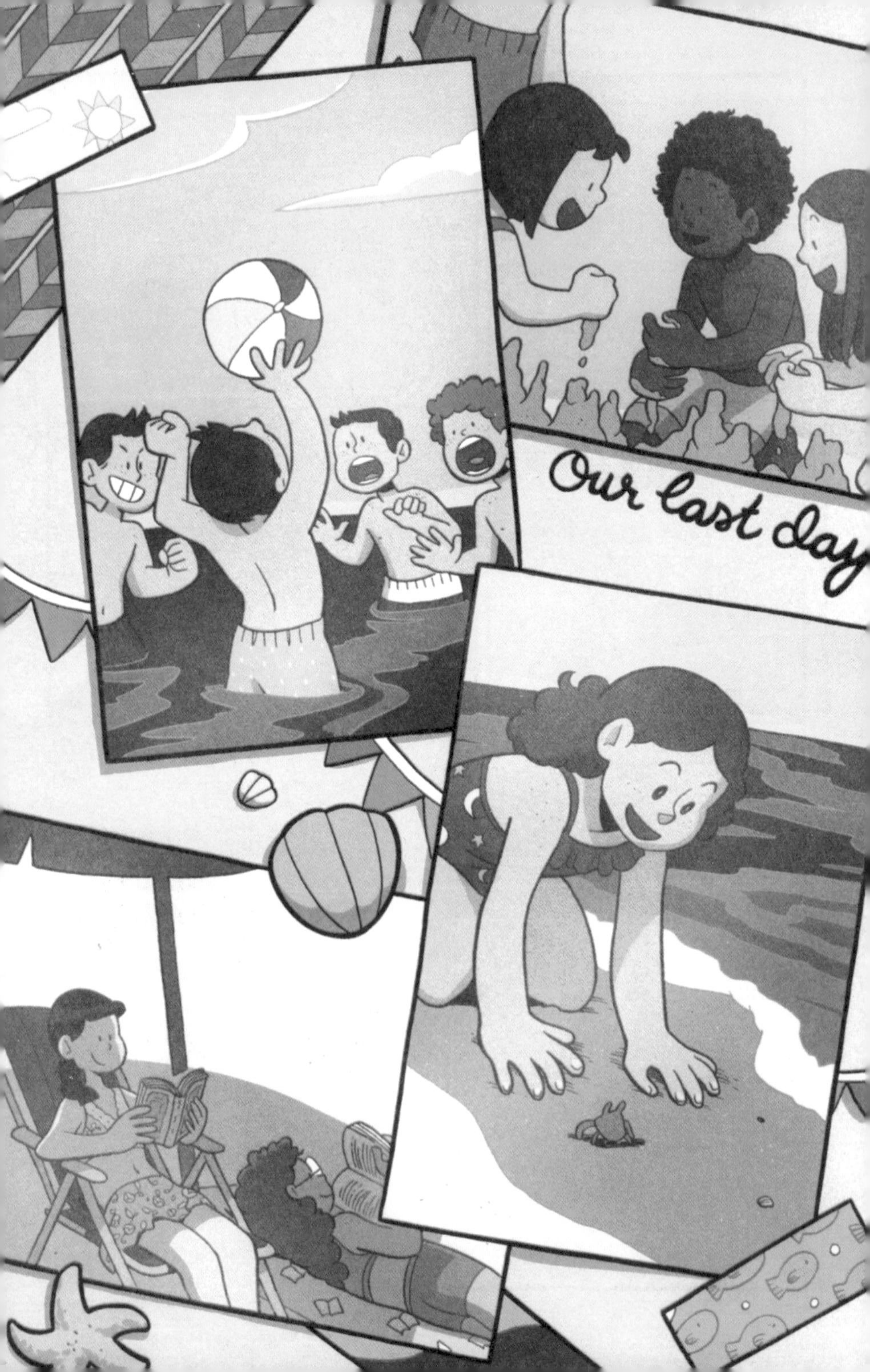
Our last day

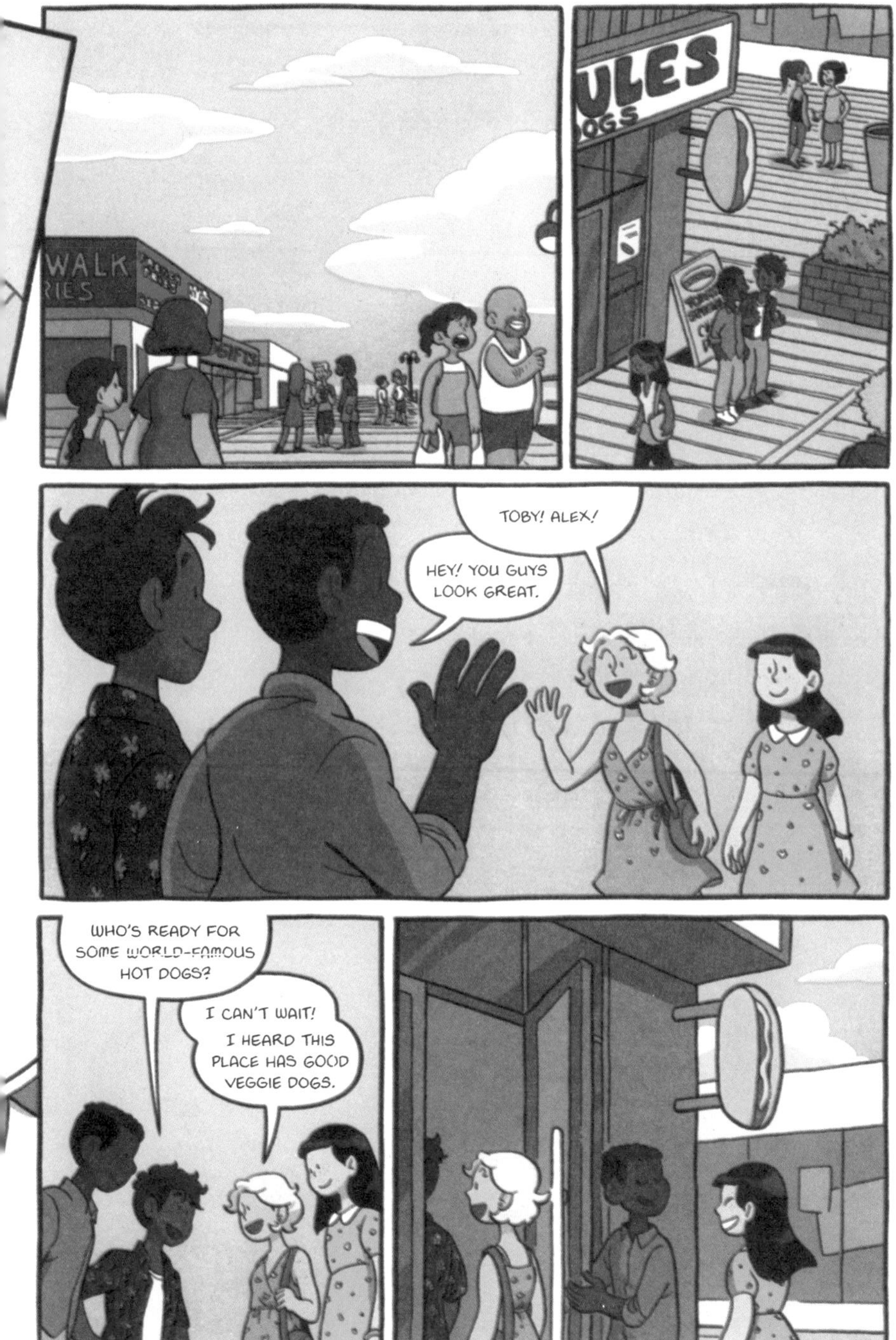

WALK
RIES
GIFTS
ULES
DOGS
TOBY! ALEX!
HEY! YOU GUYS LOOK GREAT.
WHO'S READY FOR SOME WORLD-FAMOUS HOT DOGS?
I CAN'T WAIT! I HEARD THIS PLACE HAS GOOD VEGGIE DOGS.

JUST LIKE WITH THE FLOWERS, JIMMY HAD TO WAIT BEHIND A LONG LINE OF OTHER PROCRASTINATORS TO GET HIS SUIT. BUT, THANK GOODNESS, HE FINISHED JUST IN TIME TO TAKE AMY TO THE DANCE.

THE FIRST THING SHE DID WAS ASK HIM TO GET HER A DRINK, SO HE WENT UP TO GET HER A CUP OF PUNCH...AND WOULDN'T YOU KNOW IT? AFTER ALL THAT, THERE WAS NO PUNCH LINE.

HEY... MARY ANNE?

ha

PLEASE TELL ME YOU DON'T KNOW ANY MORE JOKES.

ha ha

WOULD IT BE OKAY IF WE SPLIT UP AFTER DINNER?

I MEAN, WOULD YOU FEEL OKAY ABOUT BEING ALONE WITH ALEX?

YEAH. YEAH, LET'S DO IT.

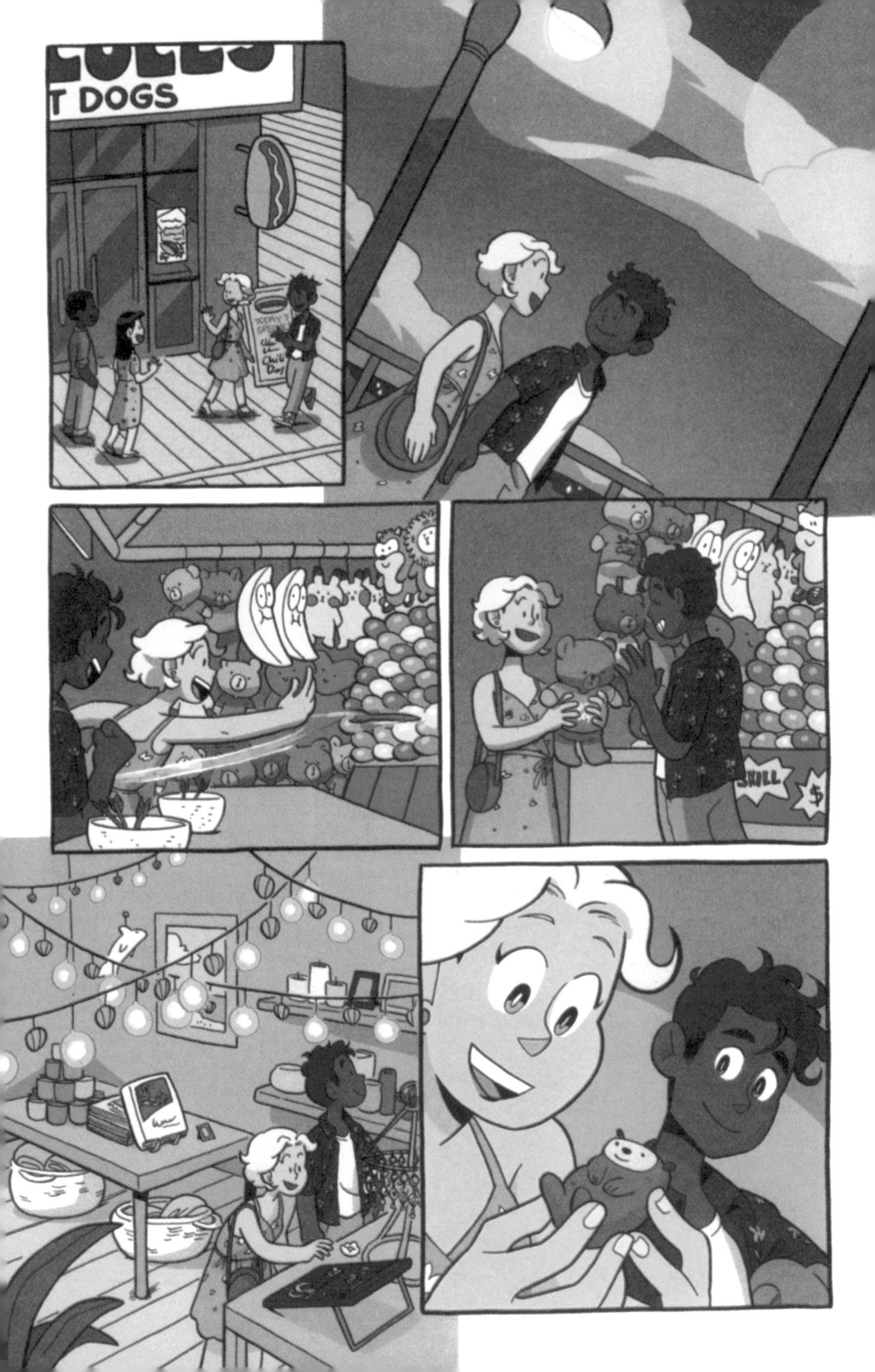
T DOGS
SKILL
$

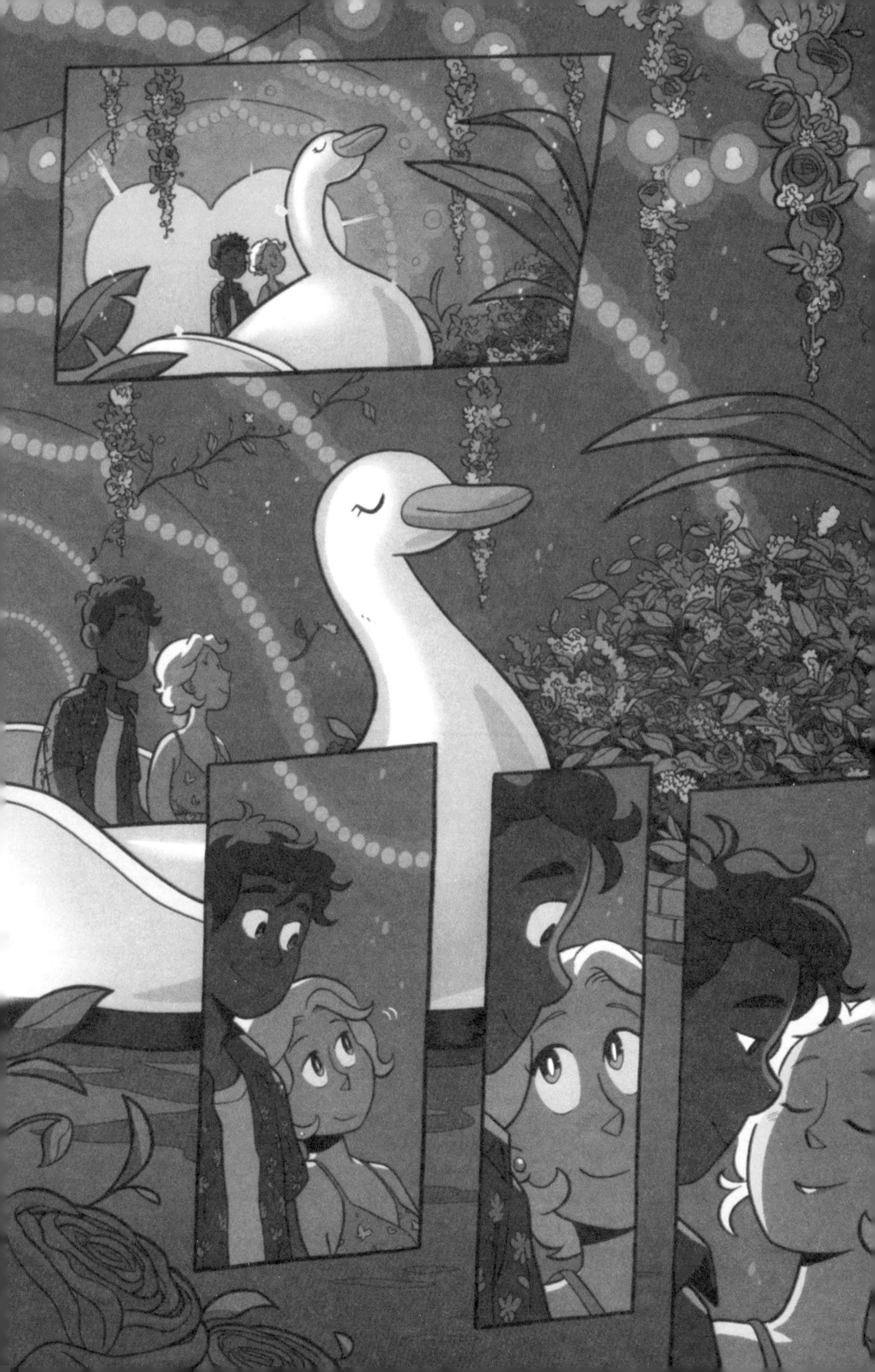

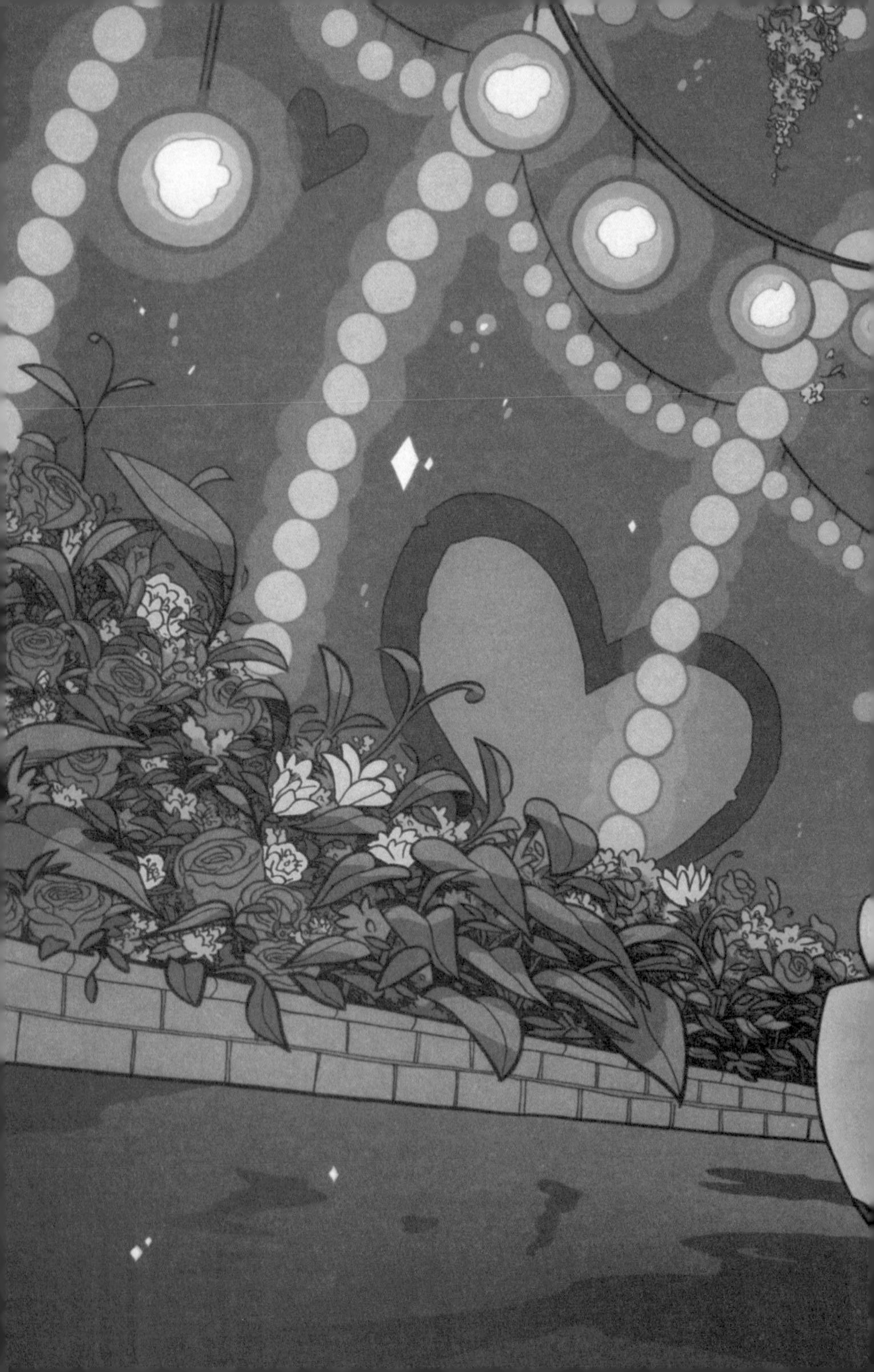

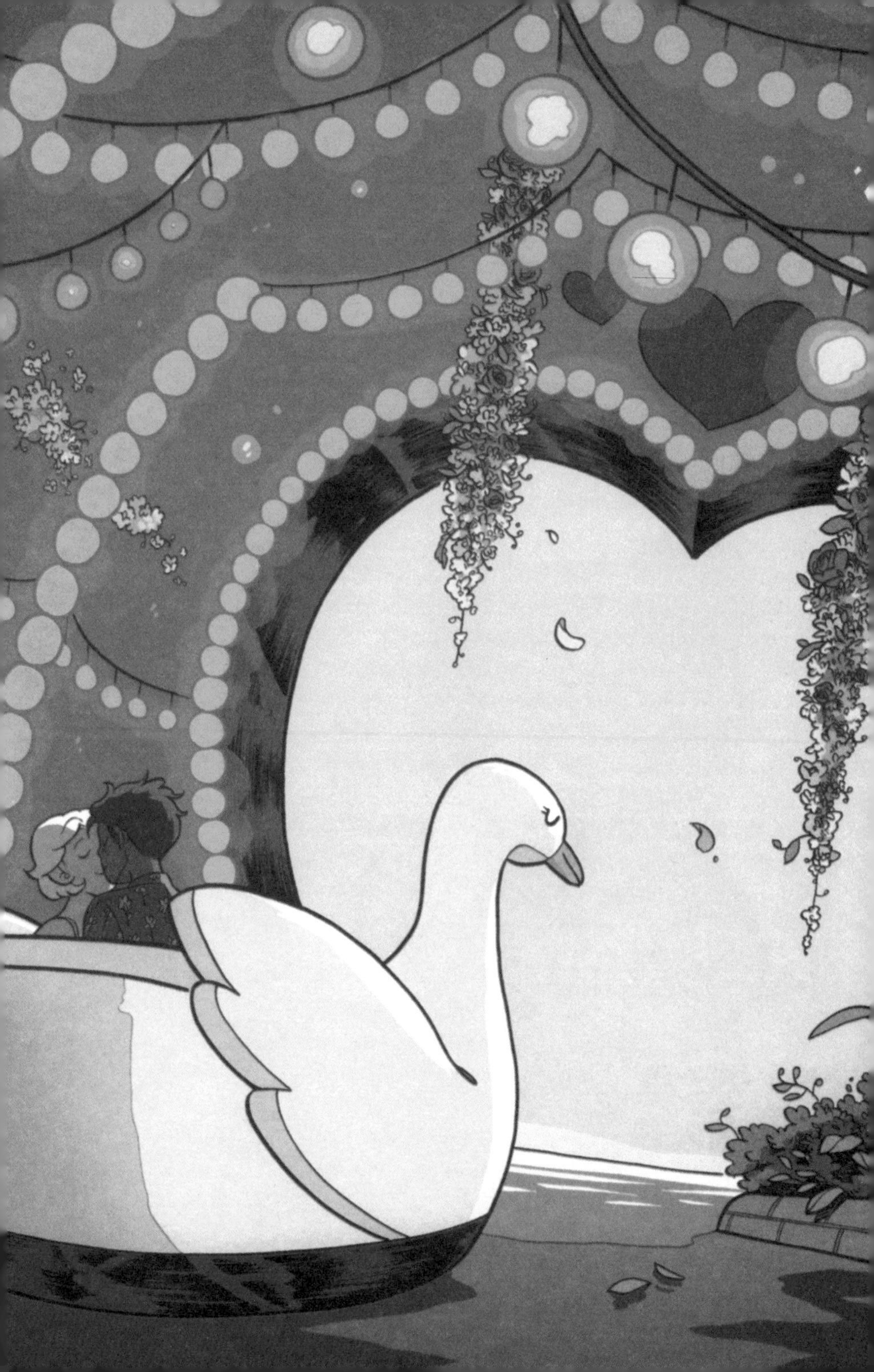

Sea
City

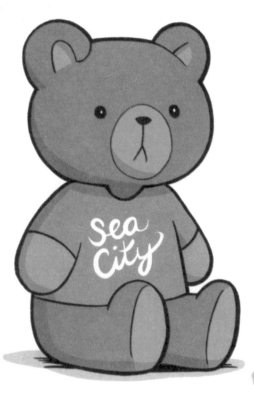

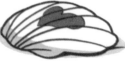

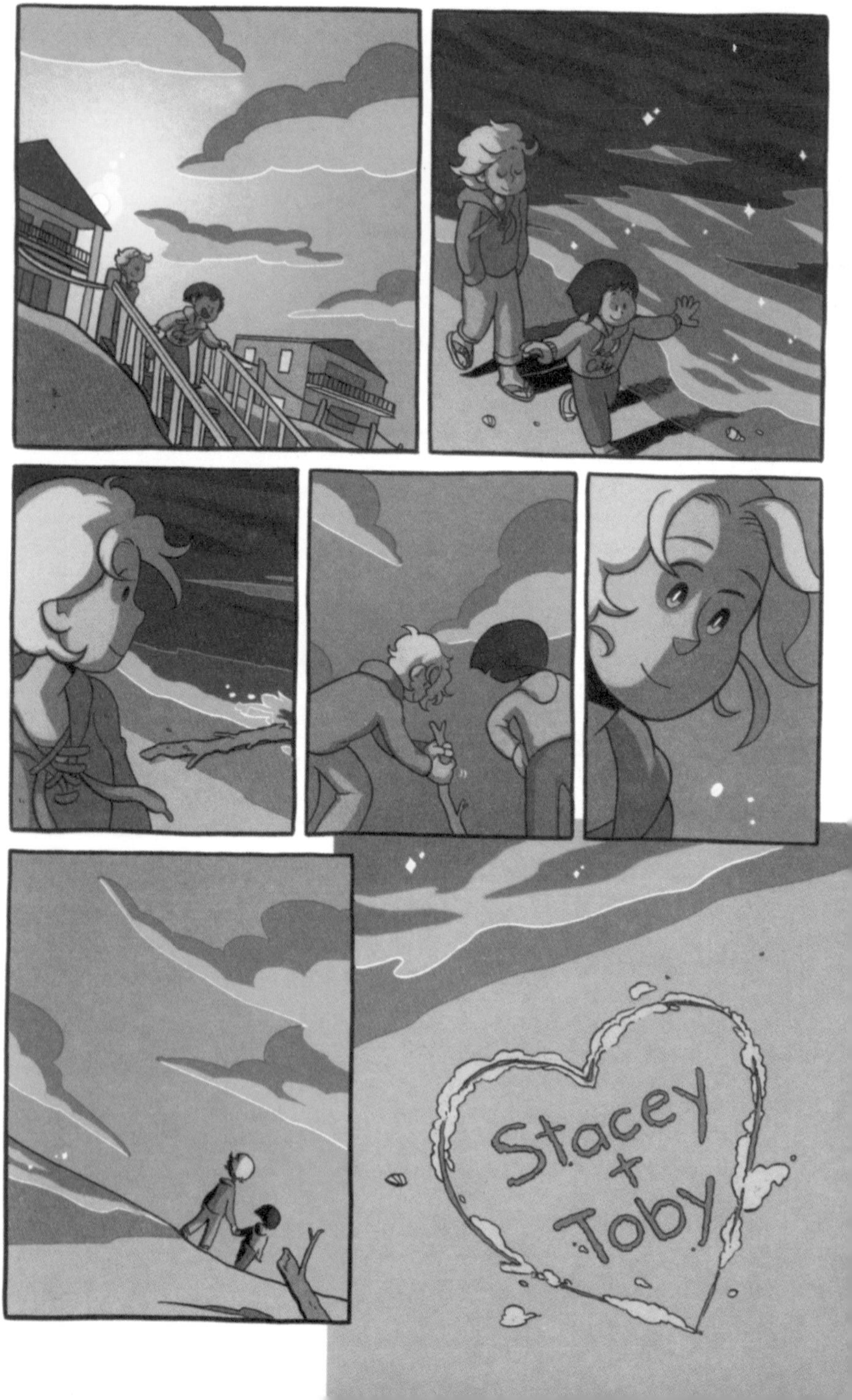
Stacey
+
Toby

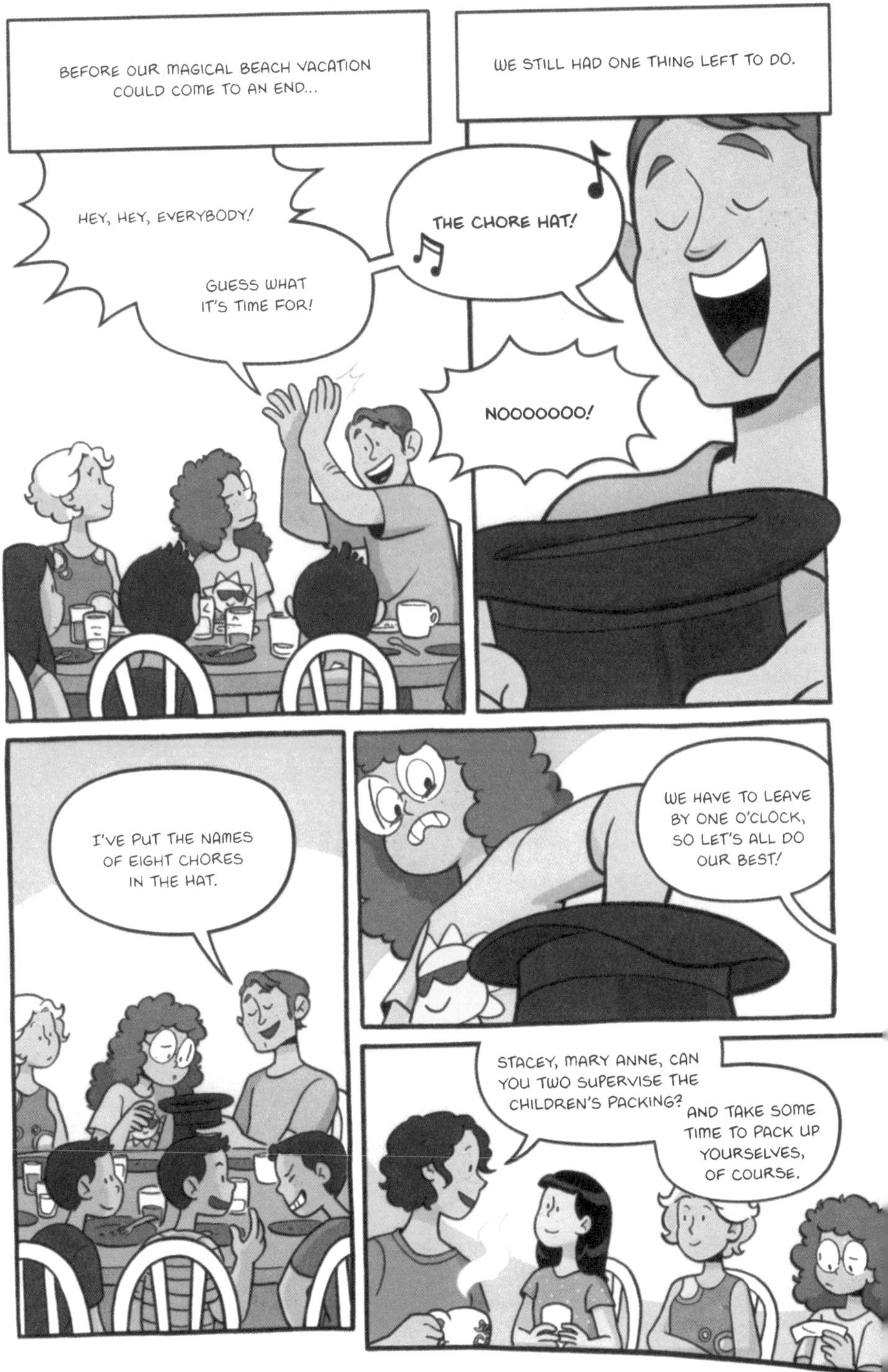
BEFORE OUR MAGICAL BEACH VACATION COULD COME TO AN END...
WE STILL HAD ONE THING LEFT TO DO.
HEY, HEY, EVERYBODY!
GUESS WHAT IT'S TIME FOR!
THE CHORE HAT!
NOOOOOOO!
I'VE PUT THE NAMES OF EIGHT CHORES IN THE HAT.
WE HAVE TO LEAVE BY ONE O'CLOCK, SO LET'S ALL DO OUR BEST!
STACEY, MARY ANNE, CAN YOU TWO SUPERVISE THE CHILDREN'S PACKING?
AND TAKE SOME TIME TO PACK UP YOURSELVES, OF COURSE.

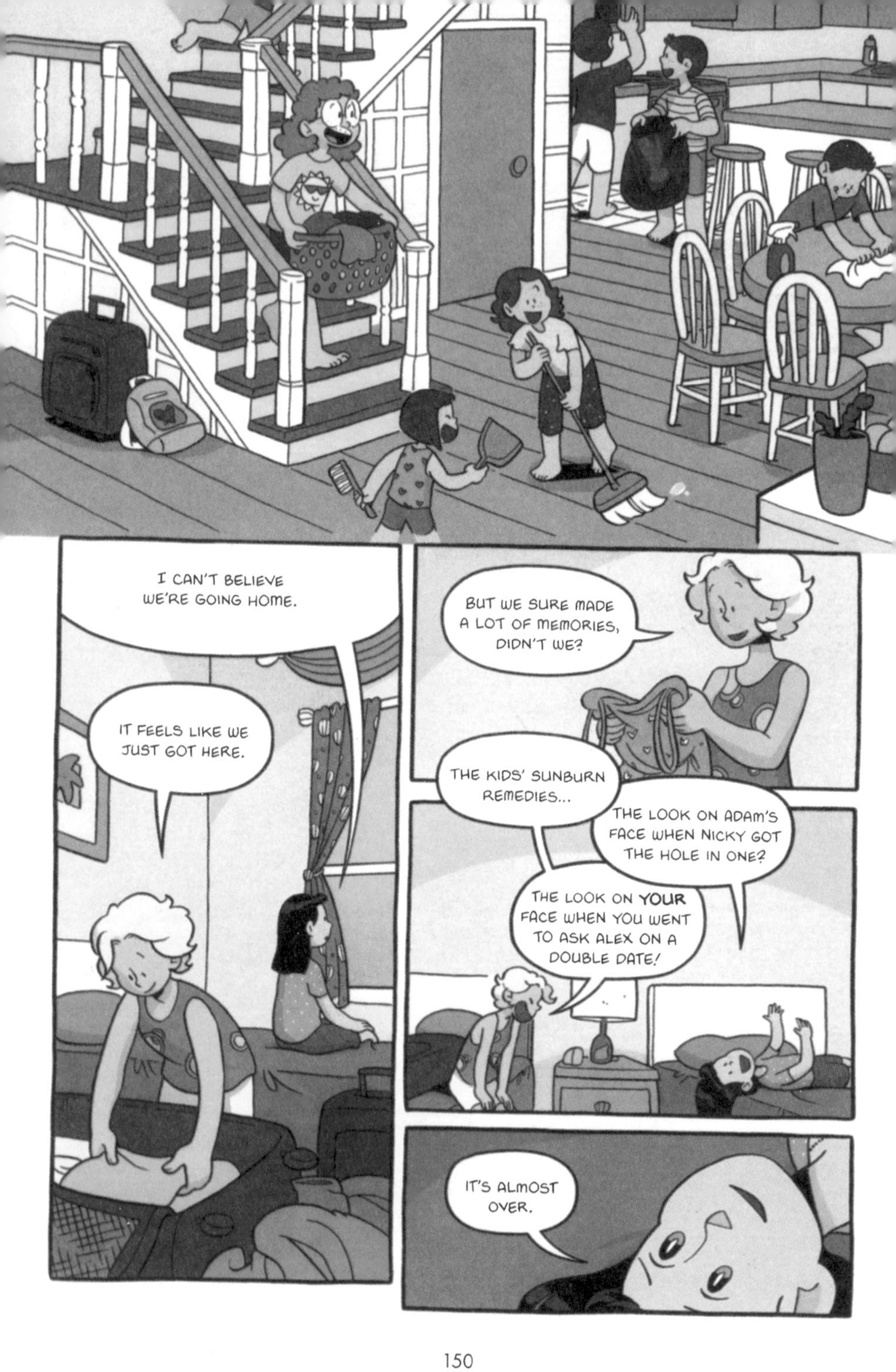
I CAN'T BELIEVE WE'RE GOING HOME.
IT FEELS LIKE WE JUST GOT HERE.
BUT WE SURE MADE A LOT OF MEMORIES, DIDN'T WE?
THE KIDS' SUNBURN REMEDIES...
THE LOOK ON ADAM'S FACE WHEN NICKY GOT THE HOLE IN ONE?
THE LOOK ON YOUR FACE WHEN YOU WENT TO ASK ALEX ON A DOUBLE DATE!
IT'S ALMOST OVER.

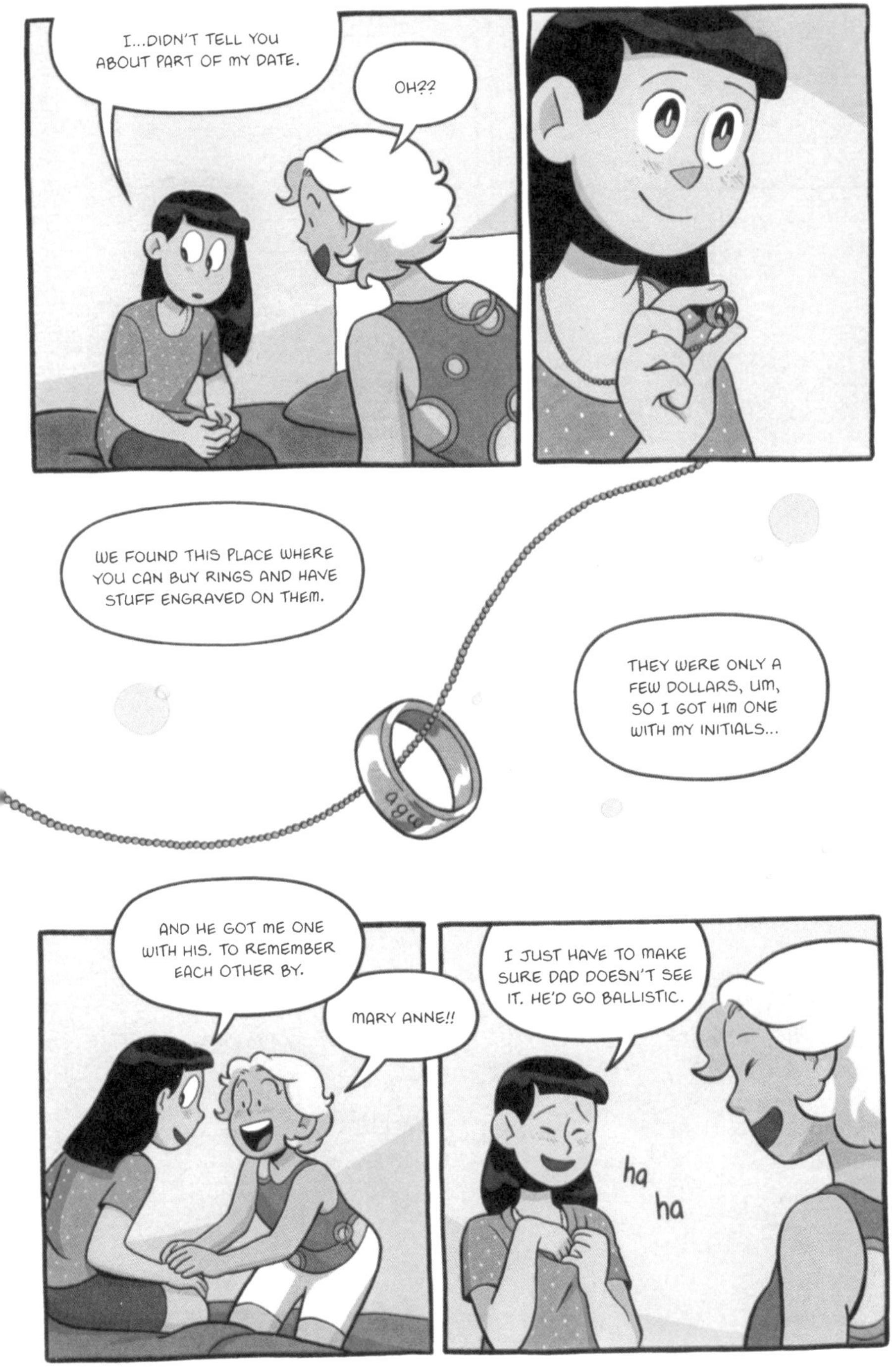
I...DIDN'T TELL YOU ABOUT PART OF MY DATE.
OH??
WE FOUND THIS PLACE WHERE YOU CAN BUY RINGS AND HAVE STUFF ENGRAVED ON THEM.
THEY WERE ONLY A FEW DOLLARS, UM, SO I GOT HIM ONE WITH MY INITIALS...
mga
AND HE GOT ME ONE WITH HIS. TO REMEMBER EACH OTHER BY.
MARY ANNE!!
I JUST HAVE TO MAKE SURE DAD DOESN'T SEE IT. HE'D GO BALLISTIC.
ha
ha

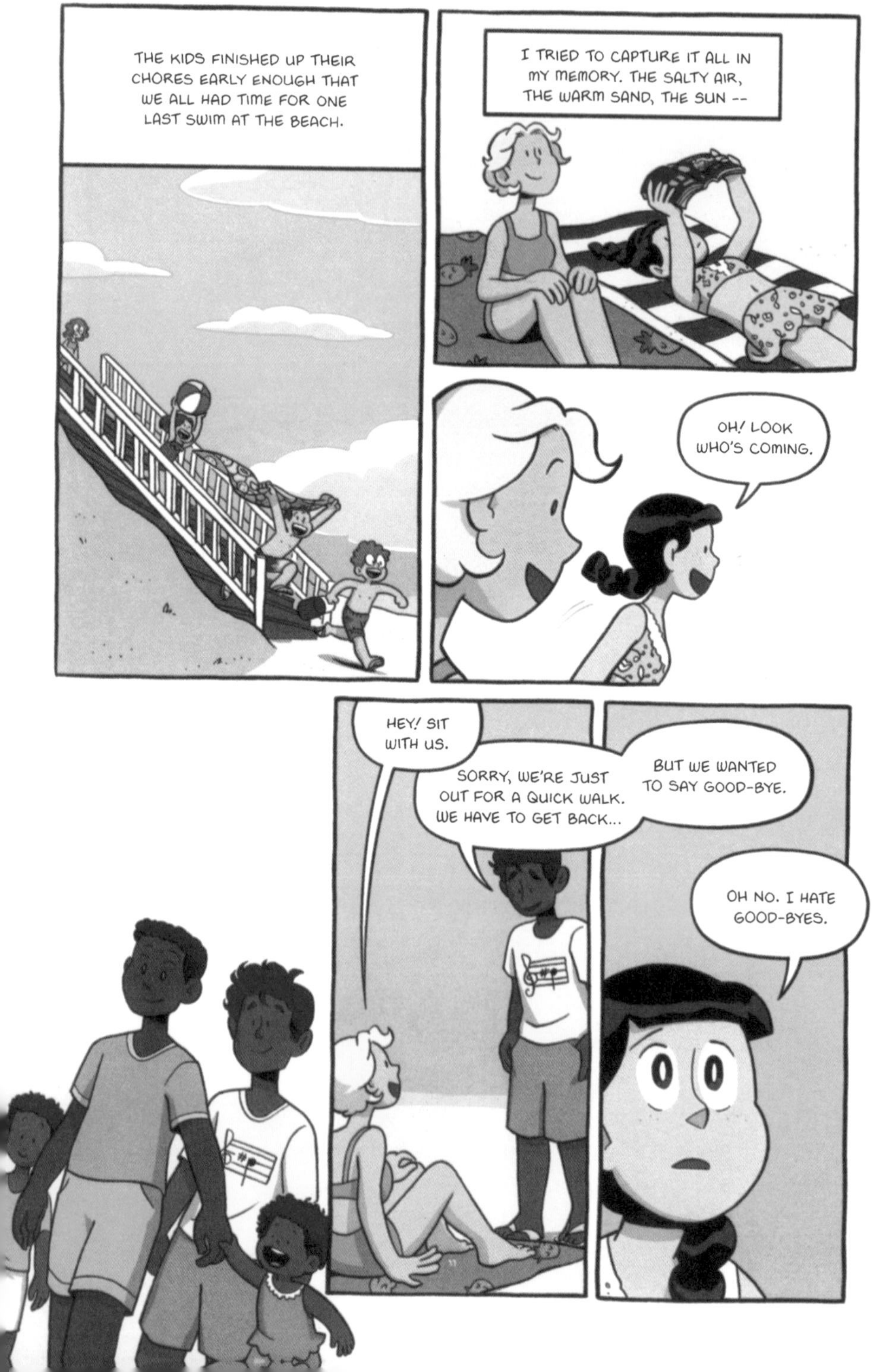
THE KIDS FINISHED UP THEIR CHORES EARLY ENOUGH THAT WE ALL HAD TIME FOR ONE LAST SWIM AT THE BEACH.
I TRIED TO CAPTURE IT ALL IN MY MEMORY. THE SALTY AIR, THE WARM SAND, THE SUN --
OH! LOOK WHO'S COMING.
HEY! SIT WITH US.
SORRY, WE'RE JUST OUT FOR A QUICK WALK. WE HAVE TO GET BACK...
BUT WE WANTED TO SAY GOOD-BYE.
OH NO. I HATE GOOD-BYES.

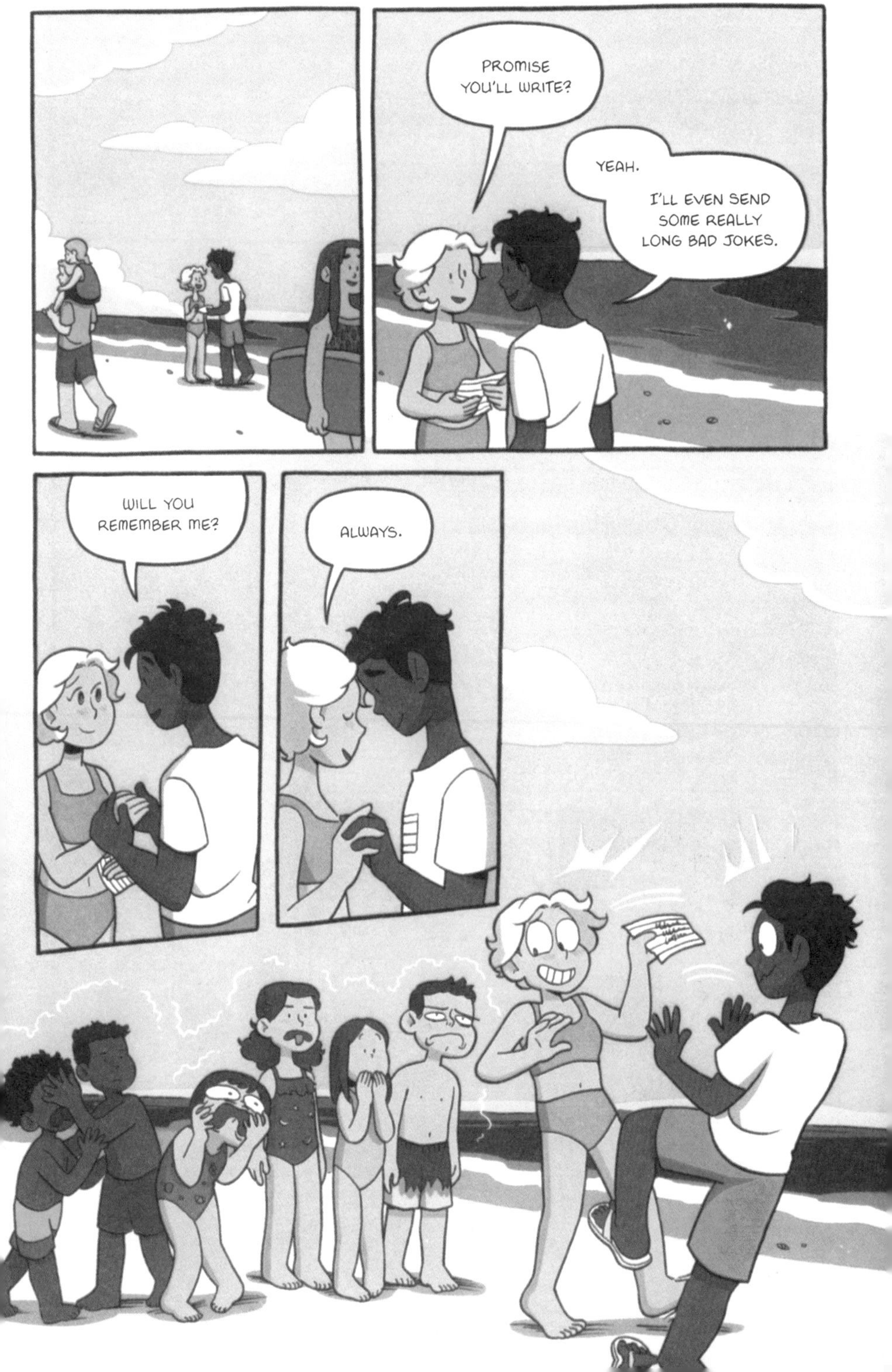
PROMISE YOU'LL WRITE?
YEAH.
I'LL EVEN SEND SOME REALLY LONG BAD JOKES.
WILL YOU REMEMBER ME?
ALWAYS.

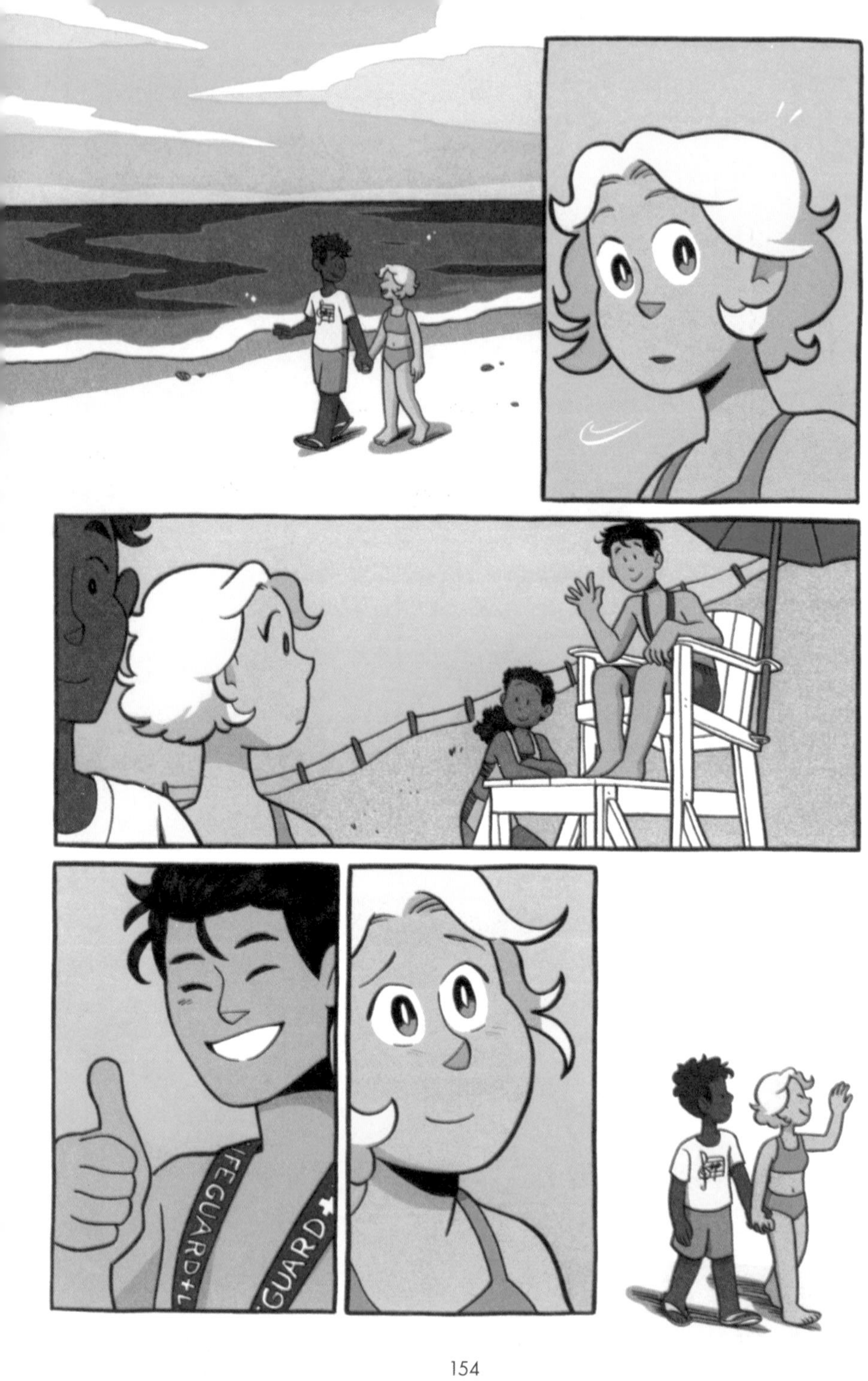

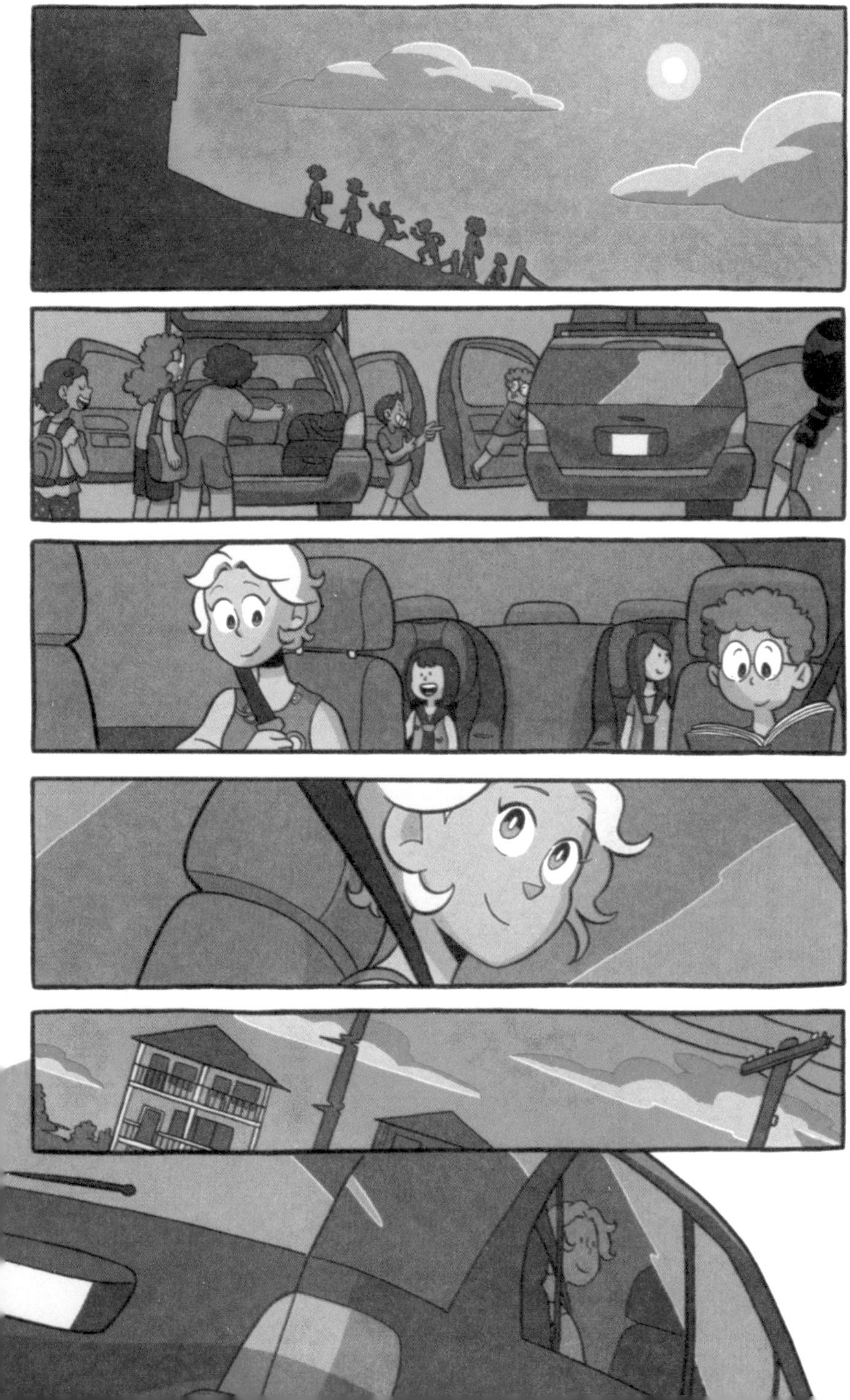

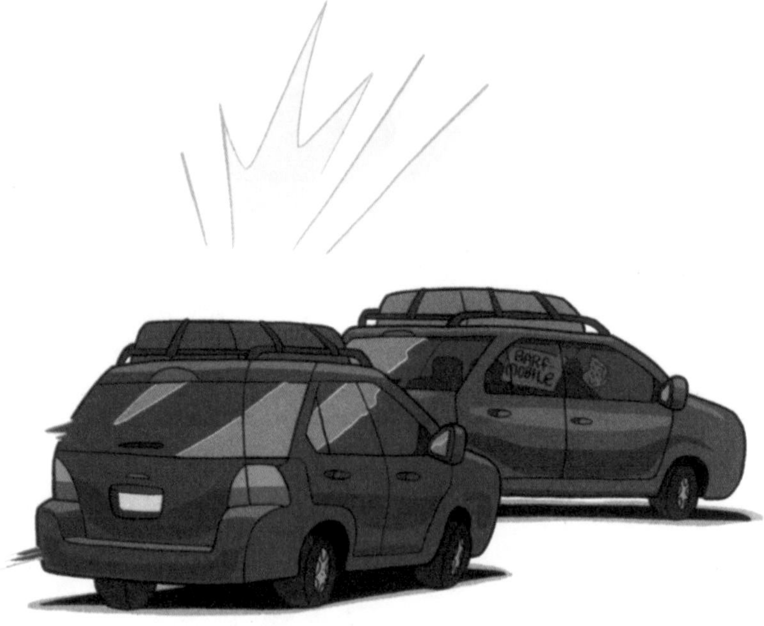
BARF
MOBILE

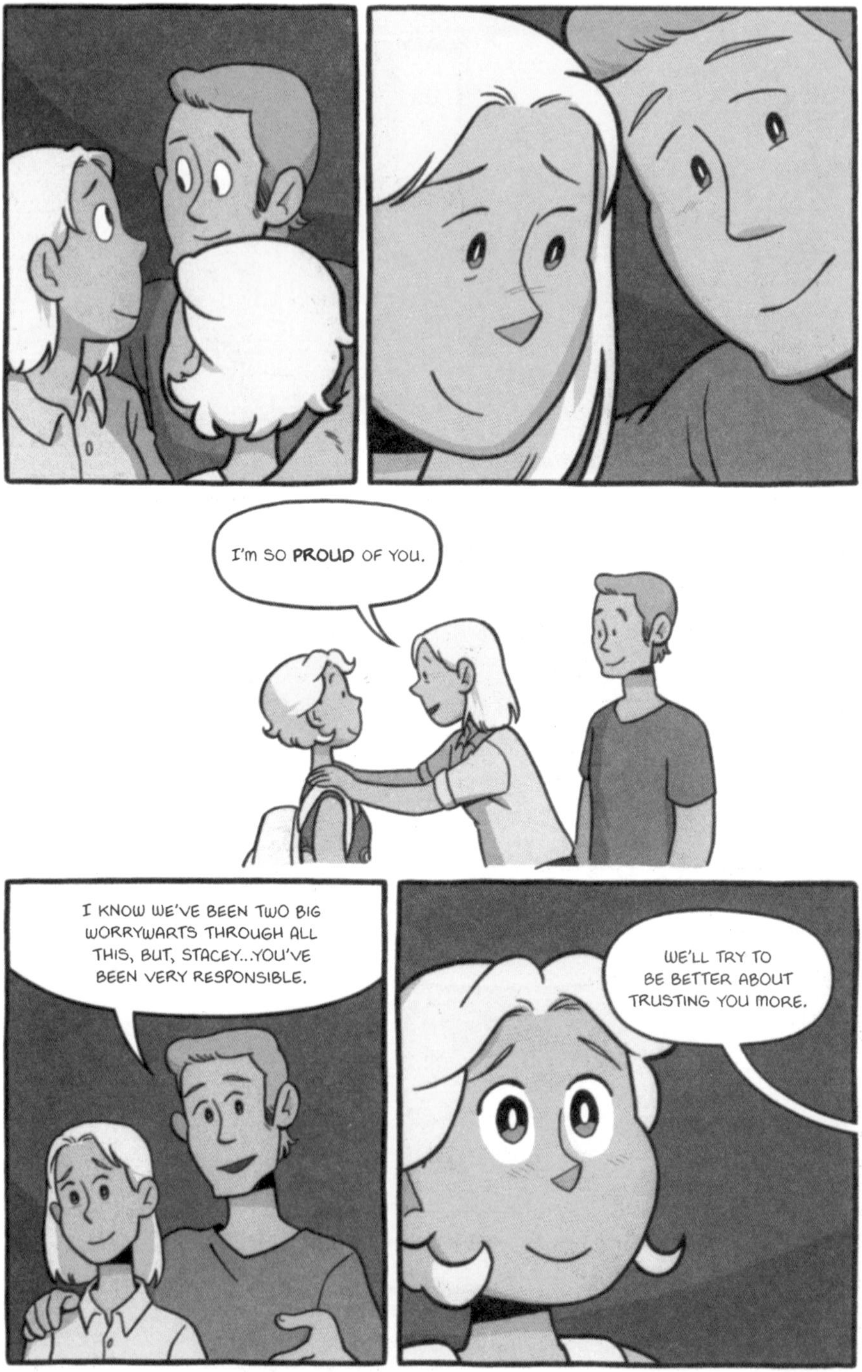
I'm SO PROUD OF YOU.
I KNOW WE'VE BEEN TWO BIG WORRYWARTS THROUGH ALL THIS, BUT, STACEY...YOU'VE BEEN VERY RESPONSIBLE.
WE'LL TRY TO BE BETTER ABOUT TRUSTING YOU MORE.

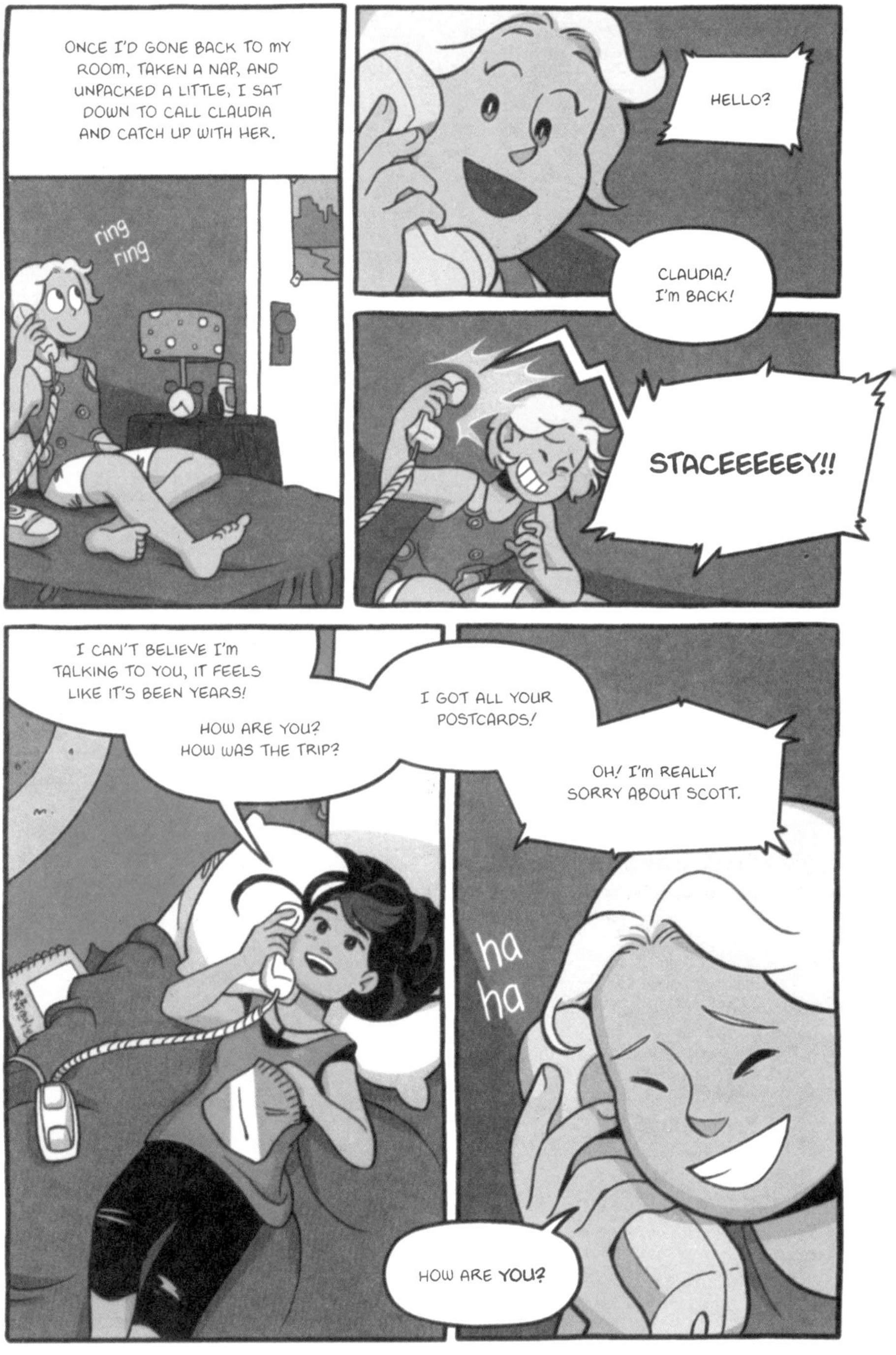
ONCE I'D GONE BACK TO MY ROOM, TAKEN A NAP, AND UNPACKED A LITTLE, I SAT DOWN TO CALL CLAUDIA AND CATCH UP WITH HER.
ring ring
HELLO?
CLAUDIA! I'M BACK!
STACEEEEEY!!
I CAN'T BELIEVE I'M TALKING TO YOU, IT FEELS LIKE IT'S BEEN YEARS!
HOW ARE YOU? HOW WAS THE TRIP?
I GOT ALL YOUR POSTCARDS!
OH! I'M REALLY SORRY ABOUT SCOTT.
ha ha
HOW ARE **YOU?**

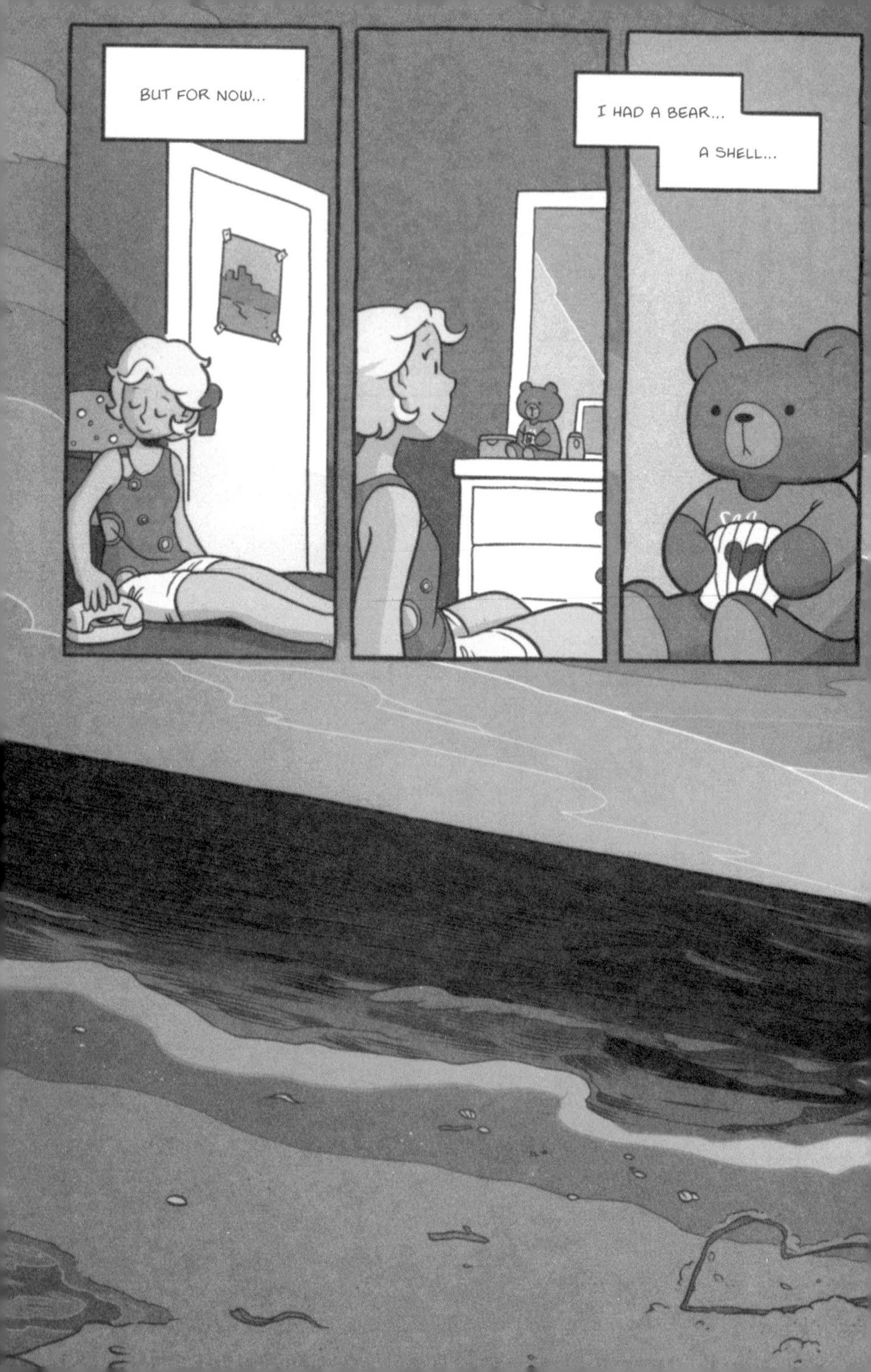
BUT FOR NOW...
I HAD A BEAR...
A SHELL...

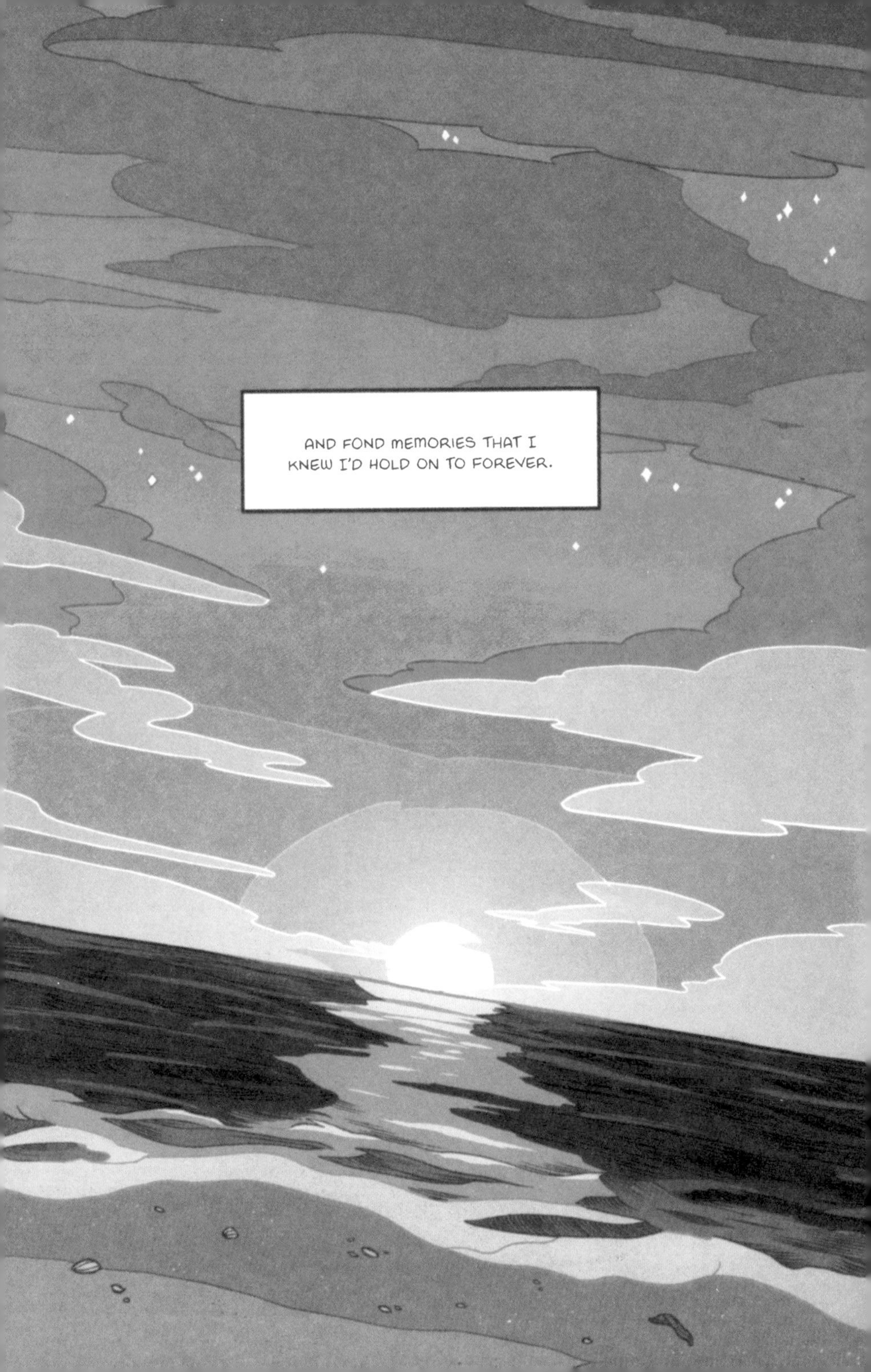
AND FOND MEMORIES THAT I KNEW I'D HOLD ON TO FOREVER.

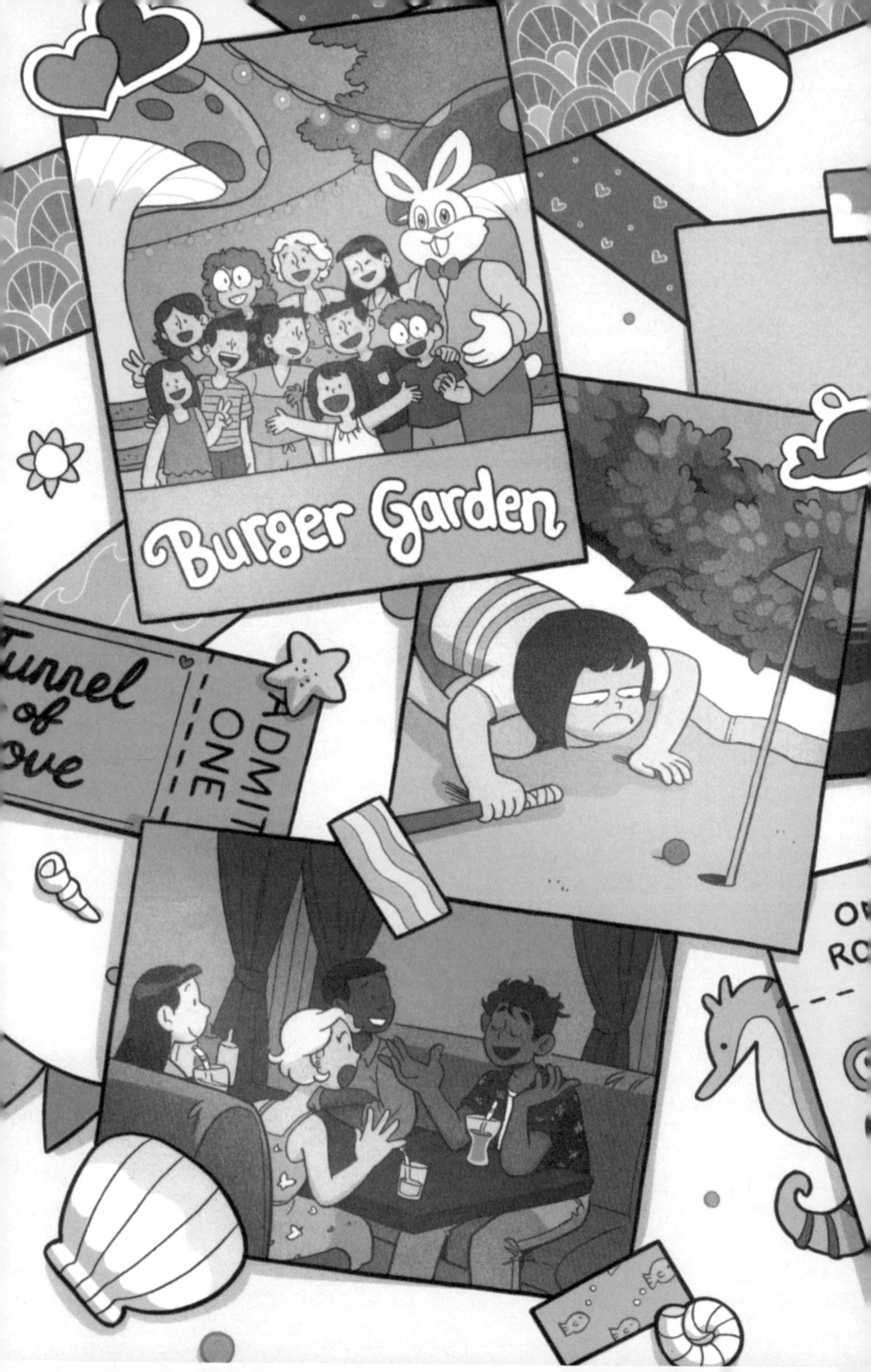
Burger Garden
unnel of ove
ADMIT ONE

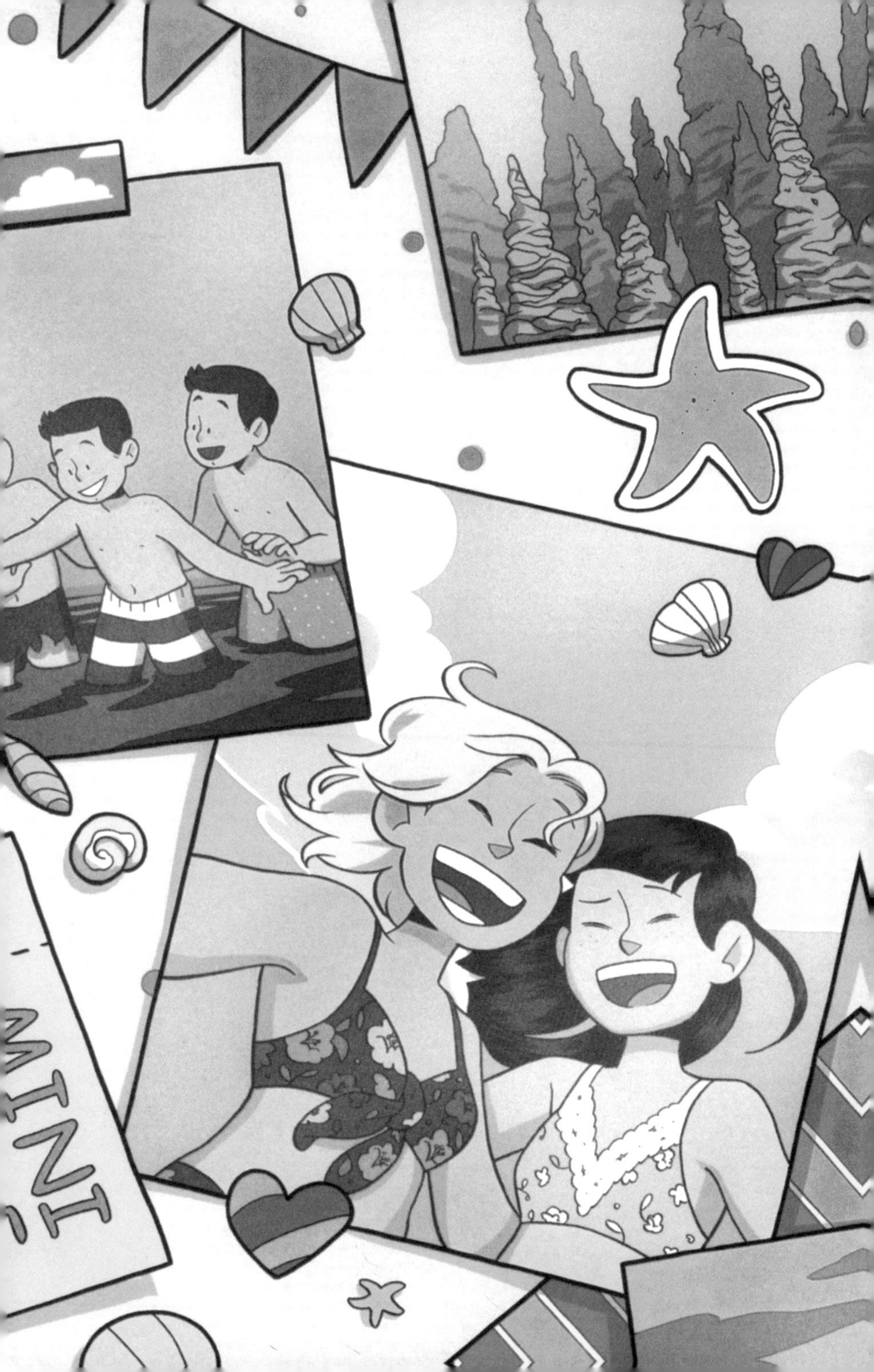

GALE GALLIGAN is the creator of *New York Times* bestselling graphic novel adaptations of Dawn and the Impossible Three and Kristy's Big Day by Ann M. Martin. When Gale ins't making comics, she enjoys knitting, reading, and spending time with her adorable pet rabbits. She lives in Pleasantville, New York. Visit her online at galesaur.com.

DON'T MISS THE OTHER BABY-SITTERS CLUB GRAPHIC NOVELS!

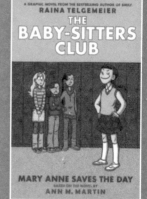